SYLVIA MERCEDES

DAUGHTER OF SHADES

THE VENATRIX CHRONICLES BOOK 1

This story is for Papa:
With thanks for the many hours of brainstorming
and the many gallons of "bad" coffee.

THE VENATRIX

Drauval Borou

Skada Mountains

Aalis River

Castra Brocar

Wodechran

Sang River

Aehanor City

CHRONICLES

Aldreda Borough

The Great Barrier

Dulimurian

The Witchwood

Sang River

KINGDOM OF PERRINION

Dulimurian

The Witchwood

The Great Barrier

Cro Ular

Grimaud

Sang River

GLOSSARY OF SHADES

Shades: Disembodied spirit-beings who have escaped from their hellish dimension—the Haunts—and entered the mortal world. They cannot exist in a physical reality without mortal hosts, whom they possess and endow with unnatural powers. If left unchecked, they will gain ascendancy within a host-body and oust the original soul, taking full possession.

The following are the known varieties of shades as catalogued by the Order of Saint Evander:

ANATHEMAS
Abilities pertain to blood and curse-casting.

APPARITIONS
Abilities pertain to mind control and manipulation.

ARCANES
Mysterious entities with abilities not fully understood, but which seem to pertain to energies such as heat, motion,

light, magnetism, and electricity.

ELEMENTALS
Abilities pertain to the natural elements of wind, fire, water, earth.

EVANESCERS
Abilities pertain to *evanescing*, or instantaneous distance-travel.

FERALS
Abilities pertain to heightened senses, augmented strength and agility.

LURES
Abilities pertain to enchanting voices and siren calls.

SEERS
Abilities pertain to visions, foretelling, and predictions. May also look into the past.

SHIFTERS
Abilities pertain to temporary transformation of host-bodies.

TRANSMUTERS
Abilities pertain to the transformation and manipulation of material substances.

PROLOGUE

THEY'D PLACED A CURSE ON THE ROAD.

The witch drew rein on her horse, pulling it up short. Her eyes widened as she stared ahead. The darkness of night closed in around her, the shadows of the looming mountains pooling together to obliterate everything from sight. But she was not limited to mortal vision alone. Shadow-light glowed in her eyes, and she could see clearly.

Furthermore, she could *sense* the curse. Woven with

expert skill, it pulsed with a faint musical quality that struck her perceptions in such a way as to make her see a humming web of magic blocking her path. A venator's curse. A snare set to entrap her if she dared draw near. Somehow her pursuers must have discerned her escape route, and one of those Haunts-blighted venators got ahead of her and planted this curse here. On the only safe road over the Skada Mountains, the only safe road to freedom.

The witch spat foul words between her teeth, gripping her restive horse's reins with one hand, while in her other arm something squirmed. A thin cry filled the deepening gloom. The witch looked down and gently pulled aside the flap of her dark cloak shielding the small bundle she carried.

"Hushaby, my love," she whispered to the baby, who blinked owlishly huge black eyes up at her. "Hushaby, my darling. I won't let them hurt you."

The baby quieted, though its little mouth pursed in a quivering frown. The witch gazed back over her shoulder. The road she followed had led steadily up through the foothills of the mountains, forsaking civilized countryside for the wilderness of these forested slopes. Her current position offered a commanding view of her backtrail for at least half a mile. Those pursuing her wore dark clothing to blend into the landscape, but they could not hide their souls, which gleamed bright to her shadow vision.

There they were. Approaching swiftly, urging their horses up the rough path, heedless of potential pitfalls in the fading light. They knew they were close to catching her. And they knew the curse blocked her way.

The baby cried again, wringing the witch's heart. She had to act, and fast.

She dismounted, her boots crunching on the rocky path she followed. Clutching her baby close to her breast, she left the horse behind and fled into the dark forest. The curse could not extend far, and if she took care and did not lose her sense of direction in the dark, surely she could find a way around it. There was still hope. There was still a chance. She might save her child.

Her lips curled back in a determined snarl as she climbed the difficult terrain, deeper into the forest. She was exhausted. For many nights she'd fled without rest, pausing only to change horses or to feed and tend the baby. None of this mattered. She called upon the being inside her, using the supernatural strength it offered to drive herself on, harder and harder, faster and faster. If she could only get across these mountains, she'd be free. The venators wouldn't follow her there. They wouldn't spread their numbers so thin now, not with the war having come to its head.

"Princess Olecia!"

The witch flinched, her breath catching in her throat. She should not turn. She should plunge onward, push herself to the very limit of her shade's powers. But at the sound of her name, she whirled and saw a figure appear suddenly between two trees. A figure whose face was hidden beneath a low red hood. To the witch's shadow sight, the color of that hood seemed to blaze like fire in the darkness.

The figure lifted its arm, and a trace of stray moonlight through the trees flashed on the metal fastenings of a wristbow and the sharp tip of a poisoned dart. The witch saw this all in a blink and dodged to one side. Not fast enough.

The dart bit into her thigh. Just a small prick of

pain . . . but she knew what it meant. She'd seen the effects of the poison now coursing through her system.

With a roar the witch hurled herself, not away in flight, but straight for the figure, who struggled to reload. The fury of her inner shade blazed in her veins like fire, and even as she tucked the baby tight against her, she reached out with her free hand, caught the venator by the throat, and, with a single twist of extraordinary strength, broke his neck. He fell like a straw doll to the ground at her feet, and she stepped back, watching with satisfaction as his spirit, and his shade's, struggled free of their mortal confines.

But she could not linger over this kill.

The lonely howl of a wolf filled the forest, wild and vicious, eager for blood. She cared nothing for that; wolves were no threat to one such as her. But her shade-heightened senses discerned the pounding of boots in the forest. At least two more shade hunters were on her trail. Now that their poison flowed through her veins, she would not be able to outrun them.

She staggered on, feeling the slow paralysis taking over. It would overcome her completely in a matter of minutes, possibly sooner, leaving her alive, awake, but utterly unable to fight. Then they would find her and deal her their Gentle Death, driving her soul and her shade on to eternal damnation.

And once that was done, they would burn her baby alive.

Her vision blurred. Her shade already succumbed to the poison, and she herself would follow soon. "No, no, no," she whispered desperately, wishing she dared to pray, wishing she dared hope the Goddess would hear the plea of a witch.

But she was cursed, forsaken. A creature born of blasphemy. The Goddess offered no mercy to her kind.

Even as her vision doubled, she saw a hollow tree loom before her, one good windstorm from falling over in ultimate ruin. She forced herself on toward it, feeling her arms slacken, fearing she would drop the baby.

"They don't know I have her," she told herself, her words slurring. "They don't know she's here. I won't let them find her."

She fell against the tree. A jagged opening at the swollen base of the trunk gaped like a monster's ravenous and shift? Why had she not taken time to clothe herself properly before making this sudden bid for escape? Strange . . .

The lifeless fingers did not resist as the venatrix pulled the knife free. It was a good blade, made of pure oblidite. The Order would want it submitted to the artisans for possible repurposing.

Footsteps behind her, and the voice of her comrade called out, "Hollis! Hollis, are you there?"

"I'm here, Nane," she answered without looking around. Her fellow shade hunter drew alongside her, panting hard. He was taller than her by a head, but he could not run as swiftly through the mountain forest. As he gazed down at the corpse, she sensed the questions he lacked the breath to ask.

"She killed herself," the venatrix said. "Violently."

"Haunts damn," Nane managed, puffing the curse through clenched teeth. A violent death empowered a possessing shade with a sudden and terrible burst of magic as it was expelled from the host body. "Did you catch it?"

The venatrix shook her head. "It was too powerful. It

escaped into the wood."

Nane laid a hand on her shoulder. "It doesn't matter. It's unlikely to find a new host body out in the wild like this. Certainly no human host."

"But we don't know for sure." The venatrix wiped sweat from her face and pushed the red hood back from her head, allowing a little breeze to cool her flushed skin. "I don't understand it, Nane," she said, shaking her head. "Why would Olecia leave her mother's protection at this time? Surely Odile would want to keep all of her children close now that the war is turning."

Nane shrugged. "Maybe the princess could see that the prophecy is about to be fulfilled. Dread Odile must fall to the Goddess's chosen champion. Perhaps Olecia thought she could escape her mother's fate."

"Perhaps." Hollis sighed heavily. "I suppose we'll never know."

She and her comrade gathered up the witch's corpse and carried it away through the trees. Soon, after the sounds of horses' hooves faded into the distance, the dark pine forests of Skada were quiet once more.

Deep in the hollow of a dead tree, a baby stirred. She

whimpered, kicking at the swaddling that bound her limbs to her little body. Then she opened her mouth and uttered a heart-wrenching cry.

In the forest shadows, a deeper shadow moved. A wolf approached the hollow tree, eyes gleaming strangely in the darkness. It sniffed and caught the scent of a small, frail human, alone and abandoned.

Its lips curled in an eager snarl.

CHAPTER I

NINETEEN YEARS LATER

THE MILLER HAD JUST LOADED THE FINAL SACK OF freshly ground flour into his wagon, preparing for a trip into the village, when he saw the Red Hood ride down the main road past his mill. He drew in a sharp breath and let it out in a curse, then stepped away from the cart, staring hard, willing that figure on horseback to ride on by, not to stop, not to look his way.

Instead, she turned her horse's head and headed up the path straight for him.

He'd never seen the Red Hood in person before. Rumor abounded throughout the borough, and he'd even spoken with those who claimed to have glimpsed her out riding her solitary circuit trails. A figure of dread, but a necessary evil. Without her presence the countryside would be plagued by shades and shade-taken. The miller knew he should be grateful.

But this didn't make him less afraid.

"Ebern. Come here, boy," he barked.

His son appeared in the mill doorway, his face, hair, and hands white with the flour he'd been cleaning from the great millstone. "What—?" His voice broke off as he, too, saw the figure approaching. Without another word he hastened to his father's side, tucking his small body close as though to hide behind the miller.

"Stay quiet and don't draw her eye," the miller muttered. "You don't want what lives inside her looking at you directly."

The boy nodded solemnly and clutched his father's hand.

The Red Hood rode her tall brown horse right up to the miller's wagon. The miller couldn't see much of her face under the shadow of her hood, though he got the impression she was younger than he'd expected. Her right arm boasted a leather bracer and a folded wristbow. From her left bracer, a sharp iron spike protruded like a fang. Strung across her chest was a series of small quivers filled with darts. From her belt hung three sheaths, one of which held a long knife, but the others . . . they held weapons stranger by far.

"Are you Miller Roch?"

She had a deep voice for a woman, with a slight roughness like a growl on its edge. The miller felt the intensity of her gaze fixed upon him.

"I am." He swallowed, trying to wet his dry throat. "How can I . . . How can I be of service?"

The Red Hood dismounted, swinging lightly down from her saddle. With her horse on a loose rein, she moved several steps closer. The miller resisted the urge to back away. His son whimpered and pressed into his side.

"Word has reached me of a shade-taken dog hereabouts," the Red Hood said. "The local bailiff tells me the dog belongs to you."

The miller shook his head quickly. "Our dog's gone.

Five days now. Shade-taken or not, it's not here. We have . . ." He swallowed again, struggling to speak without trembling. "We have nothing to do with any shade-taken."

The Red Hood tilted her head to one side. Then, to the miller's surprise, she pushed back her hood, allowing the sun to shine full upon a strangely lovely, strangely terrifying face. Her skin was pale but freckled from long hours out riding in the sun, despite the protection of her hood. Dark hair pulled into a long braid draped across one shoulder. Her brows were thick and slightly drawn together so that a faint line puckered between them, giving her an unconsciously ferocious expression.

However, it was her eyes that struck fear into the miller. They were utterly black with no discernible difference between pupil and iris. And behind those eyes gleamed strange light and movement.

His knees shook. He hoped he wouldn't disgrace himself in front of his son.

"I am told that the dog spoke," the Red Hood said.

"Not that I ever heard." The miller felt his boy's fingers clench his hand still tighter.

As though drawn by that almost imperceptible movement, the Red Hood's gaze dropped from the miller to the boy. "And what is your name?" she asked.

The boy drew a choking breath and looked up at his father, whose attempt at a soothing smile came out more like a grimace. "Answer the lady."

Unwilling to meet the Red Hood's terrible eyes, the boy stared at his shoes. "Ebern," he muttered so softly, the miller himself could hardly hear him.

"Tell me, Ebern," the Red Hood said, "did the dog ever speak to you?"

The boy shook his head, frowned, then nodded. He added all in a rush, "Silky never meant no harm!"

The Red Hood narrowed her eyes, and her head tilted slightly to one side. "How did Silky speak to you? Did you know the words she used?" When the boy didn't answer, confused by the question, she tried again, "Did Silky speak in Gaulian, or was it some other language you heard?"

The boy turned his face into his father's side, unable to answer for terror. The miller drew him close, wrapping his arm protectively around the child's bony shoulders.

"The boy's untaken," he said. "You can test him."

"Don't worry. The boy's soul is not my concern." The Red Hood dropped her horse's reins, took three steps closer, and crouched, bringing her face level with Ebern's. The child twisted, wanting to escape her gaze, but then somehow her eyes caught his, and he couldn't look away. He stared at her, unblinking, tears forming but not falling.

"What did the dog sound like when she spoke to you, Ebern?" the Red Hood asked in what was possibly meant to be a gentle tone, if such a thing were possible for a voice like hers.

The boy sniffed. "She . . . she sounded like my sister."

At this, the stern line between the Red Hood's brows deepened. She stood once more and faced the miller. "You have a daughter?"

"Aye. Heldy is my girl."

"May I speak to her?"

The miller shook his head. "Heldy run off with her sweetheart a month ago now. No one's seen them since."

Her mouth pursed into a thin line as she considered this information. The world was silent other than the sound of the river flowing and the mill wheel creaking as it turned. "Tell me," she said at last. "Why did Heldy run away with her young man? Did you not approve the match?"

"I . . . I don't see how that has anything to do with the dog."

"Answer the question."

The miller rubbed the back of his neck, his jaw clenching. No matter how he wished to, he didn't dare curse in the presence of this imposing young woman, not while those black eyes of hers were fixed on him. "I had promised her hand to Farmer Malger," he admitted at last. "She didn't favor him, though he'd have been a better match. Owned his own land and all, not like that boy of hers."

"Farmer Malger. The man who was killed three nights ago?"

The miller nodded slowly. "So, you heard of that." He hastened to add, "It had nothing to do with me or mine, I swear to you."

"Malger's brother claims to have seen your dog over the farmer's body. He told the bailiff that its eyes glowed with magic."

The miller's mouth twisted with anger. "He's trying to cast a slur on me because my daughter didn't fancy his brother. That's all. It's wild talk and naught else."

The Red Hood said nothing. She only looked at him.

"You can search my house, search my mill." The miller swung an arm to indicate the whole of his small domain. "Search all my grounds hereabout. You'll not find hide nor hair of the dog. If she had anything to do with Malger's death, if she be shade-taken as they claim, we know nothing about it. You've got to believe we'd give her up to you at once if we had her. We want no trouble with . . . your kind."

Still, her eyes refused to leave his face. He lowered his gaze and bowed his head, like a man waiting for the executioner's blow to fall.

"Tell me the swiftest route to Farmer Malger's farm."

With a shuddering gasp, the miller looked up to find that she was no longer looking at him but turning her horse about and preparing to mount. All in a rush he told her the road to take, his heart lifting with hope that she would go, that she would remove her malevolent shadow from his doorstep.

The Red Hood mounted, then paused to adjust the various sheaths dangling from her belt into more comfortable positions. She pulled the hood back up over her head, hiding her face from view. "Thank you, Miller Roch," she said. "I've got what I came for."

She turned her horse's head back to the main road. Just as she spurred it into motion, the boy broke away from his father and called out, "Are you going to hurt Silky?"

"Hush! Hush!" the miller cried, but too late.

The Red Hood paused and looked back around, fixing her stare on the boy. The miller's breath caught, and he clutched his child by the shoulders.

But the Red Hood only said, "I'm going to liberate your dog. And save all of you."

With that, she rode away.

Hollis was absolutely going to kill her.

A grim smile twisted Ayleth's mouth as she left Roch's mill behind and entered the main road. She could only hope the miller's directions were accurate. She was unfamiliar with this part of the borough, and it wouldn't do for her to become lost on the way to her very first solo hunt.

Two days ago, she'd received the summons to investigate these shade rumors, packed up, and left her mountain outpost. During the long ride she'd had plenty of time to consider the undeniable fact that Hollis was going to kill her. And she probably deserved it. She had set off on this hunt without her mistress's permission, and when Hollis found out . . .

Ayleth winced but nonetheless firmed her jaw. How many times had she begged for a chance to hunt on her own, to prove her abilities? She wasn't some green apprentice anymore. She was a venatrix—a shade huntress, trained and ready.

Besides, Hollis was away when the bailiff arrived with word of the shade-taken dog. She'd been out on another hunt and might not return for weeks. Meanwhile, the dog, which had already killed one man, might kill again. It must be dealt with.

Ayleth's grip on the pommel of her saddle tightened. Maybe this was the opportunity she'd been waiting for.

She shaded her gaze, peering across the fields of barley and rye to a distant farmhouse. If she carried back the carcass of a shade-taken dog, the spirit inside successfully ousted and the world made a little safer, then maybe . . . maybe . . .

"Maybe Hollis will see that I'm ready for a posting of my own. Maybe she'll let me present myself to the Golden Prince."

The words slipped between her lips in a whisper so soft that her horse's sensitive ears didn't even flicker at the sound. She flushed, however, and her eyes darted to either side, as though someone in the surrounding fields might have heard her. Might even now mock her for imagining she could win the approval of a prince.

But why not? Ayleth sat straighter in her saddle and drew a breath through her nostrils. Perhaps she was audacious. But if she didn't try, she'd never know. She'd end up stuck out here in this backwater borough for the rest of her life and never discover all she was capable of accomplishing.

She pictured herself wearing a crisp uniform, its buckles bright with polish. Her cloak, unstained by years of hard use, would sweep dramatically behind her as she marched along a pillared hall to the base of a high pedestal on which stood a throne. The figure on that throne . . . Her mind couldn't quite envision him, but the Golden Prince, the prophesied heir to the kingdom, could be nothing less than glorious and golden and shining. She would salute him with her scorpiona arm, vowing her service, and he would stretch out his right hand over her and say—

Her imagination came to a lurching halt as painful realities closed in. What would he say? Probably something along the lines of "So, what exactly are your credentials again?"

Ayleth chewed the inside of her cheek and, with a shake of her head, refocused on the landscape around her. It was a stupid daydream. Besides, until she brought down this shade-taken dog, she wasn't going anywhere.

Time to focus on the business at hand.

According to the miller's directions, the farmhouse just ahead had belonged to Farmer Malger. It was a sturdy structure built of local stone, its roof boasting fresh thatch. Several large barns stood beyond it, also stone.

Farmer Malger had done well for himself.

Until a shade-taken dog tore out his throat five nights ago.

Ayleth scanned lush, golden fields nearly ready to yield a good harvest. Shading her eyes with her hand, she searched the well-ordered crops for signs of disturbance. Farmer Malger had been killed in one of his own fields, and . . . Ah! there it was. The farmer's remains had long since been carried off, but signs of a struggle remained, barley stalks broken and bent.

Ayleth dismounted and tied her horse to a fencepost. "I'll be right back, Chestibor," she murmured to her mount. He gave her a placid look, and she patted his broad cheek before climbing over the fence to wade in among the tufted stalks.

Something stirred inside her. As she approached that place in the field where violence had been done, something dark shifted in her soul, strained at its tethers.

The hunt, a voice growled in her head. *The hunt, the hunt.*

"*Soon,*" Ayleth answered, speaking in her mind, not with her mortal mouth.

Wind, sun, and rain had already erased the dead man's

blood. Ayleth stood in that place of recent death, looking round at the broken stalks, her eyes bright and alert, her senses keen. Her mortal senses . . . and those other, stranger senses reaching out through her awareness.

I smell shade, said the voice in her head.

When it spoke, Ayleth inhaled and believed she smelled it too. Only *smelled* wasn't the right word. This was no mortal sense burning through her blood and bones. This was shadow sense—a perception of spirit. In her mind, she could almost see what was no longer there. She could almost see the phantom shape of Malger's body lying in ruin as he struggled to breathe through a ripped-out throat, blood pouring from the arteries and soaking the ground.

She could smell the desperation of Malger's soul. The fear. And . . . and what was that other scent?

Ayleth crouched to place her hands over the broken stalks, right where the dead man's torso must have crushed them as he fell. Breathing in deep, she closed her eyes, allowing those powerful senses to work. What was this? Fear and desperation and . . .

"Guilt?" she whispered.

Her eyes opened. She frowned at the ruined barley over which she crouched. Straightening, she sat back on her heels and looked around the lonely field.

Shade! Shade! growled the voice inside her.

Yes, she could faintly catch a trace of a dark spirit. But not enough to follow it.

Even as she considered her options, the fingers of her right hand moved almost unconsciously to one of the three sheaths on her belt. Coming to a decision, she stood and drew the weapon. This was no ordinary weapon, no dagger or cudgel. It was her Vocos—a double-headed pipe carved from animal bone. An ancient instrument, slightly yellowed with age, but highly polished and still perfect in pitch and tone.

With a quick, proficient motion, Ayleth snapped the two pipe heads open so that they formed a V from the mouthpiece. Drawing a breath deep into her gut, she blew. The drone burst into life, its skirling voice plunging down into her soul like the roots of a mighty tree, twisting and turning into the soil, into bedrock.

The fingers of her right hand moved lightly along the five holes of the recorder, picking out the opening lines of melody—the Summoning. The powerful spell song spilled out into the air, winding around the deep reverberations of the drone then spreading out in a burst of wild music. All beyond the range of mortal hearing. Music meant for the spirit world alone.

As she played, Ayleth closed her eyes and concentrated, not on the mortal world around her, but on the realm of spirit. The realm of her own mind. Here there were no fields, no farmhouses. In this realm, dark pines loomed tall, casting long shadows cut with brilliant rays of sunlight.

The Song of Summoning whirled around her, then swept away through this mind forest. In response to its call, the deepest shadows cast by the pine trees coalesced, shifting, writhing, solidifying to form a hulking shape shrouded in a coat of dense midnight fur. Red eyes glared at Ayleth, flashing like newly sparked embers.

Let me go. Let me hunt, the growling voice in her mind demanded.

"You will hunt, Laranta," Ayleth answered, speaking in spirit while her mortal mouth continued playing the Vocos pipes. *"But you will obey me."*

The being approached through the forest until it stood before Ayleth. Its head was nearly level with hers, its hackles raised with tension, its claws digging into the dirt of this mindscape.

Laranta. Her nearest companion. Her greatest enemy.

This was the dire truth behind the skills she practiced. This was the truth for all who dedicated their lives to the Order of Saint Evander. As a venatrix, Ayleth battled shades: forces of the Haunts which invaded this world and plagued mortal beings. But she could not fight shades if she were not herself a shade-taken.

Ayleth was possessed of this spirit which endowed her with tremendous power . . . and threatened her life and soul every minute of every day.

In the mortal world, Ayleth's fingers shifted the melody of the Summoning into a new melody, the Song of Command. The spell of music lashed out at the deadly spirit.

Laranta cringed. *Why do you hurt me? I want to help. I want to hunt.*

Ayleth steeled herself against these protests. She must keep her shade in line, must control it with care. This was her first solo hunt, and she dared not make a mistake.

"*Find the scent, Laranta,*" she spoke in the spirit world. "*Find the trail.*"

She played a new variation on her pipes, shifting the spell's focus, and her shade poured out of her mind in a dark stream of magic and malice to manifest before her in the physical world as a huge black wolf. This was only an illusion—beings of spirit have no physical body—but to Ayleth its appearance was completely convincing in every particular. She could see every hair of its shaggy coat, every muscle rippling beneath its hide. Every sharp tooth as it curled its upper lip.

Obedient to her command, the shade wolf lowered its head and began sniffing about. Ayleth, meanwhile, played an end to the spell song and let the pipes drop from her lips. She watched as Laranta, ears pricked, nose still close to the ground, moved away from the place where Malger's body had lain.

Suddenly the wolf shade drew up short, a growl of excitement reverberating in its throat. *I have it.* Then it lunged forward, crying, *The hunt! The hunt!*

In its eagerness, the shade pulled Ayleth several steps

in its wake, dragging her along by the soul tether connecting them. "*Wait,*" she commanded, yanking back control. Her wolf shade dropped to its belly, obedient to its mistress's command.

Ayleth snapped her pipes shut and tucked the instrument back into its sheath. She couldn't wear her red hood while on the hunt. It was a symbol of her Order, too well known in these parts. She couldn't risk having her prey spot her at a distance and recognize what she was, so she tucked the hood out of sight before drawing her scorpiona from its holster at her hip. With practiced ease, she fixed the small crossbow to her right arm bracer and loaded it with a poison-tipped dart.

"*All right, Laranta,*" she said, turning to her wolf shade. "*Find the shade. Go!*"

With a savage growl, Laranta leapt up and streaked across the field, following the dark spirit's trail. Ayleth sprang into action, racing along behind her shade, and her heart gloried in the exhilaration of her first real hunt.

CHAPTER 2

SHE'D BEEN TOLD HER NAME WAS AYLETH DI FEROSA, but she was fairly certain it was a lie.

Hollis had said that Ayleth's people, the di Ferosas, were from a northern kingdom, and that she was an orphan taken in by a local castra to be brought up in the Order of Saint Evander.

"The north sent many young trainees to Perrinion following the Witch Wars," Hollis explained to her when she was old enough to start questioning these things.

"Dread Odile left our kingdom so decimated, there was a dire shortage of potential recruits. We had to draw from the other four Gaulian kingdoms. Thus, you were sent to me."

It was a good enough story as stories went, and it was impossible to either prove or disprove. Ayleth had never had opportunity to travel north and look for signs of any di Ferosas who supposedly lived there. In truth, though she searched her mind with great care, she could remember nothing about the time before she lived at Gillanluòc Outpost with the short, taciturn woman who was her mistress.

"The Order gave you to me to train," Hollis told her when pressed. "That training is where your life begins and ends. Your past is done. Your future is the hunt. Always and only the hunt."

But Ayleth had not come to Hollis until she was seven years old. She should have some memories, however vague, of a life before then. If not of family, then of the castra where she had lived with other initiates chosen by the Order. Surely, she must have some memory of the venators and venatrices who had cared for her, of the conservator who ran the castra, of the dormitory in which she slept, of the training, the prayers, the ceremonies of indoctrination. Something. Anything at all.

There was only Hollis in her memory. And when she tried to look farther back, nothing except . . .

With a quick head shake, Ayleth forced her concentration back to the present, focusing on her wolf shade ahead. Laranta pursued the shade's trail, following a trace undetectable to mortal senses. Sometimes Ayleth wondered at how eager her shade was to pursue others of its kind. But shades generally cared nothing for other shades, and Laranta existed to hunt any and all prey.

Soon they left the fields behind and entered wilder country beyond the farmlands. Here the fertile valley gave way to the rolling foothills of the Skada Mountains, where boulders bulged through the soil and trees grew tall with sparse undergrowth. Ayleth loped along behind her shade, her gait unconsciously matching the wolf's easy, long-legged stride, not quite a run, but a pace she could maintain for long distances without tiring. The shade's strength coursed through her limbs, adding to her speed and agility. This was all second nature to her. She could not remember a time before her Possession, could not imagine what such a life must have been like—a life without access to magic.

When the soul tether connecting them pulled taut, Ayleth put on more speed to keep up with her shade. She would have liked to use her Vocos pipes to give Laranta even more freedom, but such was not the Evanderian way.

"Your shade is always your worst enemy," Hollis had told her more times than she could count. "They are spiritual entities of pure malice and mayhem. You must never be tempted to think otherwise. The power inside you is a weapon to be used in our ongoing war against the Haunts . . . a weapon that will turn on you in an instant if you ever let down your guard."

Like any other shade, Laranta would snatch at every opportunity to gain ascendancy, to take control of its host body. Eventually, if her shade grew strong enough, it could oust Ayleth's soul entirely, leaving her spirit to wander revenant in this world until she faded into oblivion, unable to ascend to the Goddess.

But that fate was preferable to damnation; and

damnation alone awaited a soul whose body perished while still shade-taken. Separated from its physical host, the evil shade spirit would be drawn inexorably into the Haunts, dragging with it the spirit of its host body . . . unless a venator or venatrix could first perform the necessary spell song to separate the two souls.

Regarding her current hunt, Ayleth knew she needn't worry about the saving of souls. A dog's soul was not considered important enough to merit the complex spell of separation. She must simply find the shade-taken animal, kill it quietly, and then drive the shade soul into the Haunts. The fate of the dog's soul was not her concern.

The grade became steep, and Ayleth used her hands as much as her feet to navigate a treacherous ridge, though Laranta moved ahead of her with ease, her heavy form seeming almost to float up the rock-strewn slope. After hauling herself up a particularly steep crag, Ayleth was relieved to find more level ground ahead. Her keen ears caught the sound of running water.

Laranta suddenly stiffened. A jolt of excitement rippled back through their soul tether. *"What is it?"* Ayleth demanded. *"What do you smell?"*

Shade! Near! The wolf shade brimmed with eagerness, but instead of dashing on ahead, it transformed into little more than a shadow slinking beneath the trees.

Ayleth dropped low and crept after her shade. She'd already armed her scorpiona with a dart dipped in the deadly venom called **mòrder** by the Evanderians. Ayleth knew the poison better by its colloquial name, the Gentle Death. If she was lucky, she could take a shot before her prey ever knew she was near. One bite of the Gentle Death, and a shade-taken would doze off and peacefully die in its sleep. Thus, the possessing spirit inside would be eased out of this life, and driving it into the Haunts would be a simple matter.

If she missed and the dog attacked her—if she was forced to deliver a violent death—the shade, empowered by violence, would burst from its fallen host body with a force so great that she would never be able to catch and subdue it. It would escape and likely find a new host body many miles away, and she would have to begin the hunt all over again.

A violent death was her very last resort.

Ayleth crept up a slope, almost on her belly, moving with precision. Reaching the top of the rise where Laranta lay in wait, big and dark and ready to burst with the zeal of bloodlust, she peered into a rocky dale through which ran a sparkling stream.

On the banks of that stream lay the body of a deer. A huge dog tore into its abdomen, staining its white muzzle red with blood and gore. Its savage grunts echoed off the valley slopes, a sharp contrast to the placid burble of running water.

"*Give me your sight,*" Ayleth commanded.

Laranta complied, and Ayleth felt the shift behind her eyes. She still perceived the mortal world, but now a world of spirit overlaid all. She could not have used words to describe how she experienced this alternate reality, but in many ways it was more like hearing. A pulse of music and of light, shimmering strands of song and energy.

She studied the dog. No trace of any dog soul remained. Silky herself was no more; her body had been utterly overtaken by the shade spirit in possession.

Now came the difficult part. She must try to determine

the type of shade hidden in that dog body. This was never easy, for shades were incredibly varied in their powers and abilities. The Order had classified them into ten primary categories, but within each category were endless variations and expressions of magic. If she used the wrong type of poison on the shade, she risked enraging rather than subduing it. In the critical moment, this could mean disaster.

But even after years of practice using Laranta's vision, she never could identify the shade by sight alone. Unless she witnessed a demonstration of its particular magic, she couldn't know for certain.

Ayleth's brow constricted in concentration. If she could strike the dog with the Gentle Death, there would be no need to categorize the shade. The Gentle Death worked efficiently on all shade-taken. And untaken too, for that matter.

She adjusted her position on the ground, stretching out her right arm and sighting along the scorpiona. The dog kept moving, shifting around its kill in the effort to sate its ravening hunger.

"*Still your breathing.*" Hollis's words came back to her,

words she'd heard a hundred times while she practiced hitting targets with her scorpiona. "*Still your breathing. Take no risks. One shot, and one shot only. This is not a game—it's life or damnation.*"

Though her heart raced with the desire to fire, Ayleth drew a long, silent breath and held it. She held it until she felt her heartbeat slow, the pulse in her veins leveling out. She focused her vision, aiming straight for the dog's heart. Her thumb moved, rested on the triggering mechanism, began to squeeze.

Suddenly the dog looked up, straight at her.

Ayleth flinched. It wasn't a dog at all. How had she not seen it before? It was a young woman—a girl younger than Ayleth herself, with fair hair braided and pinned up on her head, wearing a rough-woven but neat shift and smock. Soft, kind eyes looked up to the place where Ayleth now crouched.

"I see you there," she said in a gentle voice, lisping slightly due to a gap between her front teeth. "Won't you come out?"

Ayleth stared. Somewhere in the back of her mind, she thought she heard Laranta growling, *Take the shot! Make the kill! Shade, shade, shade!* But she couldn't quite focus on those words. Not with that young woman gazing at her with such a beseeching expression.

"Please," the girl said, "come down here. You frighten me, hiding there in the shadows."

Ayleth gasped, realizing she still had her finger on the trigger, still had the Gentle Death aimed at the young woman's heart. She quickly released all pressure and turned the scorpiona away. She got to her feet, her hands up, and stepped out of the forest shadows into full view. A thought came to her, though she couldn't say for certain from where.

"Are you . . . are you Heldy? The miller's daughter?" she asked.

The girl's face crumpled with sorrow. "She was my host. I was with her for many years, silently, in secret. I loved her dearly, and she loved me." Tears formed in those gentle eyes, spilling over. The girl wiped them away with trembling fingers. "She was killed."

"Killed?" Though she knew she should keep her distance, something compelled Ayleth to edge down the slope into the valley. Her boots skidded on the loose stony soil, but she kept her balance and didn't take her eyes off the girl. "How was Heldy killed?"

At that question, the gentleness of the girl's face vanished in an expression of sudden ferocity—an expression that looked strangely like the dog, its muzzle covered in blood. "Violently," she answered. Then, "Let me show you."

Ayleth catches her breath, blinking hard.

She is no longer standing in the afternoon light under the shadows of trees. It is night, and before her lies a crossroads where a girl waits, the same gentle-faced girl with the gap-toothed smile, clutching a small bundle of belongings in her hands.

A boy appears, hastening down the road. He calls out, "Heldy! Heldy, I'm here!"

The girl turns to him and, with a glad cry, runs and flings her arms around his neck, crying, "Kuno, dearest!"

They embrace, and Ayleth looks away, embarrassed by the intimacy of the scene. But where her gaze turns, darkness moves.

Emerging from the hedge where he has hidden, a tall, heavyset man brandishes a pitchfork. Before Ayleth can open her mouth to cry out a warning, he steps onto the road and drives the cruel prongs straight into the boy's back. The middle prong pierces his spine, the other two drive through his gut—straight through into the girl he holds in his arms.

Ayleth's vision swims with blood. She tries to move, tries to shout, but her body is utterly frozen with shock. She watches the two lovers fall, still pinned together in their final embrace, gasping and choking as their deaths take them.

And she watches their souls struggle free of their bodies. A single soul orb rises out of the boy . . . but two entwined souls spring out of the girl, one mortal and one shade. The shade spirit blazes with the light of a raging inferno, red and angry and empowered by the violence of death. It tears away from the mortal soul, leaving it to quiver in the air above the body in which it had been housed. The shade spirit shoots off into the night, seeking a new host.

All this Ayleth beholds in the space of an instant. In that same instant, the man pulls his pitchfork out of the two bodies and stands over them, panting hard. Then he bends, catches up the girl's corpse in his arms, and carries her away into the night. No doubt he will return soon for the boy.

Ayleth blinks . . .

The stream and the valley swam back into focus.

Ayleth swayed on her feet, her breath rough in her throat. The dead girl stood across from her, sweet and wholesome and alive. But nothing more than a projected memory. An illusion.

"I took the first host body I could find," she said. "Heldy's father had set his dog on her trail, trying to catch her before she and Kuno escaped. I found an opening in the dog's eye, and I entered and took possession." She met Ayleth's searching gaze, and her gentle features once more twisted with wrath. "I lost my Heldy. But I could take vengeance on her slayer."

Ayleth stared into that face, which was so human and yet so not. Again she heard Laranta at the back of her mind, growling warnings. The shade inside the dog was manipulating her mind, making her see things that were not there. She was in grave danger, standing here. She should raise her scorpiona and shoot the image of the girl in the chest.

Only the image was not the reality. Shooting an illusion would do no good. She had to see the dog itself. But for the moment, her eyes were not her own.

"Do not send me back to the Haunts," the girl said,

tilting her head to one side. "I escaped that realm, and I have known true joy in this world. Joy with my Heldy. I do not wish to return to the darkness."

Ayleth didn't answer. She reached into herself, searching for the soul tether that connected her to Laranta. If she could find it, she might be able to pull Laranta close. Her wolf shade would have the power necessary to break whatever spell held her mind in its grip.

"I will do no harm in this body," the girl persisted, taking a step nearer to Ayleth.

"You . . . you killed Farmer Malger," Ayleth said as she struggled to tear her gaze away from the girl. "*Laranta!*" she called in her mind, desperately. "*Laranta, come!*"

"I took my vengeance. For Heldy," the girl said, smiling softly. "I have no reason to kill again. I will drive this new host body deep into the wilds. No one will see it. No one will know."

Ayleth shook her head. "You do not belong in this world. You do not belong—"

She broke off with a cry as something huge hit her in the chest, knocking her to the ground. The girl vanished, and suddenly Ayleth's vision was full of bloodied teeth, and her ears roared with wild snarling. On instinct alone she got her left arm up between her throat and those snapping jaws. The iron spike on her bracer tore through fur and down into flesh, and the dog shrieked, an unnatural, hideous sound.

Shades cannot abide the touch of iron. The spirit inside the dog recoiled, and Ayleth was able to push herself upright and into a defensive crouch. The dog, its head low, barked savagely at her as blood dripped from the wound in its neck. It crouched, ready to spring.

"*Laranta!*" Ayleth cried.

Here, the wolf replied. Her shade, a being of spirit, could not physically strike the dog. But this didn't matter.

The shade-taken dog leapt for her throat just as a surge of magic shot through Ayleth's limbs. She sprang up and caught the dog by the neck and muzzle, bracing herself so that she would not fall over again. The dog writhed and tore at her but could not break her grip. Its teeth snapped and scraped at her cheek, trying to find and rip out her jugular.

Ayleth let go with one hand. It was almost her

undoing. The dog felt her grip weaken and lunged at her with renewed fury. Her right hand sought the quivers strung across her chest, found one. She only had one chance. Her guess had better be right. Let it be right, let it be—

She drove the dart straight into the dog's eye.

The dog shrieked again, a sound that should never come from an animal's throat. It ripped itself free of her hold, backing away, shaking its head. The dart fell to the ground, but its poison coursed into the dog's veins.

The paralysis was begun.

Feeling its host body weakening, the shade inside lashed out at Ayleth. She saw again not the dog but Heldy . . . only Heldy with three gaping wounds in her gut, blood pouring down her shift, out from her mouth, out from the corners of her eyes.

"What have you done to me?" she screamed, her hands reaching out as though to tear Ayleth's face to shreds. Ayleth danced back out of reach. Though the girl was only an image in her mind, she did not doubt the shade's power to kill. But that power was fading fast.

She'd guessed correctly. The shade was an

Apparition—a manipulator of minds. And the poison she'd chosen now worked through both its mortal host and its spirit.

Ayleth watched the paralysis take effect. The dog body could not resist long. It fell over in a matter of moments, its heavy breathing easing into a slow, steady rhythm. The shade struggled longer, knowing what would happen next. It struck at Ayleth, using the girl's shape in her mind but without strength enough to reach her. Ayleth simply waited.

At last the poison worked through to the core of the shade. The image of the girl faded away and vanished. Ayleth looked down on the sleeping form of the dog and saw the spirit inside it, no longer raging but humming peacefully.

The Gentle Death was still slotted into place on her scorpiona. She took aim for the dog's heart and shot the dart straight to its mark.

While the deadly poison took effect, lulling the mortal frame into death, Ayleth folded her scorpiona and reached for another of the three sheaths on her belt to draw a second set of pipes—the Detrudos. Like the

Vocos, it was carved of shade-taken bones. Like the Vocos, it was double-headed, drone and recorder. But the Detrudos boasted eight holes on its recorder rather than five, and the drone was pitched much lower. With the Vocos she crafted spells to influence her own shade. Using the Detrudos, she might, with care, influence other shades.

The air trembled with a ripple of, not heat, but . . . horror.

Ayleth felt it. And her gut twisted in response.

The Haunts. The Haunts were opening.

Overhead, the sky trembled like a veil of fine silk being clawed from the other side. Reality itself ripped apart; the empty beyond gaped wide. Ayleth blinked, and her mind balked against the insanity of what it perceived, trying to create reason where no reason existed.

With an effort of will, she tore her gaze away. But a terrible need threatened to overwhelm her, a need she fought with every fiber of her being. Don't look! Don't look! Long ago, Hollis had warned her: To look into the mouth of the Haunts was to gaze upon madness itself. Few could survive.

Yet despite the terror, despite the dread shaking her to her core, that strange and dreadful curiosity called her . . . to see . . . to know . . .

Don't look! Don't look!

She focused her very soul on the shade rising from the dog's body. Lifting the Detrudos to her lips, she called the deep, groaning drone to life. It bloomed from the pipe head like an ebony flower, filling the world with an aroma of deeper places on the far side of midnight. Her fingers danced over the recorder holes, playing the Song of Expulsion.

The shade could not resist—not without the violence of death to empower it. The spell song wrapped around it like chains. Ayleth's fingers moved naturally to the correct notes, picking out a harsh variation, and she wound those chains of magic tight.

The Haunts pulled, tugging at her soul. The void sought to drag all spirits to its center, there to compress them at last into nothingness. But it could not take her so long as her soul still clung to its mortal frame. Nor could it take her shade.

So, it took what it could. As Ayleth offered up the soul

of the shade bound in the spell song, the Haunts opened wide and swallowed it whole, deep into the crushing, consuming chaos.

Then, with a clap of darkness that knocked Ayleth to her knees, the gate snapped shut.

CHAPTER 3

"YOU'RE . . . YOU'RE QUITE SURE IT WAS HELDY? AND young Kuno?"

Ayleth stood in the long shadow cast by the tall millhouse, facing the village bailiff. Over his shoulder she saw Miller Roch in the doorway of his millhouse, watching her closely from a good thirty paces away. The great millwheel creaked, gushing river water as it turned, and she was certain its noise prevented the miller from overhearing anything she said to the bailiff.

Still, she didn't like the way he watched her. As though he somehow knew that she brought word of his dead daughter.

She focused her attention back on the bailiff's runny eyes. "I can't know for certain," she said. "I've never met either. I know only that you'll find the two bodies somewhere near the crossroads I described, not far from Malger's farm. I believe them to be Heldy and her young man."

The bailiff rubbed a hand down his face. "Ah, it's a sad business!" he sighed and cast a quick glance back over his shoulder at the miller. Both men had taken pains not to look at the huge dog she'd carried back with her, slung over her shoulders. It lay at her feet, a lifeless carcass covered in deer blood. The bailiff had asked for no details of the hunt. Neither did he ask how she'd come by her knowledge of the dead bodies. He didn't want to know.

Instead, he bowed and made the sign of the holy blessing to her, touching forehead, heart, and lips in turn. "We are in your debt, Lady Venatrix, and the debt of Saint Evander. If there is any way we can repay what we owe . . .?"

He left the sentence hanging. He knew perfectly well that the Evanderian Order forbade accepting payment for hunts. He also knew that, in lieu of payment, the Order accepted—sometimes demanded—certain "donations to the cause." He wrung his hands, blinking fast, his teeth bared in what might have been meant as an ingratiating smile.

"A cart," Ayleth said. "I need a cart. To carry the remains back to my outpost."

The bailiff let out a huge sigh. This request could be managed with very little trouble or expense to himself. He made the holy sign again and offered assurances that a cart should be brought at once.

Within the hour, Ayleth found herself back on the road astride Chestibor, her big brown gelding, who also pulled the rumbling two-wheeled cart without visible effort. A two-day journey up the mountains to the outpost lay before them, but Ayleth didn't mind. She was glad to be going.

This hunt had been . . . not what she'd expected. The battle had left her body bruised, but worse than that, it had left her mind shaken. The Apparition had penetrated her mind, manipulated her thoughts, made her see and hear things that weren't there. The experience now took a toll.

She shuddered. The image of the miller's daughter shimmered in her memory. And she heard again the words spoken through the girl's mouth by the Apparition:

"I have known true joy in this world. Joy with my Heldy."

It was probably a lie. A manipulation. In all likelihood the shade had long ago ousted Heldy's soul from her body and taken complete possession. Even the vision it had shown Ayleth of Heldy's death—the moment when she watched the two souls rise out of the girl's ruined body—could easily have been a false projection of the event. One couldn't trust a shade, particularly not one desperate to continue its own existence in this world.

And yet . . .

There had been a compelling truthfulness in the shade's voice and words. A shining in its spirit that spoke of deep emotions—love and loss, heartbreak and vengeance. Was it possible the shade had felt all these things? Or were they merely the remnants of stolen emotions taken by force during its possession of Heldy's body?

A shade cannot love. A being of pure malice cannot comprehend such noble feeling, such purity. So Saint Evander wrote in his holy script, and who was Ayleth to doubt the teachings of a saint?

And yet . . .

While riding along on that lonely road under the fading warmth of the setting sun, Ayleth drew a long breath and reached down inside her consciousness. Down into the world of her mind, the cool, dark forest of pine spice and shadows. Down where Laranta crouched, quiet and satisfied, pleased by the success of the hunt. The wolf shade had been irked when Ayleth pulled out the Vocos pipes and played the Song of Suppression. But she hadn't fought the song, had allowed herself to be driven back into the mind forest that was her home.

"Not *her*," Ayleth corrected herself out loud, startling Chestibor so that he flicked his ears and tossed his head. "Not her. *It.*"

She was always making that mistake—referring to her wolf shade as gendered. Hollis never failed to reprimand her for even that tiny slip. Shades were beings of spirit and had no gender. To perceive her shade in such personified terms was to begin to trust it, which was the first step on the road to ultimate ruin.

Nevertheless, in light of these recent experiences, Ayleth couldn't help asking herself the secret, dangerous question: Was it possible for a savage shade such as Laranta to feel love?

A memory pricked at the back of Ayleth's mind. A memory so deep and so dark, she could not quite lay hold of it. She half saw herself in the forest of dark pines. Only it wasn't her as she now was—this was her child self, naked and dirty yet smiling. Running with an abundance of strength, filled with raw power and joy. And in that vision, Laranta bounded along beside her, a projected image of her mind yet so very real, with her jaws gaping and her tongue lolling in a ridiculous, happy wolf grin.

The image faded, vanished. Though Ayleth searched within her mind, she could not find it again, and after some moments she frowned, unable to recall what it was she had thought she had seen. Only a sort of hollowness remained inside. A sense that something was missing . . .

The world around her had grown dark without her

realizing it. Chestibor, uncertain of the path ahead of him, slowed to a reluctant amble. It was time to halt for the day and make camp. Ayleth grimaced. She could force her horse on through the night up this steep mountain trail, dragging the rickety cart behind him . . . but that wouldn't be fair to faithful Chestibor.

The horse eventually slowed to a stop, letting her know he was done. She didn't try to urge him on but slid from her saddle and unhooked the cart. After seeing to Chestibor's care and feed, she spent less time on her own needs. She was a venatrix. A bite to eat and a warm cloak were all she required.

As the moon rose high above the towering Skada Mountains, Ayleth wrapped herself in the folds of her cloak and, resting her head on her saddle, dropped almost immediately into sleep.

She opened her eyes and saw pine needles overhead. That was odd. She could have sworn she'd fallen asleep beneath the spreading arms of a large oak. She sat upright and realized in a flash that she was naked—no jerkin, no cloak, no boots. At the edge of her vision she saw movement, and a figure of pure darkness materialized into a massive black wolf beside her.

You are dreaming, Laranta said.

"*I know,*" Ayleth answered. This was the forest of her mindscape. She got to her feet, shaking pine straw from her long, loose hair. Unless she took the time to envision clothing for herself, she was always naked here. She wrapped her arms around her bare stomach, shivering, but not with cold.

Something moved in her peripheral vision.

Ayleth turned sharply, but though she was fast, it was faster. Other than a sense of movement, she caught no other trace. She narrowed her eyes and tightened her grip around herself. This dream felt familiar. Too familiar.

Another movement. Ayleth was quicker this time, ready to snatch a glimpse. But again, by the time she turned, whatever it was had gone already.

"*What was that, Laranta?*" she asked, looking to her shade. "*Did you see it?*"

Laranta growled. She offered no other answer, but Ayleth sensed a deep unease rumbling in the center of her shadowy spirit.

Ayleth swayed on her feet, momentarily indecisive. Her body was tired after the hunt and the long ride. The last thing she needed was to wear herself out, mentally chasing elusive dream images. If she had any sense, she would curl up under the pine tree, burrow into the red straw, and ignore all else. Let her mind rest, let her body recover.

A third flicker of movement darted past the edge of her vision. That decided it—the lure of the chase was too great.

Leaping into motion, Ayleth hastened through the forest, moving in the same direction those three shadows had fled. Her bare feet kicked up pine straw behind her, and her long hair wafted against her shoulders and back. She ran faster and faster, almost certain she saw other shadows around her, all flowing in the same direction. Laranta followed at her heels, still growling her reluctance, but Ayleth ignored her and concentrated on running.

The trees closed in, rough pine boughs scratching at her arms and legs. She ought to slow down, ought to take the time to envision clothing for herself, some kind of protection. But Ayleth couldn't slow, wouldn't hesitate. If she did, the shadows would get away.

There were more of them now. Always out of sight, nothing more than figments, flickers of movement. But so many of them, dark, long, and low.

Ayleth gritted her teeth and redoubled her speed, determined not to let them outpace her. Laranta followed close behind, a reassuring presence. Nothing she could discover in her own mind could possibly be worse than Laranta, and Laranta was under her control. At least for the moment. Feet pounding, heart throbbing, Ayleth hurtled onward. A tangle of branches blocked her way, and she tore through them with a ferocious snarl and—

Her heels skidded to the broken edge of a precipice, and her arms wheeled in an effort to catch herself, to keep from careening over the brink.

A gasp.

A roar of open air.

The sickening plunge in her stomach, the thrill through her limbs.

Then powerful jaws caught the snarl of her hair. Pain

burst through the back of her head as Laranta hauled her back from the edge of that terrible plunge and flung her down upon the rocky outcrop.

For a moment Ayleth could only lie there, gasping to reclaim her stolen breath. Slowly she sat up again, peering round at her surroundings. The forest had given way to a ledge of stone that extended on either side as far as her eye could see. Above her hung a heavy gray sky, and below . . .

She crept to the edge and peered over. Through curling shreds of mist, she saw a gorge wall plunging down, down. A few scraggly trees gripped the rock face with roots like gnarled fingers, pulling and tearing in a hopeless effort not to fall. She couldn't see how deep it went.

Slowly Ayleth drew back, becoming aware once more of the shadows—the very shadows she had just chased. Though she still could not catch a clear sight of them, she felt them slithering to that brink and pouring over, streaming down the chasm, down into the unseen darkness far below.

"*What is this place?*" she whispered. "*Why does it seem* . . .

familiar?"

Laranta whined behind her. *Come away, Mistress. This is not a good dream.*

Her breath tight in her throat, Ayleth got back to her feet and moved closer to the edge. Were those . . . were those her memories down there? All those memories of the life she'd known before Hollis, down beneath her conscious awareness?

And these plunging shadows . . . were they the family she'd forgotten?

The names, the faces . . . so close, and yet . . .

Please, Mistress, Laranta whined again. *Please, please, come away.*

Ayleth took a step. She paused, drew a deep, steadying breath. Then she crouched and swung out over the gorge, her bare feet stretching out to find purchase on the rough wall. She lowered herself over the side, found a handhold, a foothold, inched down.

The rock broke. She fell.

Ayleth woke with a gasp, her hands outstretched to catch

herself from a fall that had never happened. Her heart pounded wildly against her breastbone, and for one horrible instant she believed she felt all her bones broken, pulverized.

But no. No, her limbs were whole. Her trembling fingers quested along her forearms, up to her shoulders, and she hugged herself tight. With a gasp, she sat upright and drew a breath of sweet air.

Then a thin cry squeezed up through her throat. "Remember," she gasped. Clutching the hair at her temples, she shook her head, desperately trying to hold onto those images in her brain. The shadows through the pines. The gorge. The dark, impenetrable depths. "Remember, Ayleth!" she growled through clenched teeth. "Remember! Remember . . ."

Her heart rate calmed.

Her vision clarified, taking in the world around her. A stream chattered down the mountainside somewhere near. The sky paled with coming dawn, and the forest of hardwood trees surrounding her stirred with bird wings and the first sweet voices of the morning chorus. Chestibor cropped on patches of grass beneath the trees, his tail swishing.

She was back on the circuit road in the mountains, back in the waking world.

She let go of her hair, dropped her hands into her lap, and took slow, cleansing breaths. That must have been some nightmare to wake her so violently. She blinked, trying to call to mind the images, but they melted away like mist.

Probably just as well. No good could come from dwelling on unpleasant dreams.

"*Laranta?*" she spoke inside herself, her awareness reaching down in search of her shade. She felt the hum of the binding song spells, felt the wolf shade stir beneath them. "*Laranta, did I . . . Was there something I should . . . ?*"

She couldn't form a coherent question. What was she trying to ask, anyway? And why would she ask her shade?

With a perplexed line creasing her brow, Ayleth pushed herself into motion. She checked Chestibor's legs and back for puffiness or sore spots, then gave him a friendly slap on his haunch and led him back to her campsite, such as it was. A nosebag of grain kept him happily occupied while she heaved the saddle onto his back and cinched the girth and chest strap. Then, after checking to make certain the dog's carcass had not been disturbed during the night, she backed her horse between the cart's shafts and hitched him up.

At last, after snatching a hasty meal herself, she swung herself into the saddle. "Walk on," she murmured. Chestibor started forward at his comfortable, rhythmic walk, and the cart creaked into motion behind him. With good luck, they would reach the outpost by the end of the day.

Ayleth watched the morning brighten around her, the rising sun chasing back shadows beneath the trees.

CHAPTER 4

EVENING CAME EARLY THIS TIME OF YEAR IN THE high country above the valley of Drauval Borough. The sun set behind the peaks, and gloom crept along the forest floor. Ayleth called up her shadow vision and guided Chestibor with care along secluded trails familiar to them both as they neared the end of their journey home.

Peering up through a break in the trees, Ayleth spied the ramshackle tower, the highest point of Gillanluòc

Outpost. A light in the window told her the venatrix was at home, awaiting her prodigal's return. Ayleth winced at the sight but braced herself. She hadn't really thought she could make it back before Hollis returned from her circuit ride . . .

"Haunts damn!" Ayleth gasped, the fingers of one hand tightening into a fist around her reins, the other hand rising to her forehead. Something plucked at her mind—Hollis, no doubt, reaching out with her Apparition shade. She'd sensed Ayleth's coming and now checked to make certain her former apprentice was well and whole. Ayleth shuddered, hating that sensation of shade presence slithering around the edges of her awareness. Hollis didn't ordinarily use her shade's powers on Ayleth, respecting her privacy. But in this instance, she couldn't very well blame her mistress.

With a last quivering sensation, the shade pulled back, and Ayleth sighed in relief, her fingers relaxing. The worst was yet to come, however: facing Hollis in person. All too soon the narrow circuit road brought her to the outpost. The gates swung wide, and a silhouetted figure stood in the opening.

Hollis, Venatrix di Theldry, looked like a doll woven out of twigs, so short and slender she was, with limbs that looked spindly enough to break at the slightest pressure. But this impression was utterly false. No other venatrix in all Perrinion was as hardy and tough as this woman. Hollis had spent her early years of service to the Order fighting the shade-taken armies of Dread Odile during the Witch Wars. Though countless venators and venatrices had lost their lives during those bloody years, Hollis had survived and gone on to take the borough of Drauval under her keeping. Here she'd served for nearly twenty years, protecting the denizens of the borough from innumerable shades, hunting down every rumor of magic doings with an intensity of focus that earned her a fearsome reputation.

Hollis said nothing as Ayleth rode Chestibor up to the gate. When Ayleth pulled her horse to a stop, the venatrix merely stepped back and motioned for her to continue. Swallowing hard, Ayleth complied. The two-wheeled cart rumbled over the threshold of the gate and into the outpost yard.

All of Gillanluòc appeared to be on the verge of

collapse, from the ten-foot wooden fence that encircled it, to the gate listing heavily inward, to the main stone blockhouse itself. This building hunched on the sloping landscape as though ashamed of itself, shedding shingles and slats every time the wind picked up, its three-story tower swaying like a rotted tree. Evanderians had built the original structure centuries ago, long before the Witch Wars. But during the two-hundred-year span of Dread Odile's reign in Perrinion, it had fallen into disrepair; and with a whole borough to care for between them, neither Hollis nor Ayleth found time to do much by way of restoration. After a big storm they would work hard to shore up the worst of the damage but otherwise made do with leaky roofs and drafty walls.

A venatrix's life was never meant for luxury, after all.

Ayleth halted Chestibor in the middle of the yard and dismounted. Hollis approached the cart, her face an expressionless mask. Ayleth could hardly bear to look at her, yet she observed her mistress from behind Chestibor's comfortingly large back, watched her peer into the back of the cart. For an instant so brief that Ayleth half wondered if she'd imagined it, she thought she saw a flash of surprise cross Hollis's face. Was she impressed by the size of the dog? Impressed by Ayleth's hunting feat?

Still without speaking, Hollis reached into the cart, pulled back the blankets Ayleth had wrapped around the dog as a shroud, and investigated the carcass. Searching for a death wound, Ayleth realized. For some indication that this inexperienced huntress had resorted to a violent death when faced with such an alarming foe. She smiled a little, knowing her mistress would find nothing.

At last Hollis looked up at Ayleth, still not speaking.

Ayleth swallowed, trying to wet her dry throat. "An Apparition," she said, the words cracking slightly with tension. "I dealt the paralysis and followed it with the Gentle Death."

Hollis blinked. Once. Slowly. Then she turned on her heel and marched for the blockhouse, calling back over her shoulder, "Take the carcass to the bonehouse. Then, inside for evaluation."

Ayleth sucked in a long breath, relieved to be free of her mistress's probing gaze, at least for the time being. She'd survived this first encounter. Maybe Hollis wouldn't flay her alive after all.

Obeying the venatrix's command, she lugged the dog's body into the bonehouse, which stood to the left of the main building. The corpse was heavy, but she managed it in her own strength without summoning extra power from her shade.

The bonehouse was little more than a glorified shed in which Hollis stored the bodies of those shade-taken she brought home from the hunts. Here she prepared and processed their bones, sinews, intestines, and any other vital parts the Evanderians of Castra Breçar deemed useful. Once every two months the supply man from the castra made his way up to Gillanluòc, bringing with him shipments of food and necessities, restocking Hollis's poisons. In return, Hollis sent back vinegar-packed casks full of shade-taken remains, along with detailed logs of each hunt. Tribute to the castra and proof of her labors in Drauval.

Ayleth hauled the dog's body onto the broad, bloodstained table used for dissections. Following her evaluation, she would return here and begin the gory work, checking which parts of the corpse were still good and which were too far gone to shadow blight. It would be a long night, but she didn't mind the prospect. This would be her first time sending her own tribute to Castra Breçar.

Before venturing into the blockhouse to face her mistress, she settled Chestibor into his stall for the night, across from Hollis's own gray gelding. She puttered about, lingering as long as she dared before at last giving her horse's nose a rub and whispering, "Wish me luck?"

He lipped her fingers affectionately then returned his attention to his feed. A generous-hearted horse was he in all regards except moral support. With a sigh, Ayleth made her way from the warmth of the stables, across the cold outpost yard, and into the blockhouse.

Warm light from the fireplace filled the main room downstairs. Rafters supported the low ceiling strung with various herbs, tools, weapons, and cooking gear, all dangling from hooks in a haphazard order only the two venatrices could possibly understand. Beneath these stretched a long table that took up most of the room. On one end lay scattered a dozen or more hand-carved darts, newly fletched and awaiting their poisoned tips. Piles of music scrolls mounded in the middle, various song spells for Vocos and Detrudos that both Ayleth and her mistress constantly pored over as they sought to improve their skills.

At the far end, nearest the light of the fire, Hollis sat with her logbook open before her, writing an account of her own most recent hunt.

Ayleth pulled the door shut, removed her hood, and hung it on a peg beside Hollis's, turning just in time to see her mistress lift her gaze from the logbook, set aside her quill, and lean back in her chair. Hollis said nothing, but her eyes lowered briefly to the chair opposite hers at the table.

Ayleth slid into the seat, her spine straight, her shoulders square and still, her hands resting on her knees. She drew long, even breaths, refusing to let the faintest quiver betray her taut nerves. Hollis held Ayleth's gaze for a long while, keeping her captive in that dreadful silence. The fire on the hearth crackled with heat, but it wasn't the blaze's warmth that caused sweat to break out across Ayleth's forehead.

"Report," Hollis said at last.

Ayleth struggled for a moment to find her voice. "A messenger from Flore arrived five days ago with word of magic doings in and around the village. A shade-taken dog was accused of killing one Farmer Malger."

Hollis nodded without comment, so Ayleth continued, describing her conversations with the bailiff of Flore and Miller Roch. She told of investigating the site of Malger's death, and went on to detail the hunt itself. With absolute precision she told which powers she summoned from her shade and how she used the Vocos to command them.

When she came to the part where the Apparition shade in the dog assaulted her mind, she paused. She didn't like to admit this moment which almost led to her undoing. But Hollis would smell a falsehood, so she gave a full report, accurate and honest, with no attempt to justify her actions or choices. What was done was done, and Hollis would either deem her decisions right or wrong. One way or another, the shade was ousted to the Haunts, which meant the hunt was successful.

Hollis asked a few crisp, clarifying questions along the way. Nothing slipped past her. Her face was wooden, utterly unreadable. Though a tiny woman—when standing, her head scarcely reached as high as Ayleth's chin—she seethed with the force of her own nature, not to mention the well-honed powers of the shade she carried inside.

Ayleth came to the end of her story and waited for more questions. Hollis said nothing. Her gaze never shifted from Ayleth's, and though Ayleth wanted desperately to look away, she would not allow herself that luxury. At last, unable to endure a moment more, she worked up the nerve to ask, "Well?"

"Well, what?"

"Have I . . . have I satisfied the requirements?"

Hollis tilted her head slightly to one side. "That would depend on whose requirements you mean. And for what purpose."

Blood pounded in Ayleth's temples. She felt she would explode with impatience, with her need to know her mistress's thoughts. She kept her voice even, however, determined not to betray the passion simmering in her soul.

"I know that a post has come available at Wodechran Borough," she said. "I know that Nane, Venator du

Vincent, has disappeared, and they need someone to take his place, at least temporarily."

Hollis said nothing. She didn't even nod.

"The Golden Prince himself will appoint the replacement," Ayleth continued. "Which means it's not a castra appointment. Which means anyone with the proper credentials can apply for the post."

"And how did you come by this information?"

Ayleth's stomach turned over. She flushed and looked down at her hands folded neatly before her on the table. "I . . . I read the letter you received. From Venator du Tam."

"Did you, now?"

Ayleth didn't quite know how to continue. News from the outside world beyond their borough was extremely rare, so when the message arrived, Ayleth had been struck with irresistible curiosity. She'd watched with interest as her mistress opened and read the scrawled lines. And she'd seen Hollis's face go very pale and still, which only served to increase her curiosity tenfold.

At first opportunity, she'd sneaked the letter out from the front of Hollis's logbook and read its contents with great interest.

"You . . . you didn't say not to," she said lamely. Then she drew her shoulders back. "It's a great opportunity, and I would like to present my candidacy. I would like to be considered for the position."

Though Hollis's face remained as closed as ever, Ayleth could feel the seething of her spirit—not her shade spirit, which the venatrix kept suppressed down inside her mind, but her own potent inner force.

"So," she said, her voice too soft, "you believe you're ready for a borough of your own, do you?"

A muscle in Ayleth's jaw tightened. "I do."

"After a single solo hunt."

Several sharp words sprang to her tongue, but Ayleth bit them back. Instead, she asked quietly, "How many hunts are required before I may present my candidacy?"

Hollis leaned her elbows on the table and steepled her fingers, resting her chin thoughtfully against them. "No set number. But I should think you'd wish to pursue several more at least. Unless you truly believe liberating one minor shade from one dog has taught you all you need to know going forward as a venatrix."

The pounding in her temples increased as her blood boiled. Ayleth swallowed hard. "That Apparition was not insignificant. And neither was the dog." She hated how defensive the words sounded. But they were the truth, Haunts damn it!

"And do you believe there is no difference?" Hollis's eyes burned into Ayleth's.

"What do you mean?"

"Do you think you'll just as easily hunt down a man? A woman?" The venatrix's lip curled. "A child? Are you ready for everything this role requires of you, all the deaths you must deal in the name of the Goddess, all the bodies you must destroy so that the souls may be saved? Are you truly ready, Wild Girl?"

Ayleth cringed at the name, one Hollis had given her long ago when she was still a small girl newly come to Gillanluòc. She used to think the venatrix meant it with fondness, proud of her apprentice's ferocious nature. But in this context, it felt like an insult.

In a still, quiet voice, she responded, "Were *you* ready, Hollis?"

Silence answered her. Hollis did not move, not a

fluttering eyelid.

Ayleth persisted. "Were *you* ready the first time you hunted a man? Were you prepared to deal death to a . . . a child?"

With those words, she watched the blood drain from Hollis's face. How vividly she recalled that night, a mere three years ago, when the venatrix returned from a hunt, her gray gelding dragging a little two-wheeled cart much like the cart Chestibor had drawn from Flore. She'd driven the cart directly to the bonehouse door and, without a word for her apprentice, dismounted and gathered the corpse out of the back. A human corpse, Ayleth could see from the shape of the shrouded body. But so small.

Hollis had entered the bonehouse and shut the door firmly behind her. Ayleth, knowing her duty, took the horse to the stables, unloaded the hunting supplies, cleaned and mounted the weapons. Over the next few hours, she several times approached the bonehouse door with food or drink but never could bring herself to knock.

It wasn't until dawn the next day that Hollis emerged,

only to go directly to her own bedroom. Once more she shut the door fast. This time she did not appear for three days, during which time Ayleth scarcely heard her move in the chamber, even when she pressed her ear to the door. Only once did she hear a sound—one that she first thought was the venatrix murmuring prayers, but which transformed into a low, wordless moan.

Ayleth had slipped out of the blockhouse and gone to the stables, staying well out of earshot of her mistress's door for hours afterward.

Studying the face across from her now, Ayleth could discern no emotion whatsoever, only the stone hardness of a venatrix. A hardness she would have to develop in herself if she hoped to survive in the Order.

Hollis stood so suddenly that her chair fell over behind her. She did not pause to right it but strode to an alcove in the wall by the fireplace in which rested long weatherproof cases. Pulling out one of these, she undid the strap and withdrew a rough parchment map the length of her arm. Her boots thunking on the fieldstone floor, she returned to the table and, with a single sweep of her arm, brushed aside a huge stack of spell-song scrolls, letting them fall to the floor. She unrolled the map, grabbing a long knife to weigh down one end and snatching a copper pot from overhead to weigh down the other.

Then she stood back, her arms folded, and fixed Ayleth with eyes sparking with shadow-light. "Tell me, girl, what do you see?"

Ayleth, swallowing to wet her dry throat, looked down at the image spread before her. It was an old map of the Kingdom of Perrinion, but with adjustments made by Hollis's own hand over the years as borough borders shifted and cities rose. She saw the almost childish sketch of a castle with the label *Telianor*, indicating the Chosen King's capital city, and she spotted the blocky fort-like structure drawn in beside the label *Castra Breçar*.

But her eye was inexorably drawn to the enormous black blot of ink spread in the center of the map. At first glance one might think it was a mistake, that the inkwell had spilled. A second glance, however, revealed Hollis's spidery script just above the blot, spelling out the name.

"The Witchwood," Ayleth whispered.

"Louder, girl, so I can hear you."

"The Witchwood," Ayleth repeated, the word like bitter poison on her tongue.

There it lay, right in the kingdom's center—right in that fertile land where the glorious palace of the Priestess Queens had stood in centuries past. Before Dread Odile rose to power, killed the last of the Goddess-marked line, and established herself as deity and queen over Perrinion for two hundred years. She'd built her city of Dulìmurian over the ruins of the Holy City and established a vast idol to her own glory on the very site where the Goddess's altar had once stood.

Now all were gone. The Holy City, Dulìmurian, the altar, the idol. All swallowed up by that dark expanse marked in black ink.

"And what exactly is the Witchwood?" Hollis pressed. "Or have you forgotten these things I've taught you over the years?"

"I haven't forgotten."

"Then tell me!"

Ayleth drew a sharp breath, her jaw tensing. "It is the final curse of Dread Odile."

Dread Odile—dead and gone nearly two decades now.

But within a year of her death, the Witchwood had grown from the heart of her kingdom. A poisonous forest made up, not of trees, but of . . . something else. Something dire.

Something from the Haunts.

"A curse, Ayleth," Hollis said, leaning over the table and planting her finger in the center of that mark. "But a curse like you've never seen. And tell me what this says?" She shifted her finger out of the black mark to the land lying just west of the Witchwood.

"Wodechran Borough," Ayleth said. The very borough which now sought a new venator to reinforce the undermanned outpost.

"The venators of Wodechran Borough are responsible for more than just the care of the borough itself," Hollis said. "Venator du Vincent and Venator du Tam have labored for years to maintain *this*." She slid her finger a third time, marking a double-thick line of red ink which ran along the westernmost edge of the forest. "Do you remember what this is?"

"The Great Barrier," Ayleth answered at once.

The branching Sang and Aiga Rivers, sacred waters

said to have sprung from the Goddess Herself in ages long ago, bound the Witchwood on the north, south, and east sides. But on the western front, only the vast Barrier song spell kept the curse at bay, preventing it from devouring all of Perrinion. Hollis had drawn it into the map with aggressive strokes, somehow communicating despite her poor drawing skills a sense of urgency and power, using ink the color of dried blood. Ayleth could almost believe her mistress had cut a finger and pressed it to the page to apply the vigorous lines.

"This song spell was established nearly twenty years ago by Fendrel du Glaive himself," Hollis said. "No Evanderian of lesser power or skill could have done such a work. But Venator du Vincent, my hunt brother, was trained by Fendrel to maintain it. Whoever takes Nane du Vincent's place will have to shoulder that responsibility."

"I know the Barrier song spell," Ayleth said. "You've taught me, and I've learned many variations."

"Not like this you haven't," Hollis answered. "The Great Barrier is huge, extending more than fifty miles, never straight, always winding. You might well be able to establish and maintain a barrier around this outpost. You might even manage to barricade an entire village. But do you honestly think you have the skill to maintain something like this? Venator du Tam cannot, and he has served in Wodechran for years!"

"I could learn," Ayleth said.

Hollis scoffed, backing away from the table and throwing up her hands. "The arrogance of the young! Do you have any idea what you're talking about? Even if—*if*, Ayleth—you had the skill with your pipes to learn the Barrier spell on this level, how can you possibly be prepared for everything else? It's not just about holding back the Witchwood, girl. There's so much more."

Once more leaving the table, Hollis crossed the room to a chest beneath one of the narrow windows behind her. She opened the lid and dug down inside before returning to the table with a poorly sewn-together book with a floppy rabbit-skin cover. She flipped the book open to the last page and slid it under Ayleth's nose. Ayleth read there a list of seven names:

Ylaire di Jocosa – The Warpwitch.
Inren di Karel – The Phantomwitch

Gillotin du Visgarus — The Corpsewitch

Zarc d'Utrehd — The Stormwitch

Zilla d'Utrehd — The Windwitch

Crisentha di Bathia — The Crystalwitch

Scias du Sibb — The Legionwitch

"Tell me, Ayleth," Hollis said, watching Ayleth's face as she read, "what do these names mean to you?"

Ayleth felt as though a fist grabbed and squeezed her heart. She knew those names all too well. She knew their histories. She knew their legends. Hollis had ingrained them in her head from the time she was small. "The Crimson Devils," she said softly. "The Crimson Devils of Dread Odile."

Hollis turned back through the pages, revealing more lists, more names, most of them crossed out.

"These were all once members of our Order," Hollis said. "Loyal Evanderians, venators and venatrices. Every one of them turned to heresy. They forsook worship of our Goddess and bowed to Odile instead. Using unholy means, they bound their souls to their shades and took control of the powers indwelling them. Not with pipes or the song spells sanctioned by the saint, but with dark arts and evil workings. When they die, their souls are damned to the Haunts right along with their possessing spirits. See how many there were, Ayleth? Some, we killed during the wars. Others, we hunted down throughout the years. But these seven . . . these devils . . ."

They escaped. Following the death of the Witch Queen, these last, most devoted of her lieutenants had fled the purging of Saint Evander's Order by crossing over the Great Barrier into the Witchwood, never to return. They preferred to live in the poisonous forest of their queen's last curse rather than be killed and damned by her enemies. The Barrier would let them enter, but they could never return.

Not unless the Barrier itself failed.

Hollis watched Ayleth's face so closely, Ayleth could almost swear she felt her skin burn under that gaze.

"Do you understand?" the older venatrix urged, leaning across the table and taking hold of Ayleth's shoulder. "You are skilled, my girl. You are fierce and you are brave. When the time is right, I will see to it that you are posted where you will serve your Goddess and your king with honor. I won't keep you here forever. But Wodechran Borough is too much for you. The Barrier, the Wood, the Crimson Devils . . ." She shook her head heavily. "No. You will trust me to know what is best for you. You will stay here in Drauval, and you will wait."

Hollis squeezed Ayleth's shoulder one last time, then stepped away from her and the table, leaving both the map and the book lying in Ayleth's view. She crossed the room to the narrow staircase leading up to the second level and there paused to look back.

"Go to bed," she said. "The dog's corpse can sit until morning. Sleep now and purge these foolish dreams from your mind. Your day will come, Wild Girl. You will prove your worth, I promise."

Ayleth made no answer, refusing to look up and meet her mistress's gaze. In her peripheral vision she saw Hollis shrug and move on up the stairs, leaving Ayleth alone with the dying fire and the maps and that list of names.

The dark expanse of the Witchwood seemed to fill Ayleth's vision.

With a throaty growl, she clenched her fist and

pounded at that blot of ink on the map, once, twice, three times, so hard that the tabletop creaked and threatened to crack.

CHAPTER 5

HOLLIS WAITED IN HER SMALL BEDCHAMBER, FULLY dressed and seated on the edge of the bed with her legs crisscrossed on the straw mattress. Her hands, holding her Vocos pipes, rested in her lap. She tilted her head slightly to one side, her ears pricked. She finally heard Ayleth's feet stumping up the winding tower stair to her room overhead. Hollis listened to the door open and shut, listened to the thump and bustle of her former apprentice readying herself for sleep.

She listened then to the silence. And still she waited with the practiced patience of a huntress, perfected to an art over the years.

At last, when she deemed the silence to have lasted long enough, she took up the Vocos pipes and softly began to play the Song of Summoning. The spell hummed down into her mind, into her soul, calling up the power of the Apparition shade she carried within. She played with care, drawing on significant power without compromising her safety, and when that spell was complete, she modulated the melody into the Song of Command.

Closing her eyes, she stepped into her own mindscape. This was a strange, dark, labyrinthine complex of stone and shadows, but she walked with confidence. She knew her own mind quite well.

Turning a corner, she came face to face with the projected image of her shade. The form it manifested was unlike anything to be found in the mortal world, a bizarre being of many wings and a lithe femininity that was neither human nor animal. Utterly unnatural, but a strange approximation of what this spirit *might* be if it were an incarnate being. It looked at her, shining eyes peering out from among feathers, its expression one of long-standing hatred converted, over time, into bored complacency.

What is your command? it asked with little interest and only mild resentment. Its voice was a multitudinous hum in Hollis's head.

In the physical world, Hollis twisted the Command song spell into a new variation. In the world of her mind, she said, "*I need to access the girl's unconscious. But she cannot be aware of my entry. You must carry my awareness with you, and we must be undetected.*"

The winged being seemed to shrug, feathers ruffling. *Easy enough,* it said, and stretched out what might almost be a hand. Hollis took it without hesitation. She was in control. Her mastery of the Vocos pipes was not to be doubted, and it had been some years since her shade dared try to fight her.

So, Hollis allowed that small piece of herself to fly out from her mind, carried by her shade's power. She flitted through the darkness of Gillanluòc Outpost, up the winding stair, through the door of the tower room and into Ayleth's bare little chamber. Ayleth lay upon her straw mattress, her boots and jerkin discarded on the floor, her linen shirt untucked from rumpled trousers. Her face was stern even in sleep, her dark brows always slightly constricted, the corners of her mouth downturned.

Hollis, carried on the wings of her Apparition, slipped into the girl's head.

They passed through clouds so thick as to feel like mounds of soft wool. Not real clouds full of moisture and electricity, but clouds as a child might envision them, as an adult might still dream them to be. They were so dense, Hollis could see nothing at first, but she followed a sixth sense, steering her shade on until they came to a gap and emerged beneath the cloud cover to hover in the air above a tall pine forest.

The landscape of Ayleth's mind. Full of secrets. Full of whispering shadows.

Hollis guided her shade to duck beneath the canopy of thickly grown pine boughs. They flitted between towering trunks, no larger than a dainty mayfly, almost undetectable. Ayleth would have to know exactly where to look to discern the presence invading her mind.

As they progressed swiftly through the forest, Hollis noticed figures flashing in her peripheral vision, deep in the darkest shadows. Long, low, wild figures, always just out sight.

Hollis grimaced. Fleeting and difficult to discern though they were, these shadow figures shouldn't be visible at all, shouldn't be this far ascendant in Ayleth's brain. If something wasn't done about them soon, Ayleth would begin to see them, to sense them. To remember them.

Urging her shade on faster, Hollis at last emerged from the trees back into open air. As her spirit and her shade hovered over a deep, ragged gorge, her brow tightened into a frown. There were footprints along the edge of the gorge: distinct human footprints.

Ayleth had been here. Recently.

Which meant the memory block was rapidly weakening.

At a silent command from its mistress, the Apparition banked and plunged straight down into the gorge. It flitted easily through the tight space where the walls nearly converged and flew down and down, deeper and deeper, until suddenly the gorge widened out again, and they emerged in a subterranean gully far beneath the pine forest.

A stream winding like a silver ribbon flowed gently along stony banks. Hollis followed its course to a place where the stream drained into a jagged opening no more than three feet wide, like a circular mouth rimmed with stony teeth. Beyond that hole, deeper and darker, lay the most remote, nearly unreachable regions of Ayleth's mind.

And, shimmering with power, an invisible webbing of spell song covered that hole—Hollis's spell song.

Hollis dismounted her shade and, moving carefully, approached the hole and the webbing. She had woven the webbing and set it in place long ago, and for many years it had hummed its powerful magic undisturbed in the darkness.

But five years ago, Ayleth had begun asking questions. Hollis, concerned by the nature of those questions, had taken the first opportunity to reenter her apprentice's mind, to seek out this gorge and check the spell webbing.

She'd found it still holding but battered, as though pounded by pummeling, raging fists. Ayleth had almost gotten through. She had almost remembered . . . everything.

Since then, Hollis had taken care to reinforce the memory block every few months.

This time, though she studied it with care, Hollis saw no sign of tampering on her spell. Still, if Ayleth had made it even as far as the gorge, the spell must be weakening, in need of attention.

Using her Apparition magic, Hollis wove strength into the spell. If it were visible, it would appear as though she'd thickened the fibers, tightened the weave, and added more threads to both warp and weft. But this webbing was more like music than anything, yet not really music at all. By the time she was done, the spell vibrated a tune of pure magic.

Satisfied with her work, Hollis climbed back onto her shade and let it carry her up out of the cold, dank gully, through the narrow ravine, and out into the open air beneath the thick layer of imagined clouds. Hollis drew a deep breath of relief.

Which caught suddenly and painfully in her throat, making her mortal body—far away in her room in the physical world—jolt where it sat.

Ayleth stood on the edge of the gorge. Staring up into the sky.

Staring right where Hollis and her shade hovered.

"*Go!*" Hollis hissed, and her shade lurched into motion, its many wings pounding the air. They skimmed the topmost branches of the pine forest, watching the sky for a break in the clouds that would allow them to escape this world. Beneath and behind them, Hollis could feel Ayleth galloping through the trees, hunting them with wolf-like intensity, pursuing the invaders of her unconscious.

Light streamed up ahead, a rent in the thick clouds. "*There! Hurry!*" Hollis shouted to her shade. It put on a burst of speed, found the opening, spun up, out—

And burst free into the small tower room in the mortal world.

Hollis hovered in the air, a disembodied projection above Ayleth's bed. She watched as the girl sat upright, choking on a scream, her hands clutching at the straw mattress, her eyes wide with a mixture of terror and hunter's lust. She looked frantically around the room, her gaze skimming over Hollis and her shade. Had her own shade been ascendant, Ayleth would easily have detected Hollis's presence. But Ayleth knew better than to go to sleep with an unsuppressed shade.

Still, Hollis worried as she watched, half afraid the girl would stumble out of bed, pound down the tower stair, and burst through her mistress's door, demanding to know what Hollis was doing, penetrating her mind uninvited.

Slowly the ferocious expression faded from Ayleth's face. She cursed irritably then turned over in her bed, planting her face in her pillow and curling up into a ball. Hollis whispered a grateful prayer. Her mortal body down in her room, still playing the spell song, sagged in relief.

Carried on invisible wings, Hollis's awareness flitted back down the winding stair and into her room. For an instant she hovered outside of herself, observing her own body seated cross-legged on her bed, the Vocos pipes at her lips, her eyes closed. Her pale hair, streaked with strands of gray, straggled loose around her shoulders, and her cheeks were hollow.

With a sigh she sank back into herself, once more fully aware of her body. She shifted the melody she played from the Command into the Suppression. Her shade fluttered angrily inside her head as the spell song wrapped around its being, but its resistance was token.

Hollis swiftly resolved the song. With the drone of the pipe still reverberating in her head, she lowered the instrument and sat motionless for some moments, her eyes closed.

Then her lips moved, and she whispered into the stillness of her room, "It will hold. For a little while."

It didn't have to hold much longer. Just until Ayleth reached her twentieth year. Then, Hollis promised herself, she would tell the girl everything. Then she would lift the memory block. Then she would explain her choices, the many hard choices she'd made, one after another, from the day she'd first laid eyes on that ratty-haired, mucky-faced little wildling child.

Only two more months. So little time! Hollis clenched her fists around her Vocos pipes, drawing a deep, ragged breath. She would hold on to whatever time she had left.

Because when the truth came out . . . when Ayleth finally knew . . . that would be the end.

She would either save or damn them all.

Ayleth slouched her way back down to the main room of the block house before sunup and put a pot of water and oats over the fire to cook. She felt as though she hadn't slept in weeks. Strange dreams had plagued her throughout the night. Dreams of hunting. Dreams of chasing after a figure she could not quite see until, just at the last, she'd caught the barest glimpse of a face. Dreams of—

Footsteps sounded on the stair. Turning, Ayleth watched Hollis emerge from the stairwell into the room. She was clad in her riding boots and spurs, her red hood over her head.

"Are you going on a hunt?"

Hollis shot Ayleth an expressionless glance. "Word arrived yesterday of a shade-taken seen five days' ride from here. I waited for your return, but I can wait no longer." She crossed the room to the armoire on one wall and opened it to reveal the various quivers filled with poison-tipped darts, not to mention her knives and other implements. Her sheaths for the Vocos and Detrudos pipes already hung from her belt. With the ease of many years' experience, the venatrix slung the quivers across her breast, slapped the bracers onto her arms, and holstered her scorpiona. "I will be gone a fortnight at least. Maybe longer, depending on how difficult this hunt proves."

Ayleth watched her closely, her muscles unconsciously tensing as though in the presence of an enemy. She was ready at the slightest provocation to spring into action, but she didn't know why.

Hollis closed the armoire and stepped to the door where saddlebags full of supplies already sat in readiness. Ayleth hadn't noticed them the night before, focused as she'd been at the time on her evaluation. Hollis slung the bags over her shoulder and opened the door, pausing briefly.

"You will not leave Gillanluòc in my absence. Prepare the dog's remains for shipment to Castra Breçar." Her eyes met Ayleth's across the room.

In that moment, Ayleth thought she saw . . . she couldn't quite say what. A storm of wings in a dark, cloudy sky. A flash of recognition, there and then gone.

Without another word, Hollis passed through the door and slammed it behind her.

Ayleth remained seated on the stool by the fireplace, her boiling oats forgotten. She clenched a wooden spoon in one fist as though it were a weapon, listening until she heard a horse's hooves in the yard, heard the gate open and shut behind her mistress.

She was alone. Again. Left behind from the important work, trapped in her own home.

Her appetite suddenly gone, Ayleth pulled the pot off the fire and, after donning a cloak against the autumnal chill in the air, went out first to care for Chestibor, then made her way to the bonehouse. The unpleasant task of preparing a shade-taken carcass would certainly help pry memories of fleeting nightmares from her mind.

Hours later, covered in gore to her elbows, blood streaking her forehead where she'd unconsciously brushed away strands of hair with the backs of her soiled hands, Ayleth returned to the blockhouse. She filled the largest of Hollis's pots with water and hung it on a hook over the coals. Impatience drove her to pull it off again before it was more than tepid, but she attacked her foul skin with a slab of hard lye soap and somehow contrived to get herself clean.

This task complete, she slumped into one of the chairs at the table. She might have turned her attention to many different jobs. There were new darts to be carved, new tips to be carefully dipped in their various poisons. She could pull out her Vocos or Detrudos and practice variations on any number of song spells, or she could set up a target in the yard and practice taking shots with her scorpiona.

Instead, she sat where she was. Staring into nowhere. Seeing again that threatening sky, that strange conglomeration of wings.

And Hollis's face.

Hollis had been in her mind last night. She was sure of it. Why, she could not guess. For what purpose, she could not imagine. But her mistress had used her Apparition magic and invaded Ayleth's privacy, invaded her dreams, her unconscious mind.

Was it possible . . . ? Could Hollis be blocking her memories?

With a sudden growl, she pounded the tabletop and stood. She didn't want to think this way. She loved Hollis. Hollis was . . . everything! Her mistress, her mother, her only friend. And Hollis loved her in return, she thought, or she hoped. To the extent that Hollis could love anyone or anything. The venetrix had always cared for Ayleth, trained her thoroughly, seen to it that the possessing spirit in her soul could not overwhelm her. She'd given Ayleth purpose, focus, drive.

And Ayleth, in turn, had given Hollis her trust.

"She lied to me." The words came out unbidden and bitter. "She's always lied to me. Or she's kept something from me." It didn't matter which. The deceit was there.

She didn't even know her real name . . .

Resolve swelled suddenly, painfully, in her heart. Striding back to the fireplace, Ayleth reached into one of the alcoves along the wall. Her fingers quickly found what she searched for, despite Hollis's efforts to hide it. Hollis would have had to burn it to keep Ayleth from looking at it again.

The castra seal was already broken, so Ayleth simply slid off the thread holding the scroll shut and unrolled it to read the thrilling words once more:

Esteemed Hollis, Venatrix di Theldry,

I regret that I must write to inform you of the disappearance and presumed death of your former hunt brother, Nane, Venator du Vincent. He served with great courage throughout the years, and his loss will be an ongoing blow to the Order. Nane spoke highly of you during the past ten years we served together at Milisendis Outpost, and I believe he would wish you to be informed of his loss.

Candidates are now on their way to Dunloch Castle to present themselves to the Golden Prince. He will appoint Nane's replacement in short order, to serve alongside me at Milisendis. Rest assured that the Barrier will be maintained.

In the name of our worthy forefather, Blessed Evander,
Kephan, Venator du Tam
Wodechran Borough

Ayleth's gaze lingered over that second paragraph.

"Candidates are now on their way," she whispered, unconscious that her lips moved.

It was all there in the letter. The Golden Prince himself would choose whomever he deemed worthy to replace Venator Nane. The castra could send anyone it willed, but the final decision rested with the prince himself.

Who was to say she couldn't put herself forward even without Hollis's official sanction? She was no apprentice anymore, after all. She was a venatrix, tried and proven.

And Hollis had lied to her. Had always lied to her. Would go on lying to her forever.

Hollis had invaded her mind.

Staring down at the words on that scroll, Ayleth tightened her jaw and expanded her chest with a deep breath. Briefly her resolve wavered. She should stay here in Gillanluòc like Hollis wanted her to. And she wasn't truly qualified, was she? Not for the Barrier spell, not on that level. She was good, but good enough to impress a prince? Good enough to fight back the Witchwood, to maintain the prison that held the Crimson Devils? No, no. She should know better than to grasp at so much. She should know her place, stay where she belonged.

Ayleth blew out the breath and rolled up the scroll, clenching it in her fist. Enough of this dithering. Enough excuses, enough petty fears. She would present herself to the Golden Prince. And she would break free of Hollis's stranglehold once and for all.

CHAPTER 6

"HERVI, SEE THAT YOU SECURE THOSE BARRELS tight!" the Oar Mistress hollered across the length of her barge. "You let Master Folquet's good wine go floating downriver, I'm sending you in after it."

The boy offered a good-humored grin and salute and set about adjusting the knots. The Oar Mistress nodded in approval, watching the rest of her crew with a careful eye. They had served under her for long enough to know they couldn't get away with anything.

The wharf of the river town bustled with noise and activity, as always. This was the primary crossing into Wodechran Borough, and merchants across northern Perrinion who wanted to do business in the Golden Prince's own domain traveled here to have their wares carried across the Aiga River. There were always new clients eager to pay a willing ferrywoman, and the Oar Mistress maintained a tight schedule to keep up with the demand.

"Is that everything, Goodman Gul?" she called to her firstman, who was checking the security of a stack of crates.

He turned to answer, but when he opened his mouth, no words came. Instead, he stared over the Oar Mistress's shoulder while his face drained of blood.

Frowning, the Oar Mistress turned. A quick breath hissed between her teeth.

A Red Hood approached along the quay. The busy crowd of merchants and river folk parted quickly before her, all eager to avoid her gaze. They needn't have worried.

That gaze was fixed on this very barge.

The Oar Mistress's stomach dropped. But, hating to show even a trace of cowardice before her men, she squared her shoulders and strode swiftly to the gangplank and down onto the quay to face the approaching Red Hood on her tall brown horse.

"How may I be of service, good mistress?" she asked, touching her forehead politely in salute as the Red Hood brought her horse to a stop.

The woman sat tall in her saddle, her hood pulled low so that shadows obscured her face, and spoke in a deep, husky voice. "I seek passage across to Wodechran." She rested a hand on a pouch at her belt and pulled back the flap. The Oar Mistress's heart skipped a beat. She'd heard rumors of the Red Hoods and all their strange weapons and poisons.

But the strange woman simply produced a coin, holding it so that the morning sunlight gleamed on its surface. "I can pay," she said.

The Oar Mistress shook her head, putting up a hand. "No need. Glad to be of service to the Evanderian Order." She swallowed hard and motioned to the gangplank. "We leave on the quarter-hour. Make yourself and your horse comfortable."

The Red Hood dismounted and led her horse to the gangplank. There the animal balked momentarily, putting its ears back. The Red Hood stroked its nose and murmured something that sounded strange and dreadful to the Oar Mistress's ears. The horse's skin shuddered, but it obeyed its owner and continued up the plank and onto the flat-bottomed barge. The Red Hood found space among the loaded crates and barrels and stood beside the horse, facing the far shore.

A flurry of movement, and the brightly colored robes and feathered hat of Master Folquet caught the Oar Mistress's eye. The merchant hastened down the gangplank onto the quay, his step spritely and quick for a man of his size.

"You . . . you didn't say you'd be ferrying one of *them* along with me and my goods!" he gasped, wheezing slightly in his panic.

The Oar Mistress gave him a look. "Would you prefer I come back for you, Master Folquet? Because I'm not asking *her* to wait for the next trip, Goddess help me."

The merchant looked back along the barge, his gaze

moving from his loaded merchandise, worth a small fortune, to the Red Hood standing still and quiet in the center. He mopped his forehead, muttering a brief prayer. Then, in a thin voice, he called to one of his men, "Gaetan! See to the unloading on the far side. I'll . . . be joining you later."

With that he turned and, gathering his robes close, beat a retreat through the crowds along the shore, making for the nearest alehouse. Or anywhere else out of the Red Hood's sight.

The Oar Mistress shook her head, secretly wishing she dared join him. But she braced herself, calling commands to her men as she boarded her river craft and took her place at the tiller. The oars set into motion, and the barge began its journey over the mile-wide Aiga to the town on the far side. The river, in all the hundreds of times she'd crossed it, had never seemed so endlessly broad.

Throughout the crossing, the Red Hood stood beside her horse, her gaze upon the far shore, never saying a word to anyone.

The Aiga River shimmered under the afternoon sun, its waters deceptively placid to the naked eye. Ayleth was not deceived. She observed the oarsmen from her position in the center of the barge, noting how they strained their backs to maintain a steady rhythm and straight course as they carried their cargo across the Aiga's powerful flow.

It was cold out on the open water. Ayleth pulled her cloak tight and stepped closer to Chestibor. This was not her first time on a barge. She had traveled in similar fashion for seven days, down the Aalis River from Drauval and deep into the low country of Perrinion, cutting her travel time in half. A day's ride across country had followed, keeping off the main roads to avoid encountering strangers, and now this crossing of the Aiga into Wodechran. With any luck, she would present herself at Dunloch Castle before the Golden Prince had made his final choice for the outpost position.

The town on the far side of the river sprawled impossibly large to Ayleth's eye, its red-tile rooftops and white-washed wattle-and-daub walls reflecting the sun with stunning brilliance. According to Hollis's map, there should be no town here—but that map was a good twenty years old or more, and the only adjustments to it had been made by Hollis herself. This town, bright, new, and prosperous, must have risen after Hollis left for Drauval all those years ago.

As the barge approached the docks, Ayleth listened to the Oar Mistress call brusque orders to begin readying the cargo for unloading. The boat boys worked around Ayleth as though she might at any moment spring at them like a panther, but they had no reason to fear her. She had already cast a cursory glance over the crew using her shadow vision, and, so far as she could tell, there were no shade-taken aboard the vessel.

Ignoring the frightened stares, she stroked Chestibor's neck. "We're almost there, boy," she whispered. And, down inside her mind, she added, *"We're close, Laranta."*

Her wolf shade only growled in answer, bound under too many suppressing spell songs to offer much else.

The barge pulled into the dock minutes later, and Ayleth, without a word of farewell to the Oar Mistress or the crew, led her horse down the gangplank and on into the town. They did not wish to speak to her, and she preferred to keep to herself in any case. She wouldn't breathe easy again until she had left both barge and town behind.

She mounted quickly and rode through the winding streets, avoiding eye contact with those who stared at her, and taking the widest roads through the crowded cluster of buildings. There was something terribly oppressive about the frightened stares and terrified, trembling spirits of all those townspeople. One would think she was their enemy.

Although her red hood marked her as an Evanderian, they could never forget that she herself was shade-taken. She would always be a figure of dread to those she sought to save.

Eventually she would get used to it, she told herself as she guided Chestibor onto a likely-looking eastern road, finally escaping the town limits and gaining the open country beyond. It would take time to build up a tolerance to the fear her presence ignited in others. She would get there just as Hollis had.

With that thought, the image of Hollis's stone-hard face flashed across her vision. Ayleth winced. She didn't like to think of her mistress. It was three weeks now since she'd left Gillanluòc behind without a message to tell the venatrix where she'd gone. Hollis would no doubt guess, and Ayleth could only hope she wouldn't set out after her. If the Goddess was on Ayleth's side, then perhaps Hollis hadn't yet returned from her hunt, hadn't yet discovered that her one-time apprentice had turned runaway . . .

It didn't bear thinking on, so Ayleth concentrated on the road before her. She was so close to her destination now. She needed to focus her thoughts on the future, on her mission.

An hour after leaving the river town behind, she found a little-traveled trail that she believed to be a venator's circuit and turned Chestibor to follow it, riding uphill. The higher she climbed, the better her view of Wodechran Borough became. She glimpsed distant villages and shrine houses. Their surrounding fields were well tended, and those laborers she glimpsed from afar looked healthy and hale. The Golden Prince was apparently a good and fair master.

A sudden chill rippled through her.

At the beginning of her flight from Gillanluòc she had

focused entirely on getting to Wodechran. But now that she was here . . . now that she was within a few hours' ride of Dunloch Castle . . .

"Goddess, help me," she muttered, "I'm not ready to stand before . . . before *him*."

The Golden Prince wasn't just any prince. He was the son of the Chosen King. His father had been the Goddess's own instrument, Her incarnate right hand, used to kill Dread Odile and end the Witch Wars. And the son . . . He was the prophesied heir sent to lead the people of Perrinion into a Golden Age. A figure of myth and legend since before his birth, living proof of the Goddess's favor upon mortals.

He would laugh in her face.

Ayleth hauled on Chestibor's reins so sharply, he pinned his ears back and yanked at his bit. Her heart thundered in her throat. The foolish imaginings she'd indulged in over the last few weeks flashed before her eyes—all those daydreams of striding valiantly to the base of a mighty throne, her cloak billowing, her buckles flashing . . .

A hot flush crept up her cheeks. How could she have

been so stupid? How could she have been so arrogant? So focused on her prize that she neglected to face reality?

The Prince would take one look at her compared to the other candidates and see at once that she was an inexperienced bumpkin from nowhere. It wasn't as though she had any proof of her qualifications. She didn't even have her mistress's approval.

And what about the other candidates? The letter from Venator du Tam had given no indication how many there might be, but whoever they were, they must be the best Perrinion had to offer. Did she truly think she could compete against such high levels of training and skill? The favored candidates selected and sent directly by the castra?

Laranta shuddered at the sudden tumult of thoughts inside their shared head space. She shifted, started to growl. *Too loud. Trying to sleep.*

"*You're no help,*" Ayleth snapped back internally.

Her shade snarled and curled in on herself, tucking into a small, irked ball in a corner of Ayleth's consciousness.

Well, she couldn't just sit here in the middle of the

road. The day was well advanced, and now that she'd come this far . . . Ayleth urged Chestibor back into motion. Now that she'd come this far, she must see this foolish plan of hers through to the end. It was that or run back to Gillanluòc with her tail between her legs to grovel at her mistress's feet in hopes of forgiveness. But she would not grovel. Never. She would face the results of her own impulsiveness head-on.

"Maybe I should change uniforms," she murmured to Chestibor's unconcerned ears, which twitched in response to her voice. "My other uniform is no better than this one, but perhaps it's a little fresher—" Her voice broke off just as her horse carried her to the top of the rise. All other worries fled, and her eyes rounded with horror.

The Witchwood spread before her view.

The final curse of Dread Odile. The poisoned heart of Perrinion.

Though she'd studied Hollis's map many times during her journey, there could be no way to mentally prepare for the sheer size of the darkness spreading across the landscape. To the north she saw the river Aiga flowing, but south and east the Witchwood extended beyond the visible horizon. Although the fringe forests, no more than a half mile from Ayleth's current position, shimmered red and gold with autumnal color, reflecting sunlight from their crowns, Ayleth saw clearly the demarcation of the Great Barrier spell song.

Beyond that line, the trees of the Witchwood seemed to swallow up all color, all light, crushing it into irredeemable darkness. And deep inside, many miles past the border, a massive stone hand reached up through the canopy of the wood like a drowning man's one last grasp for life.

Once upon a time, the great idol of Dread Odile had dominated this landscape. Once upon a time, it loomed above all, impossible in its beauty, carved from pure oblidite by the power of the Witch Queen herself, erected in her own honor for her followers to worship.

The Witchwood had swallowed up Odile's city and eaten away at the idol until only the hand remained—a desperate, forsaken testimony to the power which the Chosen King had ended with a stroke of his sword.

Ayleth could not tear her eyes away from that sight. From those five pillar-like fingers tipped in long talons of stone.

Laranta uncurled from her sulk inside and pushed against the spell-song bindings, climbing up into the forefront of Ayleth's mind. *I smell shade,* she said.

With a shake of her head, Ayleth pulled her gaze away from the Witchwood. *"Many shades live in that forest,"* she said, urging Chestibor back into motion and guiding him carefully down the incline. She thought of the names listed in Hollis's book—the Crimson Devils. But how many other shade-taken had, over the years, fled beyond the Great Barrier to escape Evander's Order? Was the death they feared truly worse than an ongoing existence in that nightmarish wood?

Laranta growled softly but intently. Ayleth felt her shade's eagerness prickle under her skin. *I smell shade. Near!*

Ayleth frowned at this. *"Hush, Laranta,"* she said. *"Or I'll bind you back."*

Laranta backed down. But she continued to brim with excitement at the back of Ayleth's awareness as they descended the incline and resumed their journey on level ground. This trail, Ayleth realized, would take her close to the fringe forests of the Witchwood. Disliking this notion, she reached for her map, hoping to find a better route to Dunloch Castle. But just as her hand touched the long container holding the map, movement caught her eye.

Looking up, she saw a horse with an empty saddle wander out from the shadows of the fringe forest.

Shade! Laranta growled. *Near!*

CHAPTER 7

"LARANTA, GIVE ME YOUR SIGHT."

Her wolf shade responded at once to the command, and Ayleth's vision blazed with shadow-light. She studied the riderless horse, searching for some sign of an indwelling shade, but discerned nothing more than the basic, wholesome gleam of horse soul.

The beast, catching scent of Chestibor, lifted its head and cupped its ears forward. With a nervous nicker it started toward them, eager for companionship after its wander in the forest. Chestibor snorted a greeting, moving at Ayleth's command toward the other beast, which put out its nose to Chestibor.

Ayleth slipped from her saddle and caught the strange horse by the reins. It shied a little but calmed with a few soothing murmurs and a gentle stroke on its neck. Chestibor's presence gave it courage. Ayleth ran her hands over the beast, searching for some sign of injury or hard use. It was a handsome, well-kept horse, evidently of bloodlines more exalted than those of her own tough mountain steed. The tack it wore was unadorned but of good quality as well.

She led the horse to the nearest tree on the edge of the forest and secured its reins to a stout branch. On second thought, she tied Chestibor alongside it. Then, using Laranta's vision, she looked carefully around the countryside and into the forest itself, searching for the glimmer of a mortal soul.

Nothing. But surely this horse's rider must be somewhere close. The animal did not look as though it had been abandoned long.

Something wasn't right here.

Ayleth slipped her Vocos from its sheath and snapped it into position. Drawing a breath, she blew into life the Song of Command. Laranta sprang forward at once, brimming with excitement and ready to hunt. Ayleth played a variation of the song spell, calling Laranta out of her mind to manifest in the mortal world beside her as the great black wolf.

Shade! Laranta said eagerly, tugging at the soul tether like a puppy on a leash.

Ayleth played a sharp line of music, hauling her back. "*I need you to find a mortal soul,*" she said in her mind. "*The mortal who rode this horse.*"

Laranta curled her lip in protest. But she could not resist the bidding of the song spell. She approached the horse, which could neither see nor sense the wolf shade in any way, but which nevertheless pulled nervously against its tether. Ayleth's knot held it fast.

Laranta lifted her huge head, snuffling at the saddle. *Mortal,* she said without much enthusiasm. She turned her muzzle toward the forest and set off at a brisk padding gait. *This way.*

Ayleth finished the last measure of the spell and

tucked the Vocos into its sheath before trotting after her wolf shade into the shadows of the fringe forest. She kept Laranta's shade vision in her eyes, watching the shimmering world of spirit that overlay the mortal world. The trees shone with pulsing life, strange spirits utterly unlike those of mortals or shades but potent in their own way. Small animal and even insect souls gleamed in her periphery, but Ayleth had long since learned to drive these distractions back to the edges of her awareness and focus on her mission.

Ahead, Laranta pulled up short. Her hackles rose.

"*What is it?*" Ayleth asked, her silent voice rippling along the soul tether.

Shade, Laranta answered, but this time with an edge to her voice. Her growl was no longer eager but warning.

Using her shadow sight, Ayleth peered ahead through the trees in the direction Laranta faced. She just discerned a shimmering of . . . magic.

Laranta was right. There was a shade. Near.

"*Where is the mortal scent?*" she asked her wolf shade.

Ahead.

Ayleth pulled the red hood from her head and tucked

it out of sight. She was now officially on the hunt and dared not offer the shade-taken any indication of her identity. "*Lead on, Laranta,*" she said. "*Maybe we're in time to save this unfortunate mortal.*"

Her shade moved ahead, losing most of her wolf shape and becoming little more than an inky shadow along the ground. Ayleth, though she could not see her, followed via their soul tether. She took care how and where she placed her feet, making no more sound than was unavoidable.

The sense of magic increased from a faint shimmer to a powerful force glowing brighter and brighter. Laranta stopped behind a stand of fir trees through which light burned like a small blue sun come down to the ground.

There. Shade.

Ayleth carefully parted the needled branches veiling her vision. She gasped.

Before her stood a mighty monastery—a huge edifice that could not possibly be there in the middle of that thick forest. For a moment Ayleth's head swam with the sickness of double vision, seeing the massive building and the forest at the same time.

Then her shadow sight adjusted, and she saw that what she at first perceived as solid stone walls and arches and lead-tiled roofs was nothing more than shimmering blue illusion. Ghostly and cold yet strangely convincing—so detailed that she almost believed it. Every pillar was chiseled to perfection; every stone saint stood in its alcove. She even heard chanting—a hundred women's voices singing together in harmonies more complex than any Vocos or Detrudos song.

An Apparition, she thought, creating a vision in her mind. Baring her teeth in a vicious grimace, she drew her scorpiona from its holster, snapped it into place on her bracer, and loaded a paralysis dart. Her grimace turned to a smile. She now had experience hunting Apparitions. She wouldn't let one manipulate her again.

Creeping forward, forcing herself to see through the shimmer of illusion, she beheld instead the forest itself. Massive ruins lay around her, covered in earth, grown over with moss and trees. Crumbled walls, broken doorways. Statues of the saints disintegrating into ruin. But where was the shade?

A door shimmered before her, a pulsing blue illusion

so convincing, she almost stopped in front of it, believing she could not pass. But behind lay the reality, nothing more than a pile of rubble. She pushed on, climbing over the broken stones—and hit a wall of ice-cold air.

It was so sharp, so sudden, it nearly froze the blood in her veins and shattered her bones. For a moment her senses were totally overcome. In the back of her brain she knew she was experiencing spirit bind, a temporary but absolute freezing of her soul which simultaneously transfixed the body. She could move nothing save her eyes.

Then she saw the shade.

It was a huge, wafting, hideous thing of no definite shape. She could not discern the host body through the haze of misty spirit shrouds. She thought she saw hair, reaching hands, two enormous eyes fixed, not on her, but on something kneeling before it.

A man, his spirit shining bright inside him, blazing with abject fear.

Out of the writhing shrouds, one skeletal hand moved, reaching down to catch the man's spirit out of his chest.

"*Laranta!*" Ayleth cried inside.

Her shade's powers surged through her, breaking the spirit bind. The impact of that break rippled back to the enormous shade, which looked up from its prey and fastened two dreadful, cold eyes on her.

Ayleth dropped to a crouch and, without stopping to think, moving on pure instinct, shot the dart.

It sped through the air and struck home. The vision of the wafting spirit vanished, revealing an ancient, withered person of indeterminate sex. The dart protruded from a hollow, emaciated throat, its fletched end quivering. For an instant, mortal eyes stared across the distance, catching Ayleth's gaze.

A blinding flash of heat.

Ayleth flew backwards and landed hard, striking her head. Darkness closed in around her vision, but her conscious awareness fought against it, screaming, *"You fool! You fool! You used the wrong poison!"*

This shade was not an Apparition.

Through the darkness of threatening unconsciousness, a wrathful light leered into her tunneling vision. An illusion of seething, roiling spirit stuff, blasting not heat but ice into her face. Ayleth stared up, unable to move. A piece of the roiling spirit substance separated from the mass, a huge, many-jointed limb lifting high, prepared to strike.

The blow never fell. Suddenly, out of the shadows, Laranta leapt. While the wolf shade could not directly influence physical bodies, her spirit form was perfectly capable of hurling itself at another spirit. She grabbed hold of that long, weirdly jointed limb and, with a wrench of her powerful jaws, broke it.

From the depths of the roiling rage sounded a soul-searing scream. The shade lashed out, striking at Laranta's head. But as claws manifested and tore through her fur, the wolf shade lunged again, this time aiming for the center of the spirit. The blow struck the shade to its core, and the spirit shuddered. With a boom that rumbled the ground on which Ayleth lay, the spirit folded in on itself and retreated into its host body.

The shimmering walls of the monastery vanished. Ayleth, her head still spinning, pushed herself up in time to see the naked, withered person leaping over ruined walls and fleeing into the forest.

"Haunts damn!" Ayleth swore through her teeth and

pulled herself into a crouch, determined to give chase. But then her gaze fell upon the man still kneeling where the shade had left him. His face was slack, his arms limp at his sides, his head bowed to his chest.

"My good sir!" Ayleth stood upright too quickly, and the world spun and went black on the edges. She braced her legs, drawing several long breaths. Once her vision cleared, she cautiously approached the man, mindful of the shifting rubble under her feet, and dropped to her knees before him.

He was breathing—a hopeful sign. And when she studied him with her shadow vision, she could see that his soul was still present inside. The front of his shirt was burned away. Ayleth pulled back the ruined fabric and found the imprint of a hand over his heart, pulsing faintly with magic but swiftly fading, much to her relief.

Ayleth took the man's face between her hands, tilting it up to her own. She tapped his cheeks, gently at first, but with increasing force. "My good sir. My good sir!"

The man's brow pulled into a tight knot. His lips parted, drawing back in a grimace, revealing strong white teeth. Then his eyelids fluttered, opened.

And Ayleth found herself gazing into a pair of amber eyes rimmed with long lashes, set in an extraordinarily handsome, fine-boned face.

"Who . . . who the Haunts are you?" the man gasped, his voice thick in his throat.

Ayleth hesitated, momentarily at a loss for words. Then, with a little shake of her head and an uplift of her chin, she said, "I'm the new Venatrix of Wodechran."

CHAPTER 8

THE ANCIENT MONASTERY BOASTED A SINGLE standing wall—part of the central shrine house, Ayleth guessed. Most of the clustered buildings lay in ruin, overgrown by forest. In that one wall, the frame of what might once have been an incredible stained-glass window now held only empty air, overlooking the dense growth of trees all around. This must be one of the many holy sites Dread Odile decimated early in her reign, allowing the forest ample opportunity during the past two centuries to swallow what remained.

The man, still suffering the after-effects of his encounter with the shade, sat with his back against a chunk of broken masonry and watched as Ayleth prowled the perimeter of the shrine-house chancel. She felt his gaze on the side of her face and turned to meet it. He blinked several times.

"So, tell me again," he said, speaking carefully as though afraid of saying the wrong thing. "You are . . . who, exactly?"

"Ayleth, Venatrix di Ferosa of the Order of Saint Evander," Ayleth answered, her voice crisp and confident. "I'm here under the sanction of the Golden Prince to take Milisendis Outpost. Now tell me, how did you end up alone in this forest, unhorsed, at the mercy of that shade-taken?"

The strange man frowned, opened his mouth as though to say something, but then, with a shake of his head, thought better of it. Instead, he looked down at his burned shirt and touched the place on his chest where the glowing handprint had faded. "Ow," he said, grimacing, though there wasn't a mark on his skin. "What . . .

happened to me?"

Apparently, she was going to have to answer questions before getting answers herself. Ayleth strode back to the man, standing over him and crossing her arms. She shouldn't take such an intimidating stance, but, well . . . the truth was, he unnerved her. Her experience with young men was limited to a few brief encounters with rough farm-boy types who weren't even brave enough to look her in the eyes. Which didn't incline her to pursue closer acquaintance.

This man, however, gazed up at her with some confusion but no fear. And he was simply too beautiful to be quite real.

"You were nearly taken by a shade," she said. But even as she spoke the words, she frowned. In the heat of the hunt she'd not paid careful attention to every detail, but now things she had seen came back to her with more clarity and context. "It was . . . trying to oust your spirit before possessing your body."

The man tried to stand but couldn't quite make it. He sat down again hard, one leg out before him, the other knee drawn up. "I don't think I understand. You're saying there was a shade?" He looked around then at the collapsed walls, his expression shifting from confusion to blankness to fear by turns. "This is the Abbey of Saint Godelieve." His brow cleared suddenly, and he whispered, "Oh. Now I remember."

With those words, he bowed his head, resting it on his upraised knee.

Ayleth didn't pay him much attention. Her mind whirled with too many thoughts and realizations. "I got it all wrong," she muttered. Laranta, still manifesting as a wolf, paced up to her, head tilted. "*I got it wrong,*" Ayleth told her shade. "*This is a trap. The illusion, the singing . . . This is a trap meant to entice a new host body. Apparitions don't set traps like this. Oh! Haunts damn!*"

Laranta flattened her ears and sat back on her haunches, watching as her mistress paced. Ayleth cursed again. She should have known! She should have realized the moment she heard the chanting. It was the *song*, the complex song she'd heard, that had presented her with the vision of the restored abbey. Not a perfect, clear illusion such as an Apparition would work upon the mind—no, this had been but a shimmering ghost of a vision. But the song had made her almost believe it despite the truth her eyes clearly perceived.

Had the song been directed *at* her, she might have fallen for the illusion completely. But she was not the target.

She turned to the man, who slowly shook his head as he raised it from his knee. He was terribly disheveled. His hair, of indeterminate color, was covered in dirt and spider webs, and his clothing—rough huntsman's garb, Ayleth noted—was dirty and torn. But he was clean-shaven, no shadow of beard covering his cheeks or jaw. Which meant he hadn't been here long.

"Do you know when you were enchanted?" Ayleth asked, though she knew as she voiced the question that it was useless. He was magic-addled and couldn't possibly give an accurate answer. "Never mind. We must assume it's been less than a day, judging by your appearance."

"My appearance?" His hand went to his hair, feeling the spider webs there. "How bad is it?"

This she didn't try to answer. What would she say? *Don't worry, sir. Dirty, haggard, covered in spider webs, you're still by far the most attractive man I've ever set eyes on . . .* No.

Besides, beautiful or otherwise, he was just a mortal fool who'd gotten himself snared in a shade trap.

Specifically, in the trap of a Lure—a shade associated with siren calls and beguilement for the purpose of tempting victims into their traps. Then they either feasted or took new host bodies. In this instance, Ayleth had to assume the latter. The shade must have been quite motivated to take a new body, considering the decrepit state of its current host.

She crouched before the man, bringing her face level with his. Telling herself firmly not to be distracted by those amber eyes blinking at her with such bewilderment. She had a job to do.

"Tell me what you remember," she said.

He flinched at her brusque tone but answered readily enough. "I remember a song. I was riding on the fringes, and I heard music. It was captivating, and I felt . . . compelled, somehow. To find it, to find the source of it. I slipped away from my company and ventured further into the forest. There was a light." He shook his head. "I know it's foolish, but I believed I saw this abbey standing whole. I was awestruck. I didn't stop to think it couldn't be real. And as I drew nearer, the door opened, and standing in the doorway . . ."

"What?" Ayleth demanded, resisting the urge to shake him in her eagerness to get his full answer. "What did you see?"

His eyes flashed to meet hers, but he looked away again quickly. "Someone I thought I knew," he whispered. "I should have known better. I've been here many times over the years; I am well aware that Godelieve is a ruin. Part of me realized I must be seeing things, but I . . . I *wanted* to believe."

Ayleth nodded. It all fit her theory well enough. "Go on."

"I don't know what more to say," he answered with a shrug. "I stepped through the doorway and wandered the halls for some while, calling for . . . the person I thought was there. I kept believing I saw her, kept believing that just around the next corner she would appear. Then, when I was ready to give up, she approached me herself, speaking my name. Or rather, she didn't. But I believed she did."

It all came together. The deadly song of a Lure could

make a human mind believe all manner of things as it drew a victim deeper into its trap. "What I don't understand," she muttered, "is why it took so long. Once it had you in the trap, it should have been easy for the shade to oust your soul and take possession of your body. Unless . . ."

He gave her a wary look. "Unless what?"

Unless he was already shade-taken.

Rather than voice this thought out loud, Ayleth called up Laranta's shadow vision and turned to the man, staring into his eyes. He began to move away, but she caught him by the shoulders and forced him to look at her, studying what secrets his eyes might disclose. A cursory glance had revealed no sign of a possessing shade, but a spirit might well be crouched deep down within this man's soul, hidden from view. His prior possession would explain why the Lure had failed to oust his soul.

It would also mean she had a duty to perform.

Ayleth forced her shadow vision to look deeper and then deeper still. An ascendant shade she could detect easily enough, but in the case of a hidden spirit, the eyes were the best place to search. Shades enter their host bodies through the eyes. The Order designated a body that could be possessed as "eye-torn." This referred not to a physical tearing but to a spiritual opening into the soul.

To her surprise, Ayleth could find no sign of a tear. Though she searched long and hard, her vision glowing with shadow-light, the stranger's eyes were perfect, clear. Untorn.

This man was incapable of being possessed. One of the few. One of the blessed.

"That explains it then," she said, pulling back and letting go of his shoulders.

The man swallowed hard, still staring at her. "Um. I'm sorry?"

She realized that she'd just been gazing into his eyes without speaking for much longer than might be deemed socially acceptable. And he'd had no idea what she was doing.

A furious blush crept up her neck. She stood up and backed away quickly. "I . . . Well . . . You are untorn," she said. "That explains why the shade was unable to oust your spirit. Probably."

"Oh. Um. Good to know." The man raised his brows, his mouth twisted in a nervous half-smile. He got to his feet then, swaying a little but more stable than before. "I should probably find my horse," he said. "It was good to meet you, Venatrix—"

"Wait, you're leaving?"

The man stopped, his eyes swiveling uncomfortably sideways then back to her face. "I was, actually, yes."

"But you can't." Ayleth took two quick steps forward and placed her outspread hand directly on his chest.

The man blinked. "Um."

"Right here," Ayleth said urgently. "Right here is where it touched you. I saw the mark myself. The Lure has anchored a curse. It's not strong and will fade fast, but for the moment"—she stared into his eyes, the urgency of the hunt bright in her face—"for the moment, the connection is still there. If I can call the curse back into full potency, the shade will return. And I can kill it."

His gaze dropped from her face to her hand. She was touching his bare skin. With a short gasp, she pulled her hand back quickly.

"So, let me see if I've got this right," the man said,

looking up at her again, eyebrows high. "You want me to be . . . bait? For a shade. A shade that wants to oust my soul and steal my body."

"Well, we already know that it cannot oust your soul."

"It *probably* cannot."

"Probably. Yes. Most likely."

"And if it should fail once more, it will . . . devour me?"

"Oh. Well." Ayleth rubbed the back of her neck beneath her long braid. "It's more likely that a second touch would stop your heart. But Lures aren't all of them carnivorous. Not necessarily, anyway."

"I see."

Ayleth gritted her teeth, her hands clenching into fists. She needed to catch this shade. She couldn't possibly ride on to Dunloch Castle knowing that she'd left a dangerous spirit loose in the very borough she intended to claim as her own. "See here, my good sir, if the shade goes unstopped—"

"I'll do it."

Ayleth blinked, persuasions dying on her tongue. "You will?"

"If the shade goes unstopped," the man said, completing her argument, "it will no doubt ensnare some other unsuspecting host. One that may be more susceptible to possession. I don't want to be responsible for some poor soul's death. Or damnation, for that matter."

He drew himself up straight, running a hand through his cobwebby hair, and gave Ayleth a smile that took her by surprise. Her stomach twisted, not at all unpleasantly.

"Tell me," the man said, "what you need me to do, Venatrix."

CHAPTER 9

CALLING THE LURE'S CURSE BACK INTO FULL LIFE WAS easier said than done. It required using her Detrudos, which worked influence on shades other than her own, but Ayleth struggled to decide which song spell to try. There were no Detrudos songs specifically used to revive faded shade curses. They were all intended for breaking and suppression.

After trying and failing to use a variation of the Song of Summoning—which was intended to be played on the

Vocos rather than the Detrudos pipes anyway—Ayleth at last attempted the Song of Revealing. She thought perhaps she could use the song to reveal what remained of the faded curse and, in that revealing, call it back into power.

The minute she began the complex tune, she knew it would work. But finding the correct variation was no simple matter. She tried several before finally hitting on one that seemed to return a glimmer of spell light, the faint outline of a hand on the man's chest.

He felt it too, sucking in a sharp breath and taking a half-step back from Ayleth as she played. But he braced himself, squaring his shoulders and setting his jaw, and retreated no further, not even when the curse suddenly blazed back into full power. It hurt him, but he did not cry out. His face only flinched a little.

"There," she said, dropping the pipes from her mouth and studying the place where the glowing handprint once more shimmered over his skin.

He looked down too, but without shadow sight, he could see nothing. "It worked?" he asked.

"Can't you feel it?"

The man nodded slowly. "There's a . . . coldness."

"Then it worked." Ayleth snapped her pipes shut and tucked them into their sheath. "Now I need you to— Are you all right?"

All color suddenly drained from the man's face. His mouth went slack, his eyes, empty. He slowly spun in place, looking up at walls, arches, pillars, statues, and stained-glass windows that were not there. His lips moved, trying to speak. Nothing but a moan escaped as he sank to his knees.

The curse was definitely reawakened.

Ayleth drew a long breath. "Right," she muttered. Then, "You wait here. I'll be close." He couldn't hear her, but she felt better after leaving him with a parting word. He'd agreed to do this based on confidence that she could fulfill her part. She had better justify his trust.

As she climbed back out of the ruins, shimmers of light appeared in the air, telling her that the rest of the Lure spell was quickly repairing itself. Would it work as a reverse snare to the siren shade? She believed so . . . but this was pure conjecture on her part.

Once free of the rubble, she retreated to the forest,

away from the ruins. If she stayed too close, the Lure would sense her and not return. It would not want to risk another encounter with Laranta. Then she'd be forced to track it through this strange forest, so close to the Witchwood. Even with Laranta's abilities at her disposal, it would take time, and the shade might hurt others along the way. Better to catch it now and end this. If possible.

Ayleth hid in the grove of fir trees, pressed low to the ground. Edging in beside her, Laranta quivered with excitement. But she was an experienced hunter; she waited in absolute silence for her prey to approach.

Ayleth took comfort in her shade's proximity. Granted, the wolf shade was always with her, inside her, but she preferred to have Laranta out of her head and manifested in this form at her side. If it wasn't so dangerous to give her shade this much leeway—if it didn't risk letting Laranta grow in strength and ultimately turn on her—she would never use the Vocos to suppress her shade at all.

But those were heretical thoughts. She quickly dismissed them and focused on the shimmering Lure spell, which strengthened rapidly now. The shade must be drawing near. Ayleth checked her scorpiona, already armed with the paralysis dart. She wished she dared go for the Gentle Death directly but knew she wouldn't be able to get close enough to deliver the poison without alerting the shade to her approach. It would already be wary, having had an encounter with her. If not for the power of its own curse drawing it back to its marked prey, it would be long gone by now.

Suddenly . . . music. Voices. Hundreds of women's voices, chanting together in chorus, first a mere whisper on the edge of Ayleth's conscious awareness, slowly growing in power.

The reverse snare was working.

As the song increased, so did the intensity of the visual illusion. Rather than a faint shimmer, the walls of the monastery began to take shape once more before Ayleth's vision, all their long-lost glory temporarily restored.

Ayleth crept forward. She could not see the shade through this bright vision of magic. But she had to believe it was near now, near enough to be focused on its prey and not attentive to her approach. This time she didn't seek the door of the monastery—she knew better than to believe in that part of the spell. Rising to her feet, she crept right up to the glowing wall and climbed over the ruinous stones lying beneath the illusion. She peered into the chapel.

There below her knelt the man, his face upturned to the ghost of the great stained-glass window. Ayleth saw his mouth open, close.

Then he cried out, "Fayline!"

The shade appeared. Huge, shining, and powerful, the illusion completely shrouded the reality of its mortal host. It drifted through the window, reaching many-jointed arms out toward the man. For an instant—just the barest breath of an instant—Ayleth believed she saw neither the spiritual being nor the withered host. Rather, she glimpsed, all in ghostly blue haze, a young, beautiful woman clad in a tattered ballgown, her face shining with pure love.

"Fayline!" the man cried again, reaching both arms toward the apparition, which swept down upon him with vicious intent. A single touch to the heart from one of those hands would kill him this time. No mortal could survive that touch twice.

Ayleth leapt upright, took aim and fired, not into the wafting image, which was not her true target, but down lower, where she could barely discern the form of the host body.

The dart struck its mark. Directly between the eyes.

A gut-wrenching howl shattered the spell, breaking through the chanting voices. The ghostly walls of the abbey fell, stone upon stone, landing exactly where their physical counterparts lay.

The withered host body collapsed to its knees before the man, reaching out trembling hands, trying to grab him by the front of his burned shirt. He recoiled, horrified, his eyes still half dazzled with the enchantment. What a shock to wake from the image of that beautiful girl to find himself facing this horror of broken humanity.

"No, no, *no!*" the host body croaked. Its mouth dropped open, and a terrible, otherworldly light blazed deep in its throat. With a choking gurgle it fell on its side. The man got up hastily and backed away, then took a half step forward, reaching down as though to help.

"Don't touch it!" Ayleth scrambled down the ruined wall and hastened toward him. "We're not done yet."

"What . . . what of the mortal soul?" the man asked, drawing back but still gazing down on that wretch, his face twisted with an expression Ayleth could not name.

"There is no mortal soul left," she answered. Closing the distance between her and the shade-taken body, she slotted the Gentle Death into her scorpiona. As soon as her shadow sight told her that the shade inside was quieted, unable to resist, she shot the dart straight for the cavernous chest, into the heart.

With a shuddering gasp followed by a huge sigh as though of relief, the body died. The soul of the possessing shade rose from the mortal remains, shimmering, roiling, snarled in tangled spirit coils. As she suspected, there was no human-soul orb to be seen. Only the shade.

She quickly pulled out her Detrudos and began to play the Song of Expulsion. The air shivered with the simultaneous heat and chill of the Haunts opening wide to receive its due.

Ayleth closed her eyes, refusing to succumb to the temptation to look, focusing on her song. Her spell song ensnared the shade soul, winding tightly around it, and carried it on to the realm of its eternal torment.

The Haunts snapped shut, driving Ayleth back several paces. Nevertheless, she played the end of the song spell, bringing the melody to a conclusion. Only when it was complete did she let the Detrudos fall from her lips. Then, breathing hard, she opened her eyes . . .

And saw the man kneeling beside the corpse of the shade-taken, gently holding its hand.

CHAPTER 10

AYLETH CROUCHED ACROSS FROM THE MAN, ON THE other side of the body. Now that the spirit was gone from inside it, she could see more clearly just what the Lure had done to its host. The skin was paper-thin, translucent, the veins standing out thick and black with blighted blood. The body was utterly emaciated, the ribcage a cavern of bones. The skeleton was all too visible, displaying every sign of rot in the marrow. Only the magic of the shade itself had kept the body going for this long.

She recalled reading about Lures in Hollis's small library at Gillanluòc. Unlike most shades, they did not care for their host bodies but used them up rapidly. Thus, they were known for setting traps for new hosts, passing frequently from body to body. Human bodies when they could get them, animal when necessary.

There would be no point in trying to salvage these remains for the castra.

A bolt of horror shot through Ayleth's heart, making her breath catch in her throat. Did she really just think that thought? Crouched here beside the first shade-taken human she'd ever brought down in the name of the Order, did she truly just consider the worth of its remains? *Her* remains. Now that she was close enough, Ayleth saw that the naked, withered body was female.

Had she already become so hardened?

Shaking her head as though she could clear it of these thoughts, she looked across at the man. He still held that limp, withered hand. "Was she . . . someone you knew?" Ayleth asked.

To her relief the man said, "No. I wondered at first if

maybe . . . But I've never seen this woman before." He looked up at Ayleth, his eyes swimming. "What became of her soul?"

Ayleth hated to answer. His expression told her he was looking for the truth, however, so she forced the words out. "A soul ousted from its body wanders revenant in this world for some while afterward. Eventually it . . . fades."

"The Goddess does not take such souls into Her Light?"

"According to the writings of Saint Evander, no."

The man studied the face of the broken shade-taken. The skin was already peeling away, disintegrating before their eyes. Within minutes there would be nothing left but scattered, shade-blighted dust. "Seems an ineffectual Goddess who cannot save the souls of Her children."

This outspoken blasphemy struck Ayleth like a physical blow. She drew back from the man in an unconscious need to separate herself from him and his words. What should she do? How should she react? As a member of the Evanderian Order, her life was dedicated to the service of the Goddess. Should she say something?

Reprimand him? Correct his error?

Yet, a secret, dangerous part of her mind whispered, if the Goddess was indeed all-powerful, why would She let innocent souls be lost so pointlessly? Was She truly not so divine or so good?

Or was there some mistake in the teachings Ayleth had always believed so implicitly?

Her brows drew together, deepening the line between them. "The tragedy of ousted souls must serve as a reminder to all servants of the Order how important our work is," she spoke firmly. "How vital our duty to drive the spirits of the Haunts back into their imprisonment and out of this world." It was nearly a direct quote from the Saint's own writings. A safe fallback for when she felt out of her depth.

The man gave her a quick glance. Then the hand he was holding broke apart into nothing, and he drew back, watching the disintegration. Silently he moved his right hand in a gesture of blessing, touching forehead, heart, and mouth, symbolizing the three holy attributes of the Goddess—Head, Heart, and Soul. Bowing his head, he began murmuring a prayer for the fallen:

"May the Mother receive you, who hath called you, and may the heavenly spirits conduct you to the Gates of Light. GoddessHead have mercy. GoddessHeart have mercy. GoddessSoul have mercy."

Had he not heard what she said? The human soul was long gone. There was nothing left for the Goddess to receive. Ayleth held her tongue and stood, turning her back on him and the drifting pile of black dust that was all that remained of her prey.

The body was only a shell, she reminded herself. Just a shell. She had not hunted a human but a shade in a stolen human frame. Her first hunt of a shade-taken human with its soul still intact . . . that hunt was yet to come.

She shuddered.

"I'll take you back to your horse," she said over her shoulder to the man. "I found him wandering the edge of the forest and tied him to a tree."

"Thank you," the man answered. She heard him rise, heard him dust off his knees and draw a deep breath, letting it out in a sigh. "At your bidding, Venatrix."

She led him out of the ruins. Laranta trotted on ahead of them, guiding the way back through the forest, undetected by the man. Perhaps she ought to use her Vocos and suppress her shade, but for now Ayleth left their soul tether slack. It was comforting to have Laranta near and visible.

After some moments of pushing their way through underbrush and navigating the maze of trees, the man drew up alongside Ayleth. "So, tell me, how long have you been the new venatrix of Wodechran? Have you met the prince yet?"

Ayleth blushed. In her effort to assert her confidence and authority over the situation, she may have overstepped the mark. But then, this man was unlikely to know the doings of the Golden Prince and his dealings with Castra Breçar. "I have not officially met the prince yet, no," she admitted. "I was on my way to our first official meeting when I detected the shade presence near at hand."

"And lucky for me you did." His voice was easier, friendlier now than it had been. As they put distance between themselves and the abbey ruins, his spirit seemed to rise and brighten. He spoke with a certain courtly grace, Ayleth noted, which did not coincide with his rough garments or the serviceable tack she'd observed on his horse.

"Who do you work for?" she asked, wincing a little at how abrupt her voice sounded. She had no experience talking to ordinary people other than during interviews for hunts. She sounded like an interrogator!

But the man merely gave her a sidelong glance and answered without hesitation. "I am employed at Dunloch."

Haunts damn. This man worked under the prince himself. He might be more aware of the doings at the castle than she'd expected.

Time to deflect the conversation from this uncomfortable line.

"And what were you doing out here on the fringes? You say you were with a company?"

"Um, yes," he answered. "I rode out with a hunting party to chase rumors of a . . . a red-haired witch." He gave her another of his sidelong looks. "Prince Gerard is anxious to find out if these rumors are true. He might know who the witch is."

"Did Venator du Tam ride with you?"

"No. Venator du Tam is much occupied with the ongoing business of the borough now that his partner is gone. He was unavailable to join the hunt."

Ayleth's brow darkened. "You're telling me that the prince sent you and other men on a hunt for a possible shade-taken without a venator in your company? That is nothing short of idiotic."

"Come again?"

She threw up her hands, scoffing loudly. "However brave you and your cohorts may be, you are not equipped to deal with a shade-taken." She realized how angry she sounded and quickly tried to modify her tone. "Forgive me. I mean no offence to you or your fellows. Of course you must obey your master's commands. But he should never have put your lives at such risk. He should at least have waited until Venator du Tam could join you."

"I . . . I believe he was afraid that if he waited for the venator, the witch would disappear without a trace. He is quite keen on finding her."

"Witch hunting is no sport," Ayleth growled. "He's a fool if he thinks otherwise."

"No, of course. You're quite right." The man was

silent for several paces. "With the disappearance of Venator du Vincent, the borough has been . . . busier than usual. Shade-taken have always gravitated to Wodechran—making for the Great Barrier and escape into the Witchwood, you know. But the two venators, between them, were generally able to keep it under control. With one venator gone, du Tam is overtasked, and Castra Breçar has been slow to send a replacement."

"I understand." Ayleth gave the man what she hoped was a sympathetic look. "And your prince has been trying to deal with shade-taken by sending out you and your fellows on missions which you cannot hope to fulfill. It is wrong for him to risk your lives so."

The man gave her a half-smile, which crinkled his amber eyes pleasantly. "I trust you will tell the prince yourself when you meet?"

"Of course," Ayleth answered. "And you needn't concern yourself anymore either. I'm here now, and I'll take care of all rumors of witches or shade-taken."

The man nodded. "That is a relief." Another several paces, and he asked, "Are you trained to handle the Great Barrier then?"

A strange question. Ayleth frowned uncomfortably. What did a servant of Dunloch know about the specific tasks of a venator in this borough? Ayleth shot him a quick, sharp glare. "I am well trained in all aspects of my work," she said in a tone which implied it was none of his business.

The trees thinned around them. Following Laranta, Ayleth led the man directly to where their two horses waited. Chestibor didn't look up from his munching on a patch of weeds, but the other horse appeared frightened at their approach, pulling nervously at its ties.

"Whoa there, Nog," the man said, approaching his beast with his hand outstretched. At the sound of his voice, the horse visibly relaxed. He stroked its soft nose and checked it over for injuries, running his hands with expert, gentle skill up and down its legs and haunches. "Good boy," he murmured over and over.

Ayleth untied Chestibor but hesitated to mount. She watched the man with his steed for some moments before finally saying, "Do you need help finding the rest of your company?"

"No, no," he answered, looking round at her with

another of his half-smiles. It was so brilliant, she wondered briefly how devastating a full smile from him might be. "I can find my own way well enough. You should hurry on to the castle. You don't want to keep the prince waiting."

Ayleth nodded and mounted. She looked down at the man again, wondering if she ought to say something more. She realized she was rather reluctant to part from him. Which was stupidity itself! He was nothing more than a stranger whom she'd happened to liberate from enscorcellment. Nevertheless, she forced her stern mouth into a quick sort-of grin. "Perhaps we'll meet again at Dunloch."

With that, she quickly turned Chestibor's head away so she could hide her face and the horrible blush that flamed across her cheeks the moment the words left her mouth. Haunts damn, what was wrong with her?

"Wait a moment," the man called out.

Ayleth pulled Chestibor up and, mustering what remained of her dignity, looked coldly around, schooling her features into an utterly implacable expression, even if she couldn't hide the flush in her cheeks.

"The prince is fortunate to have such a brave and efficient venatrix come to Wodechran," the man said. He raised a hand in farewell.

Ayleth responded to the gesture in kind. Then she kicked Chestibor into a quick trot and hastened away, Laranta loping along in spirit beside them.

Dunloch Castle stood on an island in the middle of the shining waters of Loch du Nóiv—a holy lake, according to legend. Long ago, it was said, the Goddess Herself stepped down from Heaven to speak to the first Priestess Queen on those very shores. Hundreds of years later, Dunloch Abbey was built as a sacred retreat where men and women of various sacred orders might retreat for prayer and communion with the divine.

But that was long ago. Since then, the abbey had been rebuilt into a fortified castle that needed no wall. Steep, stone-lined banks would prevent any but the most intrepid of invaders from reaching the ground above, and a massive portcullis gate stood at the only bridge leading out to the keep.

Ayleth noted certain details first—the best points of defense, the weaknesses, considering what types of shades might take advantage of the lake setting and what might be done to prevent attacks. It took her several moments to notice how picturesque the castle looked, built of sun-brightened stone, standing there in the middle of that shining water. The sky reflected perfectly on the lake's surface, turning it to a bright mirror of blue, and the surrounding landscape seemed lusher as a result, its autumnal glow turned to burnished gold.

The circuit trail Ayleth had been following tapered away into nothing well before she entered the private grounds of Dunloch Castle. Finding a broad paved road leading through the manicured gardens and lawns, she followed it, meeting no one on her way save a few groundskeepers hard at work. These men and women, noting her approach, stood straight as though at attention until she had passed them by. She did not speak to them, nor they to her.

Most of the summer flowers had faded, but willows lined one shady avenue, the late sun casting golden spears of light between the trailing leaves. It was all much more elegant, far more beautiful and refined than any place Ayleth had ever seen. Laranta stalked along beside Chestibor in the spirit realm, growling irritably to herself. *We should go. Back to the forests,* she muttered, sniffing at a late-blooming rhododendron and curling her lip in distaste. *It's too . . . tame here. We belong in the wild where we can run and run and run and run—*

"*Silence,*" Ayleth said sharply inside her head. Her physical mouth formed a stony line. Her shade had only given voice to her own deep-rooted desires. But she was committed now. She would present her candidacy, come Haunts or high water. "Walk on, Chestibor," she murmured, though the horse had made no effort to stop.

They approached the gate where guardsmen in polished armor stood at perfect attention. She lifted one hand to make certain her red hood was in place, not fallen back over her shoulders. The guards, taking note of this sign of her Order, opened the gate to her. The leader saluted her with his lance and said, "Venatrix," in a crisp, respectful voice.

For the moment at least, Ayleth's heart lifted. She'd half expected them to bar her entrance, to demand explanations, proof of her station. But they took one look at her and accepted her for what she was—a Venatrix of Evander, a servant of the Goddess.

Maybe she could succeed here after all.

This thought faded the moment her horse stepped off the bridge onto the island. A green lawn encircled by a broad white drive spread before her, as perfectly manicured as the rest of the grounds. Rosebushes, just ending their summer bloom, lined the drive and bordered the massive porch steps leading up to the castle's extraordinarily ornate double doors. It was all too beautiful, too ostentatious, beyond anything she'd ever imagined. A sudden wish for the tottering tower and leaky roofs of Gillanluòc shot through her heart.

Laranta trembled. *Let's go,* she urged. *Let's go now.*

"*To me, Laranta,*" Ayleth commanded sternly. Her wolf shade tried to resist, but when Ayleth put her fingers threateningly to the Vocos pipe, Laranta gave in. With one leap, she vanished, and Ayleth felt her possessing spirit crouch down inside her head. It was a comforting, familiar sensation. It felt good to have her shade close but unsuppressed.

Her red hood made her conspicuous as she rode Chestibor around that drive. One of the keep's double doors opened before she'd reached the base of the porch steps, and an elegant man in long, wine-colored robes stepped forth. For one foolish instant, Ayleth wondered if it was the prince himself. But no—the Golden Prince, son of the Chosen King, would certainly not be answering his own front door. Besides, this man, with his long golden beard flecked with silver, was much too old.

He descended the steps at a dignified pace, watching Ayleth from under heavy eyelids as she rode Chestibor to the base of the steps and dismounted. Ayleth hesitated, wondering if she was expected to bow to such an imposing personage. But if he was merely one of the prince's servants, she technically outranked him, even though she wore her shabby huntress garments and he wore velvets and linen. So, she stood her ground and faced him with head up and shoulders back

"I am Ayleth, Venatrix di Ferosa, lately of Drauval Borough," she said with as much dignity as she could muster. To her delight, the velvet-clad man blinked and looked impressed. This bolstered her courage. "I am come to present my services to . . . to His Royal Highness, Prince Gerard du Glaive." She hesitated, then added, "Kindly take me to him at once."

That seemed to do the trick. The velvet man bowed. "If you will follow me, Venatrix."

Movement to one side, and a young servant boy in a billowing blue-slashed doublet darted up to take her horse's reins. Ayleth turned them over with reluctance. "Go on, then," she said to Chestibor, giving him a pat on the shoulder.

The velvet man swept a trailing sleeve, and Ayleth started up the white-marble steps in his wake. As they passed through the double doors, Ayleth took one quick look around before focusing her gaze entirely on the elegant gold embroidery across the velvet man's shoulders. She could not bear the opulence around her, so much more beautiful and ornate even than the gardens and grounds. It would surely break her courage, so she studied that embroidery until she was certain that, years from now, she would still remember in perfect detail how the bright threads formed an elaborate and entirely unrealistic-looking pheasant with trailing tail feathers.

Her boots made no sound on the soft carpets beneath her feet, but when the carpets gave way to polished marble floors, her heavy heels seemed to clunk all the louder, echoing tremendously off the moldings on the walls. They passed few living souls along the way, and Ayleth would not make eye contact with those they did pass. She never once let her gaze shift away from that golden pheasant, schooling her expression into a mask of perfect sternness.

The velvet man opened a door. "If you will step in here, Venatrix. His Highness will be with you shortly."

Ayleth obliged, passing through the doorway into a shadow-filled room. The windows, though open with the curtains drawn back, faced east, so little of the early evening light filtered through. An enormous hearth was prepped with logs for a fire not yet lit, and none of the candles arranged in brass sconces along the walls were alight.

Ayleth realized the velvet man was shutting the door behind her, leaving her alone in the room. She turned quickly, a flutter of panic in her belly.

"How long until the prince comes?"

"Shortly," the velvet man repeated.

The door shut with a final boom and was so thick that Ayleth, despite Laranta's augmenting abilities, could not hear his footsteps retreat down the hall. She felt like a prisoner thrown into a cell . . . albeit a bizarrely ornate cell. Laranta prowled on the edges of her mind, head low, teeth bared.

"*Hush,*" Ayleth told her shade, more out of habit than with any real conviction. Then, reminding herself that she was not some green young apprentice but a venatrix who had earlier that day successfully defeated and ousted a shade from this realm, she faced the room and took three steps in.

She froze on the third step, her careful calm crumbling into a momentary grimace of dismay. If she'd thought the passageways of Dunloch Hall grand, they were nothing, absolutely *nothing* compared to this room. The furniture was of white-painted carved wood with gold trimming, upholstered in velvets and silks even richer with embroidery than the garments of the velvet man. The floor itself boasted rugs of such intricate design, Ayleth scarcely dared look down for fear her brain might explode with the beauty of them.

Above all, the walls were lined with gilded shelves packed—absolutely *packed*—with books. The weight of words surrounded Ayleth on all sides. She shivered, feeling the pressure of ages of learning and erudition, and realizing suddenly how very small and unimportant she was in this world.

"I don't belong here," she whispered, her voice so faint she couldn't hear it.

In that moment, she realized she wasn't alone in the room.

Her first thought was that the prince himself had entered while she was too addled to notice. The figure lounging with such comfortable ease in one of the ornate chairs drawn close to the cold hearth was certainly manly. She couldn't see much more of him than long legs in tall boots and an elbow and forearm clad in a leather bracer, but the masculinity of his presence was unmistakable.

Then she sniffed, using Laranta's senses . . . and distinctly detected shade.

CHAPTER II

AYLETH'S HAND FLEW TO THE BONE KNIFE AT HER belt. But even as she touched the hilt, she noticed something more about the figure in the chair, and her heart plummeted. Protruding from that leather bracer on the stranger's arm was a sharp iron spike.

A venator. A candidate come to claim the borough.

And, furthermore, a candidate who apparently found the luxury of his surroundings not even remotely intimidating, stretched out as he was like a comfortable, long-legged cat before the hearth. His boots crossed at the ankles, his spurs gleaming. A small table to his left held a tray of crumbs and a half-empty flagon. Ayleth's stomach gave an unruly growl at the sight, as loud as any of Laranta's grumblings.

Was he asleep? Otherwise, he surely must have heard her entrance, but he'd given no indication that he was aware of her presence. While she debated approaching him, awkward moments of indecision slipped away, one after another. If he *was* awake, he must certainly sense her dithering, her discomfort, which put her at still greater disadvantage.

She couldn't keep standing there like some sort of an idiot.

Taking no care to disguise the clunk of her boots or the clink of her spurs, she strode across the room, assuming a position beside the fireplace mantel to face the stranger in his chair. He wore his hood pulled up over his head, and she could gain no sense of his features beyond a faint glitter of half-lidded eyes. So, he was awake, at least.

Ayleth drew a breath. "I am Ayleth, Venatrix di

Ferosa, lately of Drauval, and I—"

"No."

The single word, spoken in a voice as deep and dark as an echo at the bottom of a well, emerged from the shadow where his mouth should be.

Ayleth stopped, her jaw hanging open. "I'm . . . I'm sorry, what?"

"No." The repeated word, just as deep, just as dark, but this time tinged with an unmistakable trace of annoyance. "There is no point in an exchange of names or, indeed, in any subsequent conversation between us. I prefer not to waste my breath, for I have had a long day and anticipate a longer one tomorrow." Eyes flicked up to meet hers, a flash of coldest, iciest blue. "You may sit, I suppose."

Those eyes trailed up and down her figure, noting the travel stains coating her from head to toe. She had not bothered to change garments before riding up to the castle, and her mission in the abbey ruins had left her the worse for wear. She'd tried to convince herself the prince wouldn't mind, wouldn't expect elegance of dress in a venatrix.

Maybe the prince would not. But this man certainly did.

Deep shadows notwithstanding, she could see that he was perfectly put together. He wore the same tough leather jerkin, trousers, boots, and bracers of any working venator, but without stain, wrinkle, or patch of any kind. The spurs on his boots were polished to such a sheen, they might have been new, and his red hood showed no trace of fading or fraying.

"I'll bet he blacks his boots every night before bed," Ayleth spoke silently in her head.

Laranta growled a wolfish chuckle in response.

The man's gaze shot to Ayleth's face again, and those icy eyes narrowed to slits. "Your shade is ascendant, Venatrix," he snapped.

Ayleth wanted more than anything to take a step back, possibly two. But she refused to allow herself to move. *"Down, Laranta!"* she said inside, so sharply that her shade flinched and retreated without protest into the darker recesses of the mind they cohabitated.

Ayleth, never breaking gaze with the other venator, offered no excuses, made no counter remarks. She reached out with her shade-sharpened senses to try to get a better impression of his shade but found no trace revealing its type. Nothing but a deep humming of the Song of Suppression. She'd never encountered such a profound variation of the song spell, leaving the indwelling shade almost undetectable save for the shape of the song surrounding it.

The venator watched her, no doubt perceiving her inspection of him. When she finally retracted her prodding senses, one corner of his mouth turned up in a hard, mirthless grin. "Drauval, you say?" He spoke the words with such coolness, Ayleth could have sworn her skin frosted over. "And who is the venator of Drauval these days?"

This question rankled Ayleth more than any personal insult he might have thrown her way. Hollis had overseen Drauval Borough for nearly twenty years now, managing the wild, remote outpost almost entirely on her own during that time. It had never occurred to Ayleth that other venators of Perrinion wouldn't even know Hollis's name.

Trying to disguise the bitterness in her voice, she

answered, "Hollis, Venatrix di Theldry. My mistress."

"Tell me," said the venator, resting his elbow on the arm of his chair and cupping his chin in his hand as he regarded her. "Does your mistress encourage your dabbling in heresy, or is she unaware of your heretical leanings?"

The world seemed to tilt on its axis. Only a forceful mastery of her limbs kept her standing upright. She would not let a muscle on her face twitch, would not let the shocked *What?* escape her lips, as it pressed forcefully against the back of her teeth. She clenched her hands into fists behind her, meeting those cold eyes upraised to hers.

Bite him! Laranta growled from deep inside.

A tempting suggestion. But Ayleth said only, "I don't know what you're talking about."

"In that case," the venator said, "allow me to enlighten you. The fact that you would enter the Golden Prince's own hall with your shade unsuppressed is unforgivably careless. The only excuse I can imagine for you is that you must so often leave your shade unchecked that you did not realize you had done so now. Which is, I hardly need add, in direct opposition to the teachings of Saint

Evander, which urge all venators not actively on the hunt to keep their shades deeply bound." He tilted his head just slightly. "Either you are unaware of the holy teachings, which strikes me as unlikely, or you blatantly disregard them. Which is heresy."

Ayleth stared, momentarily dumbstruck.

Then, carefully enunciating each word through her own grinding teeth, she said, "I don't know about that. But tell me, Venator, is *your* former master aware that you prefer lounging about in a comfortable chair, eating crumpets all day, while shades plague the countryside? I've only just come from driving a dangerous Lure from this world, and yet you don't find me warming my heels at the hearth, do you?"

These words struck home as sure as any dart from her scorpiona. The venator sat upright, drawing up his extended legs and lifting his chin from his hand. A flash of fire blazed in the depths of his pupils, and for just a moment the hum of his Suppression spell song wavered.

"Listen to me, and listen well," he snarled. "I'll grant you are plucky to dare present yourself here as a candidate for the borough, but there is no chance in

Heaven or the Haunts of any other venator taking the empty post at Milisendis. Venator Dominus du Glaive has sent me to serve as Venator du Tam's hunt brother, and serve I shall."

Ayleth's lips twisted grimly. "I'm sure the other candidates will have something to say about that."

But the venator chuckled, leaning back once more and resting his forearms on the arms of the chair, his hands dangling from his wrists. "There are no other candidates. The castra sent only me. But sit. Stay. Meet with the prince if you must. You've wasted this much time; you might as well waste a little more."

Ayleth could only stare. No other candidates? The letter from Venator du Tam had implied a very different scenario. And wasn't the Golden Prince himself supposed to decide the appointment for this outpost? Or was this the castra's way of asserting its will? Let the prince choose the candidate . . . but send him one candidate only from which to choose.

Reality slowly pressed in, crushing her shoulders. She should march from the room at once. Find her horse and ride out from here, back to the mountains where she belonged. She'd stepped headlong into scheming and games for which she was grossly unprepared, and it was time to retreat.

Instead, she folded her arms across her chest and fixed the venator with a dagger-like glare. "So, you want to speak of wasted time? I spoke with a man earlier today who said shades are slipping into Wodechran while it is undermanned, more every day. Venator du Tam is unable to keep up with them all. One would think you'd be eager to get out there and do your job, but"—she shrugged with feigned disinterest—"some folks prefer fine speeches over action. I suppose we'll have to wait and see which of us the Golden Prince favors."

Another flash of fire in his eyes, this one fiercer than the last. The venator opened his mouth, no doubt prepared to flay her alive with his tongue. But in that moment, the door opened and the velvet man's polished voice declared, "His Royal Highness, Prince Gerard du Glaive."

The venator sprang from his chair, unfolding to an astonishing height. Ayleth was tall, especially in her hunting boots, but this man towered over her by a head at least. Yet he moved with a graceful ease as he turned to face the open doorway through which light poured and a figure stepped. "Gerard, at last," he said in an affable tone that contrasted sharply with the depth of his voice.

The chamber was too dark with deepening evening to discern anything about the prince's face or form. Ayleth blinked across the room, her heart thudding in her throat, and heard a voice that struck her as weirdly familiar. "It's dark as a tomb in here, Terryn. Why didn't you light a candle?"

"I don't mind the dark," the venator answered. Then he snapped his fingers, and all the candles in their brass sconces along the walls lit in an instant, while flames leapt to life in the fireplace. The room filled with a warm, golden glow that shone against the gilt paint and edgings of furniture and bookshelves, gleamed off the gold print on the spines of all those books.

By that light, Ayleth beheld the Golden Prince of Perrinion—still wearing the dirty, stained, cobwebby garments of a huntsman he'd worn when she'd used him as shade bait earlier that day.

CHAPTER 12

A COLD CERTAINTY FILLED AYLETH, RISING FROM THE pit of her gut as she stared across the room at that dirt-streaked face.

She drew a breath, gathered herself together, and bowed deeply.

Then, before the other venator could make a move, she strode swiftly across the room, past the prince, aiming for the door.

A hand darted out and caught her by the elbow. "Wait

a moment. Where are you going?"

Her eyes so wide she feared they might drop right out of her head, Ayleth stared down at that hand, at those long fingers holding tight to her arm. She couldn't bring herself to look up and meet the prince's gaze—those amber eyes she'd already looked into earlier today as she ranted at him with an unchecked tongue, little knowing to whom she spoke.

Had she called the Golden Prince a fool? An idiot? Right to his face! And what must he think of her arrogance, declaring herself the new venatrix of Wodechran?

"Please," she said, her voice husky with the effort to keep it from trembling, "do forgive me. I have made a mistake, and I will leave now. Sir. Your Highness." She tugged against his grip, which didn't relax.

"Don't go, Ayleth, Venatrix di Ferosa," the prince said, and there was a smile in his voice. "Have a seat, and we will talk. I see you have already met my good friend Terryn, Venator du Balafre."

He pulled, and she could either resist and risk insulting the Golden Prince or allow herself to be steered back into the room. Her ears buzzed, her brain roared, and Laranta ducked further down inside to avoid the maelstrom of panicked emotions. In a haze of embarrassment, Ayleth found herself led to a chair, seated, and staring hard at the floor as conversation went on over her head.

"You know this person?" the deep voice of the venator rumbled.

"We met earlier today," the prince replied, taking a seat across from Ayleth on a low sway-backed chaise longue propped up on gold-painted legs carved like swan wings. He relaxed with perfect ease, as though he wore a silk jacket and embroidered slippers rather than stained huntsman's garments and riding boots. One arm draped along the back of the chaise, and he crossed an ankle over his knee. "She saved my life."

"What?" The tall venator turned his hooded gaze upon Ayleth again. She could not bring herself to meet it, even when she felt those icepick eyes of his boring into her skull.

"I was riding the fringe forests north of here when I was separated from my company," the prince said with perfect candor. "Since the untimely disappearance of

Venator Nane, the shade-taken in these parts have grown in viciousness. I was caught in a shade spell and nearly lost my life. I would even now lie dead among the ruins of Godelieve Abbey were it not for this venatrix, my savior, who managed to pick up my trail and come to my aid."

"Indeed." The freezing gaze redoubled in intensity before the venator finally turned from her and addressed his next question directly to the prince. "What of the shade-taken? I will ride out at first light to see to its end—"

The prince held up one hand. "No need. Venatrix Ayleth dispatched it capably on her own. Or mostly on her own. I assisted by making most effective bait."

"*Bait?*" The tall venator whirled on Ayleth again. "You used the Golden Prince of Perrinion as *bait?*"

Ayleth firmly shut her mouth, looked up into the venator's cold eyes, and held his gaze. If she tried to speak, she would only embarrass herself. Her only hope of retaining any dignity whatsoever lay in silence.

"It worked out quite well, all things considered," the prince said, leaning back still more comfortably into the plush seat with no regard for the mud on his clothes dirtying its fine fabrics. "I quite like knowing that I did my part to make the borough safer for all."

The venator's jaw worked, and a muscle under his right eye twitched. Now that she looked at him by candlelight, Ayleth saw that, despite his pale eyes, the venator was as dark as a Noarian. Perhaps he hailed from one of the castras in southern Talmain. But while his complexion, along with his height, certainly made him stand out among the pale faces of Perrinion, what struck Ayleth's attention most keenly was a strange, vicious scar spread across most of his right cheek. Not a scar such as might be acquired in a fight or a hunt. This was a perfect circle, as though carved there on purpose, extending from just under his eye, to the corner of his mouth, to his jaw, his ear, and across his cheekbone. The skin was tight, puckered and pink.

He caught her staring, and his eyes lanced into her, blazing fiercely. He wanted her to look away first—she could feel how much he wanted it, how deeply he needed her to break his gaze, to cower before him.

She steeled her spine. The truth was, she *had* taken

care of the Lure shade. She *had* rescued the Golden Prince. And while she may have done her own pride irreparable damage in the process, what did that matter when compared to the deeds themselves?

"I take it, Terryn," the prince said, his voice breaking through the silent war waging before him, "that you have come about the vacancy at Milisendis Outpost."

"I have," the venator answered between his teeth, still without looking away. "Fendrel sent for me as soon as word arrived in Breçar."

"I thought as much." The prince tapped his foot with some impatience, regarding the two shade hunters across from him. "My uncle always had you in mind for this post. It only serves his purpose better to have had Nane meet his untimely end."

Only then did the venator at last look away from Ayleth. She drew a deep, silent breath of relief, blinking hard and shaking her head as her combatant addressed himself to the prince. "What happened to Nane?"

The prince shook his head. "No one knows. He disappeared nearly two months ago. At first I thought he'd merely gone on a long hunt, but I no longer believe so. Kephan has done what he can alone, but I am hoping the new venator will take up the task of discovering answers."

"I will certainly endeavor to oblige," the tall venator said quickly. "I will have answers for you within a week."

"Bold promises, Terryn," said the prince.

"Promises I intend to keep, Gerard," answered the venator.

"It is one thing to promise action; another thing entirely to guarantee results."

Both men turned to Ayleth, and she realized suddenly that she had spoken those words out loud. She swallowed hard, hoping the hot flush rushing into her face wasn't too obvious by candlelight.

"Are you so reluctant to promise service to your prince?" the venator demanded, a vaguely triumphant expression in his cold eyes.

Ayleth blinked once, disdainfully. She had to crane her head to look up at him, for he had not yet taken a seat, but stood looming over her. Trying to intimidate her, perhaps. Let him try; she wasn't about to back down now.

She turned to the prince. Suddenly, she did not care

that she had so hideously embarrassed herself. She did not care that she had bungled nearly every step of this dance-like interaction with her fellow venator. She didn't care about anything except the opportunity before her.

"Give me Wodechran Borough," she said quietly, "and I will hunt all shade-taken who fall under my sights, just as I hunted the Lure today. I will use any and all means available to me to see to it that shades are ousted from this world, that the Kingdom of Perrinion is made safer. I will serve you, Lord Prince, to the furthest extent of my ability and beyond. This I promise. This I swear." She lifted her chin, fixing her gaze on the prince's without blinking, like a wolf fixed upon its prey. "But give me Wodechran. Give me Milisendis."

It was as though all the air had been sucked out of the room. The tall venator did not so much as draw breath, and the prince leaned his head back a little, as though the force of Ayleth's words physically affected him.

At last, Prince Gerard broke the silence in the room, saying, "I hate to go against the will of Dominus Fendrel, to whom all Perrinion owes so much—"

"A wise view," the venator inserted.

"—but," the prince continued, raising his hand and glancing quickly from Terryn to Ayleth and back again. "But the position is mine to assign as I see fit."

"Gerard!"

The shock in the venator's voice was almost painful to hear. Ayleth realized suddenly that these two must have known each other for some time, that this tall, arrogant venator had assumed, based on years of acquaintance, even friendship, that the outpost was his. To suddenly find that assumption thwarted by an unknown venatrix from some backwater borough was more than he could bear.

But the choice wasn't his to make.

Ayleth waited, hardly daring to breathe.

"It is my decision," Gerard continued at last, "that, for the time being, *both* of you will assist Venator du Tam in the keeping of this borough. You will both ride the circuits, see to the needs of the people, investigate all rumors of shade doings. And as Kephan himself is much occupied with his ongoing labors, I charge the two of you to discover what happened to Nane."

The tall venator's eyes flashed with a sudden burst of

brilliant shadow-light. "You cannot seriously be considering her for the role," he said, fury lacing every word. "You know what I can do, Gerard! You know what I can accomplish here. Wodechran is much too important a borough to entrust to just any hunter. Fendrel intended me for this position since before my Possession, trained me to guard the borders of the Witchwood, to maintain the Great Barrier. This was always meant to be *my* borough."

Gerard's face, which had seemed so open, almost mirthful up until that moment, shuttered. He rose from the couch, assuming the bearing of a prince, ragged and worn though he was.

"I have made my decision, Venator," he said coldly. "You and Venatrix di Ferosa will operate Milisendis together with Venator du Tam. You will divide Nane's duties between you and work in tandem to get Wodechran back under proper control. Three months from today I will make the official appointment. Until then, this is the arrangement." He folded his arms. "Questions?"

The venator opened his mouth—closed it. Shook his

head.

Gerard turned to Ayleth then and repeated the last word. "Questions?"

"None, Your Highness," she replied, though something in the deepest part of her gut roiled uncomfortably.

"Very well. I invite you both to take a meal here at Dunloch before continuing on to Milisendis."

The prince said nothing more, made no move, but something in his voice and stance clearly indicated an end to the audience. The venator, without a glance Ayleth's way, bowed and strode from the room, his long legs crossing to the door and out into the passage. Ayleth sprang from her chair and offered a hasty bow of her own. All her boldness suddenly fled; she did not want to spend a moment alone in the prince's company.

She made for the door, but the prince stopped her with a word. "Wait."

Ayleth paused, looked back. How many social blunders did she commit by simply standing there? Perhaps she should bow again, perhaps there was some polite something she should murmur. But all she could think about was getting out of that room as quickly as possible.

The prince, as though reading her thoughts, smiled suddenly, a smile that seemed to fill the whole room with light brighter than candle glow. "Do well out there, Venatrix di Ferosa," he said. "Make Terryn work for everything. *Everything.*"

In that moment, under the warmth of that smile, Ayleth realized there was nothing in the world she wanted more than to make this man proud of her service.

"I will," she said, and it was as good as a vow. Without waiting for another word of dismissal, she darted from the room.

"May we speak?"

Gerard, just stepping from his office into the passage beyond, paused. Terryn leaned against the wall outside the door, his eyes bright but his face shadowed. The nearest candle sconces were too far away to illuminate his features.

"Of course, Terryn." Gerard pulled his office doors

shut and turned to face the venator. "But we must be quick. I promised Chancellor Yves that I'd come grovel at his feet in abject apology for my wayward behavior as soon as I was done meeting with my new venators. He is not ready to forgive me for riding out with the huntsmen this morning against his advice. In retrospect, advice I probably would have done better to heed."

Terryn's lip curled, weirdly tugging at the scar on his face. It would be an intimidating expression if Gerard didn't know this man so well. "Don't put me off," the venator growled. "You know exactly why I'm here."

"I do." Gerard sighed, crossing his arms and leaning his back against the closed door. "I know very well. Fendrel intends for you to take the position at Milisendis. Fendrel will not respond well to my changing of the plan. Fendrel will rain fire and brimstone down upon us all." He chuckled mirthlessly. "I'm familiar with my uncle and his moods, Terryn. You needn't remind me."

Terryn stared at Gerard as though looking upon the face of a stranger. "Everything I've been through. Everything I've done. Everything *we* have worked for together, you and I. Does it count for nothing?"

Gerard shook his head, suddenly heart-heavy. He did not like hurting Terryn. But he said, "Tell me the truth. Is this even what you want?"

The venator didn't answer. Beneath the obscuring shadows, his expression hardened.

"Fendrel has had it all planned out from the moment he set eyes on you," Gerard persisted. "You and I would grow up together. Later, you would serve me here at Wodechran. Later still, when I assume my father's crown, you would take Fendrel's role as Black Hood. Always one step behind me, always in my shadow."

"Always there to protect you," Terryn said, his voice dark and low.

"Always there to dance to Fendrel's tune. Like we all dance. Even my father, the so-called Chosen King." The words came out more bitterly than Gerard intended. As though to escape them, he pushed away from the door and strode down the hall. Terryn fell into step behind him, as he had been carefully trained to do since boyhood.

"I'm tired of doing exactly what my uncle decides for me," Gerard said. "Both of us have been forced into these roles—me as some prophesied prince, you as my protector. Just as Fendrel has always been my father's protector. He wants to recreate his own history, wants to guarantee that the world goes on working according to the pattern he himself has designed."

Gerard shook his head harshly. "But it is I, not Fendrel, who will sit on the throne at Telianor. It is I, not Fendrel, who will decide what is best for Perrinion. And I am determined to start making those decisions. Wherever I can."

Terryn stopped abruptly behind the prince. Gerard paused as well, looking back around to where his longtime friend stood in the middle of the corridor, so tall and shadowy that he seemed to fill the space. His head was bowed, and his eyes did not meet Gerard's when he said, "Do you not trust me to always serve according to your best interests, my prince?"

Gerard shook his head slowly. "I do trust you, Terryn. But I believe the borough needs more. The kingdom needs more. More than you and I can give, more than Fendrel can force us to be."

Silence answered him for some long moments. Gerard

almost wondered if he should turn and go on his way to his meeting with the chancellor.

But Terryn spoke at last. "Did that girl really rescue you from a Lure today?"

"'That girl,'" Gerard answered, "is a venatrix. You will remember as much and afford her the respect due her position."

Terryn's breathing deepened. He made no answer.

Gerard rubbed a hand through his hair. His temples throbbed with exhaustion, for he had not yet rested or eaten since his ill-fated hunt. But he couldn't very well walk away from Terryn.

"Yes," he said. "She did save me. She is capable, and she will help you as you work to restore the Barriers to full strength. There is too much that needs doing here in Wodechran for two venators alone. You should take advantage of her presence and work with her. Kephan will be grateful for extra hands."

"Tell me this, Gerard," Terryn said suddenly, an edge to his voice. "What were you doing out alone at the Godelieve ruins?"

Gerard drew a long breath, holding it for as long as he

dared. Then, letting it out slowly, he whispered, "Fayline."

Terryn cursed softly, a hiss through his teeth.

Gerard bowed his head, feeling the weight of disappointed hopes suddenly heavy across his shoulders. "I've heard rumors of a red-haired witch several times in the last six weeks, since Nane's disappearance. This time just north of here, near Godelieve. Fayline and I used to ride out to the ruins when we visited Dunloch as children. It was one of our favorite hideaways. I thought perhaps . . . maybe . . ."

"It's not her, Gerard."

The prince grimaced. Terryn's words were knives striking at his heart.

"Even if it is her—even if she somehow got back through the Barrier—it's not *her*." Terryn took a step closer to the prince, putting out a hand as though to catch him and hold him back. "Only the spirits which have possessed her. It's Inren and the shade. After all these years, Fayline herself is no longer present. You have to accept this."

"I know," Gerard breathed. "I have to accept that her soul is lost." He lifted his head, meeting Terryn's eyes.

"But on the chance—on the *chance* that she might still be in there, I must find her. *We* must find her. So that you can save her soul. I know that she is lost to me, that she will never be my wife. But . . . the idea of her being damned for all eternity . . ."

His words trailed off into an abyss of horror and sorrow. Terryn stood across from him, a looming shadow, unable to offer comfort, unable to speak false promises. Gerard knew he should value his friend's honesty, but . . . he wished that for once Terryn would lie to him. Would tell him there was still hope.

At last, Terryn placed a hand on Gerard's shoulder. "I will investigate these rumors. You have my word."

Gerard nodded, drawing a shuddering breath. "First, see to the Barrier. See that the spell song is strengthened and that nothing more gets through from the Witchwood. Nothing."

CHAPTER 13

AYLETH LEFT THE PRINCE'S PRESENCE SO QUICKLY, she did not realize until she stood in the corridor outside that she had no idea where she was meant to go next. The prince had invited both her and Venator Terryn to have a meal. A prince's invitation was as good as a command, wasn't it?

But where in the Haunts was she supposed to take this meal?

If she were in the wild forests of Drauval, she would

be able to retrace her steps well enough. But in this labyrinth of a castle she felt turned around, lost. She'd focused so intently on the velvet-clad man and his pheasant embroidery, she'd not taken the care she should have in noting her trail.

She looked up and down the corridor for some sign of the other venator, but he had miraculously disappeared. Well, good. She had no desire to tag along in his footsteps anyway. Lifting her chin and deciding that it would be best to pick a direction, any direction, she chose to turn left and see where it took her.

The corridor led to what looked at first to be a dead end, but a cracked doorway revealed a narrow staircase. Probably a servants' stair, but surely there was no harm in her using it. She was, after all a servant of the prince.

She met no one along the way and emerged a floor below in a passage with windows overlooking the lake along one wall, and pillars supporting the low ceiling. She took another left turn, stepping out of the pillared corridor into a long gallery. Here the windows were higher and narrower, casting enough light to fill the room but not enough to cause damage to the magnificent portraits displayed along both walls. In the gloom of falling evening these portraits were shadow-veiled, leaving Ayleth with only an impression of lordly men and women in various states of official dress. Gold flakes set in the paint caught what little light there was, creating an almost otherworldly shine of embellishment to elaborate collars, headdresses, and crowns.

This was definitely not where she was meant to be. With a muttered curse, Ayleth began to back out of the room, but her gaze caught on something at its far end. A single portrait illuminated by the last of the light falling through the nearest window.

Almost against her will, Ayleth stepped into the gallery, her boots clunking hollowly on the marble floor. From either side she felt the pressure of painted eyes watching her—glorious depictions of the Priestess Queens of ages past interspersed with images of the heroes and heroines of the Witch Wars. But none of these drew her attention, which remained fixed on that one image at the end of the hall.

On that one pair of captivating eyes.

This portrait was the largest of all—larger than life-size

and displayed in a place of prominence. The background was black as a void, but this served only to make the golden hues of the central two figures that much more vivid, that much more radiant. A mother holding her young child in her lap, her hands gentle and soft. The child, a golden-haired angelic creature, held its own hands in an unlikely gesture of holy blessing such as a priestess might make. Both mother and child gazed out upon the viewer with expressions of serenity and promise.

Ayleth knew exactly who they were. The mother was Queen Leurona, the Chosen King's wife, who had died during the Witch Wars before her son reached his first year of age. And the child, of course, was the Golden Prince himself, in an idealized, infantile form. Ayleth didn't fully believe the likeness, but she recognized those warm amber eyes.

But it wasn't the infant's gaze that caught and held her attention. It was the queen's. When Ayleth looked into her eyes and only her eyes, the expression she saw there was no longer one of serenity. Instead she saw—fear. A haunting desperation. And rage.

For a long moment Ayleth studied that face,

wondering suddenly what had inspired such emotion in the young, beautiful queen. She did not know a great deal about Leurona's history, only what Hollis had told her— that she was a princess from Talmain in southern Gaulia sent to marry King Guardin and strengthen his rule. That she and her entourage were captured on their way to the wedding by one of Dread Odile's lieutenants. That the Chosen King himself fought to rescue her, bringing her back to Telianor in triumph, there to wed her. That she bore the king a son. And then she died.

None of this explained the expression Ayleth now observed in the dead queen's face, a puzzle she would probably never solve. Only after some moments of contemplation did she realize that the queen's eyes looked nothing like her son's. They were the color of coldest ice. And yet they were somehow . . . familiar . . . .

Something else was not right here. Something was off. Laranta's unnatural instincts reached out to pluck at Ayleth's awareness, but she couldn't understand it, couldn't quite grasp what it was she saw. At last, after some uncounted moments, she frowned, tilting her head. Her frustrated awareness clarified suddenly and brilliantly, and she knew what it was that disturbed her.

The portrait of Queen Leurona and her son was hung upon hinges.

Forgetting the queen and her strange expression, Ayleth stepped forward as the curiosity of a huntress overcame all else. The hinges were cleverly worked in gold so that they almost disappeared amid the elaborate scrollwork of the frame. Why was this portrait mounted in such peculiar fashion? What lay behind it, a secret passage or chamber? Her hand reached out, trembling slightly with the desire to pull at the frame, to catch a glimpse of what it hid. Her fingertips touched the gold.

"Madam Venatrix."

Startled, Ayleth turned around sharply, her heart thudding in her throat. The velvet-clad man stood in the doorway of the gallery, his hands neatly folded, his face a study of long-suffering. "The prince has ordered a meal laid out for you in the second dining chamber. If you would come with me?"

"Of course," Ayleth murmured. She swallowed, and though her chin partially turned, she would not allow herself a last look over her shoulder. No, it was better that she not. She was here to serve the Golden Prince, not to pry into the secrets of his family.

So, she hastened back down the gallery, falling into step behind the man and his velvets as he led her from the room. With every step, she felt Queen Leurona's eyes burning into the back of her head.

Night had fallen by the time Ayleth finished her lonely but bountiful meal and was at last escorted out to the front drive. Torches lined the white road leading from the main keep to the bridge and the gate beyond, and overhead the sky was clear and brilliant with stars. An autumnal chill whispered through the air, but now that she was somewhat rested, Ayleth looked forward to a night ride.

Or she did until she saw the looming form of Venator Terryn standing on the broad porch steps. His back was to her, his arms crossed, and she could almost feel the wall of resentment humming around him like a spell song.

Well, she didn't want to talk to him either. So, while waiting for someone to bring Chestibor from the stables, she took a position several steps behind the venator, fortifying herself with a stony silence. Would it be possible to go the next three months without speaking to him at all?

The memory of his words raked across her brain like talons. *"Does your mistress encourage your dabbling in heresy?"*

How dare he? How *dare* he accuse her of such a thing? And all for what? Because she'd let Laranta remain ascendant rather than suppress her following the hunt? Surely he did not expect her to always bind her shade so thoroughly? Yes, as a venatrix, she must take care never to give her shade too much leeway inside. But she had worked with Laranta for years, and the two of them had established a certain . . . comfort with one another. This didn't make her a heretic.

Did it?

She refused to consider it. Not now. Not when more pressing matters weighed upon her. She must get to Milisendis Outpost. She must introduce herself to Venator du Tam and establish herself quickly as a reliable and industrious hunt sister. She must put down roots in the borough so that when the time came, Prince Gerard would know she was the one for this position.

What was it Terryn had said while they were in the prince's meeting room? He had been sent by Dominus Fendrel . . . *Fendrel du Glaive*. Of all people! Ayleth's knees trembled despite her best efforts. Who was she to think she could thwart the will of the Dominus, the most powerful, the most influential of all venators in Perrinion? The king's own brother, who held the whole of Castra Breçar in the palm of his hand.

A clack of hooves, a flash of torches. Ayleth saw two horses being led through the gloom by young stable lads—Chestibor, and a tall red mare presumably belonging to the other venator.

"I see you are ready to set out."

A shiver ran down Ayleth's spine at the sound of the prince's voice behind her. She turned and could not stop the flush that heated her cheeks at the sight of Prince Gerard descending the porch steps toward her.

"I've come to see the two of you off," he said, addressing himself as much to Terryn as to her.

"No need," the deep rumble of Venator Terryn answered.

Gerard shrugged one shoulder at this. Focusing his attention on Ayleth, he held out one hand, offering her a scroll bound with a red cord and sealed in golden wax. "This is for Venator Kephan," he said, "informing him of my wish for the two of you to focus your initial efforts on discovering what happened to Nane. No doubt Kephan will have additional tasks for you—Wodechran is a large borough with many needs—but until we know Nane's fate, it is my opinion that we cannot determine how best to protect our people going forward."

As Ayleth accepted the scroll, a whole new wave of resentment from Venator Terryn rolled over her. Was it because Gerard entrusted the message to her and not to him?

She smiled. "I will deliver your message, Your Highness," she said, shooting her competitor a swift look as she spoke.

The venator glowered, offered the prince a crisp salute and, without another word, strode down the steps to claim his horse from the stable boy.

Ayleth took a step toward Chestibor but paused when the prince spoke in a low voice meant for her ears alone.

"He doesn't see it now, Venatrix, but I do believe the two of you will achieve more together than alone." As she turned to meet the prince's sympathetic gaze, he continued, "Terryn is . . . difficult. But he is the best Castra Breçar has ever produced. If you can learn to work with him, I don't doubt the two of you will accomplish wonders here in Wodechran."

The prince might not doubt, but Ayleth had doubts enough for them both. Nevertheless, she offered a brisk salute. "I will endeavor to serve my prince in all things to the best of my abilities."

"No one could ask more of you," Gerard replied, and waved her on.

Terryn was already astride his horse and riding down the drive by the time Ayleth mounted Chestibor and hastened after him. She hated the idea of following him across the borough, but the map she'd pilfered from Hollis offered only the vaguest possible directions to Milisendis Outpost, and she could never hope to find it in the dark. She could either follow the other venator and hope he knew where he was going or stay the night at Dunloch Castle.

So, the two of them rode out, crossing the bridge and passing through the gate in single file. The venator ignored the guardsmen, but Ayleth offered them cool nods. Once the gates lay behind, Ayleth relaxed in her saddle. Although the manicured grounds still struck her as too elegant for comfort, they seemed to breathe a little more wildness in the night shadows, and scents of fallen leaves and golden grass and trees slipping into autumn slumber soothed her heart.

Once they passed from the garden onto the lonely venator's trail, Ayleth maintained a space of at least two horses behind Venator Terryn. In this manner they progressed in silence broken only by the clop of hooves on the track and the punctuating shrills of night birds.

Ayleth had no way of knowing the distance between Milisendis Outpost and the prince's hall. After the first two hours, she gave up hope that it would be near. Venator Terryn continued steadily onward, and Ayleth watched him in the moonlight, determined not to let him get out of her sight. Chestibor stopped once or twice, certain it must be time to make camp, but when Ayleth insisted otherwise, he jogged to catch up with the red mare and fell back into his ground-eating amble.

When they had been riding for nearly three hours, judging by the turn of the stars, Terryn pulled his horse to an abrupt halt. Ayleth half hoped he'd spotted their destination up ahead, and her heart lifted.

But when the venator turned in the saddle to face her, she slumped. She couldn't see his face beneath his hood, but there was a confrontational set to his shoulders. This wasn't going to be good.

"You need to know something," he said. His voice carried across the dark space between them, chilly as frost. "Wodechran is unlike all other boroughs in the kingdom. A venatrix who does not follow the laws of Evander *exactly* cannot hope to survive it. Do I make myself clear?"

A little growl in her throat, Ayleth spurred Chestibor onward. The venator shifted in his saddle, and his horse gave a nervous sidestep as she approached, but they did not back away. Ayleth rode until she was knee to knee, stirrup to spur with the other venator. From this proximity she could just discern the contours of his face, the sharp cheekbones, the long narrow nose, the deep brow under which his eyes glinted.

"Was that Venator Nane's problem then?" she asked. "Not following the laws *exactly* enough?"

He said nothing. He merely looked at her. And she looked back. Will strained against will. This man was a force to be reckoned with, but she refused to give him an inch.

His jaw clenched tight, Terryn kicked his horse into motion, continuing along the venator's trail. Feeling as though she'd won some contest, the rules of which she didn't fully understand, Ayleth urged Chestibor on behind him, allowing a little more distance than before. The venator crested a hill they'd been climbing and vanished over the far side.

Ayleth blinked uncertainly. Then she squinted into the moonlight. But no, her eyes did not deceive her . . . Venator Terryn was riding straight back toward her mere moments after he'd disappeared over the rise.

Terryn, spotting Ayleth ahead of him, pulled his mare up short. Though his face was still obscured from her vision by his deep hood, Ayleth detected startled confusion flowing from his spirit.

"Milisendis is *that* way," she called ahead dryly.

Without a word, he turned his horse around and once more vanished behind the hilltop. But just as Ayleth reached the summit, she saw Terryn riding back as though to meet her, facing the way they had just come.

He threw back his hood, turning in his saddle to look over his shoulder. Then he faced forward, looking at Ayleth, his expression utterly baffled.

If he was playing some game with her, she wasn't going to fall for it. Giving the venator a sour look, Ayleth rode on past him . . . only to find herself suddenly facing back along the road she had just traveled, climbing rather than descending the slope. She stopped, gaping much like Terryn had.

Terryn, who'd had more time to ponder the dilemma, said, "There's a curse here."

"A curse?" Ayleth repeated somewhat stupidly.

"Yes." Terryn pointed out over the landscape they had just crossed: the venator circuit trail winding like a ribbon across moonlit fields until it vanished from sight in a patch of dark forest. In the far distance, black hills against the starry sky. "Do you see that point of light on the horizon? That's Dunloch Castle. Now look behind you again."

Ayleth turned in her saddle. Her breath caught in her throat. "It's the same."

The exact same view spread before her, like some sort of reflection in an enormous mirror. A mirror preventing the eye from seeing what truly lay ahead.

"Who would cast a curse like this?" she asked. As soon as she said the words, she guessed the answer and wished she'd not betrayed her ignorance.

Terryn looked even more superior and aloof by moonlight. "Venator Nane's shade was an Anathema—a curse-caster. This must be one of his own protections to keep the outpost safe from prying eyes."

Ayleth snorted softly. It struck her as a completely unnecessary precaution—Milisendis was already so remote, one would have to know where it was to find it. She might easily have missed it in the dark had she not followed Terryn. "So how do we break the curse?"

The venator gave her another superior look. "Don't you know?"

Instead of dignifying this with a response, she pulled

out her Vocos pipes, put them to her lips, and played the Song of Summoning. At the bidding of that song, Laranta sprang to the forefront of her mind.

Hunt? she asked eagerly.

"*Not exactly,*" Ayleth answered. "*There's a curse on the road ahead. I need you to find it for me.*"

I'd rather hunt.

Ayleth altered the song into a more forceful variation. "*Obey me, Laranta.*"

With a heavy sigh, her wolf shade slipped out of her mind, manifested on the road before her, and immediately put her nose to the ground and started sniffing about for any sign of magic. She prowled up and down the edges of the road as far as she could go without running into the curse itself.

Soon enough she lifted her head and looked back at Ayleth. *It's here. It's . . . wrong.*

Ayleth finished the measure of music she was playing and sheathed the Vocos pipes, all the while aware of Terryn's close observation. He could not see Laranta in her wolf form, but he could certainly sense her spiritual presence. Which meant he could also sense the effectiveness of the song Ayleth had played, proving her ability to control her powerful shade.

Dismounting, Ayleth tossed Chestibor's reins to Terryn. "Hold him, if you please," she said.

He caught the reins but didn't answer, his eyes mere slits of silver.

Ayleth hastened to her wolf shade's side. "*Give me your sight*," she said. Shadow-light flared in her eyes, and she followed Laranta's fixed stare to a certain place in the air. Even with shadow vision it was difficult to see the glimmering threads of the Anathema curse, more like music made visible than anything else. There was a certain *wrongness* about it, as Laranta had said. The curse was turning sour, resulting in a snarl of magic so intense, one could hardly sense where it began or ended.

The simplest method to break a curse was to find the object cursed and then break that object. One strand of this curse continued down into the valley, indicating that the curse was anchored somewhere below.

But how to get down into the valley when the curse only drove her backwards?

With Venator Terryn's cold eyes intently watching her

every move, she could reveal no hesitation, no weakness.

She reached out a hand toward the curse thread. It was not something she could touch in any physical sense, but with Laranta's powers coursing through her, the tip of her finger somehow *sensed* it. Like a shivering line of coldness in the air. Like the vibration of a thin, sharp, inharmonic note of music.

Following that sensation along her finger, Ayleth started walking . . . backward. Her steps were unsteady since she could not see where she was going, and she had to feel her way carefully or lose the thread. But Laranta walked on her other side, facing forward, and with her hand on the wolf shade's back, she felt steady enough. She kept going until Terryn and the horses were dots on the hilltop, keeping her gaze focused on them. In her peripheral vision the world was hazy, and if she let herself glance to either side, her stomach pitched and heaved with sickness caused by the curse trying to assert itself.

Her boot heel struck something solid. Drawing a slow, steadying breath, she looked back and saw a gate. A great, tall venator's gate much like the one at Gillanluòc. More importantly, she could see the place where the curse thread had been anchored into one of the gate slats.

"Venator Nane was serious about discouraging unwelcome visitors," Ayleth muttered as she slid her hand carefully up to the place where the curse tangled in a deep knot. It frayed fast now that she'd found it. The keys to breaking these curses were widely varied and could be dangerously tricky. Some curses required incantations. Others simply required the anchored object to be destroyed or defaced. According to some of the reading she'd done, there were even curses that required kisses to break, though Ayleth wasn't altogether ready to believe that.

She bent close, studying the place where the curse anchored into the slat. There, unless she was much mistaken, was a streak of blood. Not much left now, but when she looked with shadow vision, Ayleth could still see traces of what had once been a patterned mark. Nane had used his own blood to anchor the curse, painting a sigil.

That was easy enough to undo in this instance. Ayleth slipped her knife from its sheath and set to work carving the sigil out of the wood. She had to go deeper than she'd initially expected, for though the blood itself had washed away over time, the anchor was deeply planted. It would be simpler to remove the slat entirely and break it, but she would then have to find a replacement board and patch up the gate. So, she continued scratching at the wood, her knife digging a deeper and deeper gouge.

Suddenly the curse broke. The strands of magic curled and vanished in a discordant hum of spell song. Immediately the landscape around her clarified under the moonlight. Looking around, she saw that she'd descended into a narrow, rocky valley with a few sparse pine trees breaking up the otherwise gloomy landscape. Beyond the gate stood the outpost itself, complete with high walls, its watchtower looming three stories into the sky.

Milisendis. Her first official posting.

Ayleth smiled.

She found the bell pull used by messengers to summon the venator inside and pulled on it three times, listening to the gong on the far side of the wall. She waited a few minutes then pulled thrice more.

She heard clopping hooves and the squeak of leather as Terryn rode up behind her, leading Chestibor.

"Venator du Tam does not seem to be in residence." Ayleth looked at Terryn over her shoulder while the echoing boom of the gong faded to nothing. "He must be out on a circuit ride."

Venator Terryn offered no response, not even a word of congratulation on her successful breaking of the curse. He dismounted and brushed past her as though she wasn't there, heading directly to the place in the wall where a secret mechanism was hidden that would open the gate from the outside. Ayleth, who had not yet thought to search for it, watched in some surprise as he pulled the lever. The gate opened with a reluctant groan. Her companion, she realized, must have visited Milisendis before to be familiar with its secrets like that. Ayleth's heart sank. Here was yet another advantage this favorite of the Venator Dominus had over her.

Without so much as a glance Ayleth's way, the venator took his horse by the reins and led her to the gate . . .

Only to sink halfway up his calves into the dirt.

His shout of surprise startled Ayleth. Her gaze shifted at once into shadow sight, and she beheld the tangled snarl of curse surrounding the venator, dragging him forcefully down.

Venator Nane had left more than one defense behind to guard his outpost.

CHAPTER 14

FOR THREE BREATHS AYLETH COULD DO NOTHING but stare, unable to believe what she saw. In those few seconds Terryn sank to his knees. The ground rippled in a pool around him, more liquid than solid, but when he tried to move it bound him fast. It would consume him completely before another minute passed.

"*Laranta!*" Ayleth cried. "*Find the anchor!*"

Laranta sprang into action. Ayleth spared a passing thought that Venator Terryn should be grateful she hadn't already suppressed her shade again—calling her back up with the Vocos would have wasted moments he didn't have. As it was, the wolf shade dove forward, nose to the ground, eagerly seeking the curse scent.

Terryn was already up to his waist. "It's . . . crushing!" he gasped.

Ayleth saw that his right hand was caught in the ground. He'd tried to get his Vocos free, to call up his own shade. Not that he would have had time to break through the intense binding spell.

Here! Here, here! Laranta barked, her smoke-like tail wagging with excitement. She pranced in place just under the arch of the gate. Ayleth, looking with her shadow sight, saw the tangled snarl, another unraveling mess of curse song. One thread plunged into the dirt. The anchor was buried beneath the gate.

Ayleth flung herself onto her knees. The ground shifted uneasily beneath her, but she was just outside the curse's reach. "*Laranta, give me your strength!*" she commanded.

Immediately her shade's power flowed through her limbs. Ayleth jammed her hands forcefully into earth which had been beaten down under many footfalls until it was hard as granite. She tore into it like it was no more than loose snow, digging up great scoops, all too aware that Terryn was now up to his chest, trying not to let herself focus on his peril.

Her hand struck something solid, and she sensed the rippling hum of the curse thread wound around it. She grabbed hold, pulling up a large stone. The curse anchor. Like the slat in the gate, it was smeared with a complex blood sigil, partially wiped away but deeply implanted. Her knife would not be strong enough to gouge it out, she would only dull her blade.

Terryn gave a strangled, choking gasp, his head tilted as far back as it could go. He'd sunk to his shoulders now.

Ayleth took the stone in both hands. With a roar, she summoned up her shade's strength, forcing all of it possible into her arms, shoulders, and fingers. Clenching her teeth, she pressed the stone, grinding it into powder between her fingers.

As the stone crumbled, the sigil broke and the curse fell into broken strands of magic, vibrating as they disintegrated into nothing.

With a cry, Terryn tore his arms free, scrabbling at the edges of the pit, which no longer sought to swallow him. He pulled himself partly out, shaking dirt from his limbs. Ayleth crawled over to him, caught hold of him by his belt, and yanked him the rest of the way out. He fell flat on his stomach, one foot still partially buried, gasping for air.

"Thank the Goddess you're so tall," Ayleth said. She sat back on her heels, resting her hands on her knees to breathe heavily. Surges of Laranta's power jumped in her muscles, fading slowly. "Anyone shorter than you would have been swallowed whole already."

Terryn lifted his head, giving her a frigid stare. Then he pushed himself up onto his hands and knees and shook his head like a dog, scattering dirt every which way. Drawing a long, long breath, he staggered upright, swaying dangerously, then walked to his horse, which watched him curiously. The curse apparently was not intended for animals, as the red mare had passed into the outpost yard without trouble.

Ayleth jumped to her feet and called at the venator's

back, "And you're welcome for saving your life!"

He paused as he took his horse's reins, his shoulders stiffening. For a moment Ayleth believed he would go on without a word. Then, much to her surprise, he called back over his shoulder, "You acted quickly and with good instincts."

Not quite a thank-you. More of an observation. Then again, acknowledgement of her capabilities might be better than thanks coming from him. Ayleth rolled her eyes, but a glow of satisfaction unexpectedly warmed her face.

They proceeded with caution across the yard. Ayleth could tell the other venator was using his shadow sight as he led his horse toward the stables. Apparently, though he kept his shade deeply suppressed, he maintained consistent use of its sight.

Milisendis Outpost looked very much like Gillanluòc. The stables stood in the same place off to the right of the blockhouse, and the low, squat bonehouse building stood opposite the stables. Everything was a little bigger and significantly better maintained, however. Milisendis received a much greater stipend from the castra for its care and keeping.

Terryn left his mare with Ayleth as he carefully entered the stables, checking for any sign of a curse. Ayleth sent Laranta on her own inspection but was ultimately satisfied that Venator Nane had left no snares in this building. He drew the line somewhere, at least.

Terryn appeared in the doorway to beckon her in, and they went about settling their horses into the available stalls. There was no recent sign of another horse, verifying Ayleth's suspicion that Venator du Tam was out on a circuit ride. They did find plenty of fresh hay and oats, and both offered their horses generous portions. Ayleth hoped more supplies were due from the castra soon. With three horses going through a supply intended for two, she and Terryn might end up having to spend their own meager earnings on oats to compensate.

Once their horses were comfortably munching and their tack was clean and hanging on pegs, Ayleth and Terryn slung their travel bags over their shoulders and cautiously approached the blockhouse. Terryn went first, not out of any sense of chivalry, Ayleth suspected, but out of sheer desire to pretend she wasn't present. Well, let him, she thought. Let him walk on ahead into any waiting curses.

Finding no curse on the front door, they stepped into the house. Using her shadow sight, Ayleth glanced around. It looked quite a lot like the main level of Gillanluòc—the same long worktable stretching down the middle of the room, piled with instruments in various states of repair and assembly. The same or similar collection of herbs strung over the dark hearth, the same, if rather brighter and newer, copper pots hung from the low rafters. A once fine but now rather battered desk stood under one window. No sign of a logbook anywhere, but stacks of parchment piled on the desk and around it. Chests lined the wall to the right of the desk, their open lids revealing more books and scrolls—many of them music scrolls. Ayleth eyed these with interest, wondering if Venators Nane and Kephan had any useful song spells not found in Hollis's collection.

Terryn took a look around, said nothing, and silently moved to the stairs, stumping up to the next level. Ayleth, after waiting a moment in case a curse caught him on the stairway, followed. There were two bedrooms on this level. While Terryn entered one, Ayleth peered into the other, noting signs of current occupancy. This must be Venator Kephan's quarters.

Turning to look through the open door of the opposite room, she was just in time to see Terryn drop his bags on the bed. She raised an eyebrow. "Who decided you would get Nane's old room?"

Terryn whirled on her, scattering dirt every which way from his clothes. His eyes flared bright in the darkness. "Make no mistake, Venatrix: This posting is mine. It was always meant to be mine. I have earned it for years, and if it takes me another three months to earn it yet again, so be it. You'll be packing your bags and turning your back to Wodechran before a week is out if I have anything to say about it."

With that, he slammed the door.

Ayleth, standing on the dark landing, opened her mouth to shout back. But really, why bother? It wasn't as though she relished the idea of sleeping in the dead venator's bed.

She continued up the stairs to the tower room—very like the tower room she had lived in at Gillanluòc, but without any of the sparse furnishings Hollis had provided for her. Setting down her bags, she pulled out her bedroll and unfurled it. Not the most comfortable way to sleep, but she was a venatrix. She could handle a little discomfort. At least the chimney stack ran up one wall of this chamber. If they kept a fire burning downstairs, it should be warm enough up here.

But it was cold now. And she was hungry. The meal she'd enjoyed at Dunloch seemed suddenly long ago. A clunking on the stairs told her Terryn had emerged from his room. Though she didn't relish his company, there would be food stores downstairs, and she preferred not to let him eat without her.

With a bracing sigh, she made her way to the main room below.

Terryn wore a fresh uniform. Ayleth smirked at this, noting the careful creases in the travel-worn fabric. Would he stay up late tonight and launder his other uniform following his rather messy episode at the gate? She pulled back a chair at the long table—letting the legs scrape so he could be in no doubt of her presence behind him—and sat in it. He refused to so much as look around from where he knelt at the hearth, stacking kindling and striking flints.

Ayleth frowned, watching the venator at his efforts. Why was he bothering with flints and kindling? She'd seen him light candles and a fire on the hearth in Gerard's stately office earlier that evening with just a snap of his fingers. Or had she been mistaken about that?

She leaned forward in her chair, trying once more to get a glimpse of his shade. His human soul shone bright enough, but the shade remained utterly suppressed under the hum of the suppression spell. Ayleth tilted her head to one side, studying him curiously. She'd assumed, based on that little demonstration with the candles, that Terryn carried an Elemental—a shade with abilities pertaining to control of fire. Elementals were considered the most powerful of all shades, and a fire Elemental would be formidable indeed. But Terryn's current struggles to light this fire didn't add up.

"What kind of shade do you bear, Venator?" she asked suddenly. A bold question, one that she probably had no business asking so bluntly. But she'd already saved his life once; he owed her something in return.

Terryn looked round at her, his expression unreadable in the darkness. No doubt he scowled, though. Something about the shadows *felt* like a scowl. He returned to his flints without saying a word, striking for a spark. At last there was a bright flare of light—

—followed at once by a burst of blue flame that erupted in his face and up the chimney.

Ayleth yelped and leapt to her feet, then let out a great bark of a laugh when Terryn turned blinkingly around, his face a mask of weird, bluish soot, his eyebrows and eyelashes singed. He wiped at his face with the sleeve of his erstwhile clean uniform.

Ayleth sank back into her seat, shaking her head and grinning like a fiend. "You certainly have a gift for finding curses, Venator du Balafre!"

Her first night in her new tower room was far from comfortable, but Ayleth was so exhausted it hardly mattered. She called Laranta close, and with her shade curled up beside her—in spirit if not in reality—managed to ward off most of the chill.

The following morning, she rose with the sun and went out at once to care for the horses. An early autumn frost glazed the ground, and Chestibor blew white streams from his wide nostrils as he looked over his stall door to greet her. Tough mountain horse that he was, he'd soon grow a thick winter coat, but Ayleth went ahead and gave him an extra blanket in the meanwhile.

Terryn wasn't up yet, apparently, so Ayleth tended to his mare's needs as well. No point in withholding a good beast's care because she couldn't stand its owner. By the time she'd finished, her blood was flowing and her limbs were warm, and she felt ready to face the cold blockhouse again.

Back inside, she stoked up a distinctly uncursed fire, grabbed a handful of barley cakes from a barrel, and stood munching, looking around the room. Sunlight poured through the eastern windows, lighting up the desk and stacks of papers.

Prince Gerard's command prickled at the forefront of her brain: She must find out what became of the former venator of Milisendis. A daunting task for a new venatrix, but the prince had no idea how inexperienced she truly was. The last thing she wanted was to let on. No, she would prove herself worthy of his faith if it killed her.

Granted, the prince intended her to work *with* Terryn. But Venator du Balafre, it would seem, preferred to sleep in on his first day. Who was she to begrudge him a few extra snores if it meant she had opportunity to snoop alone?

She pulled out the chair and sat down at the desk. Venators always carried logbooks on them during circuit rides, in which they recounted abbreviated details of their hunts. Later, they wrote out more complete accounts to be sent along with shade-taken remains to the castra. Perhaps some of the papers piled on the desk were Nane's own unfinished accounts, never sent on to Breçar.

The night before, she'd set Prince Gerard's message for Kephan on top of a stack of documents, where she assumed the venator would find it easily. Shifting the scroll to one side, she reached for the topmost page . . . but paused, thinking better of it. Instead, she pulled out her Vocos and quickly summoned up Laranta inside her.

Her wolf shade moved into the forefront of her mind. *What need?* she growled.

"Give me your sight," Ayleth said, and Laranta obeyed. Shadow vision flared in her eyes, and she scanned the desk with care, checking for any curses. Nothing stood out, so she went ahead and grabbed a page, drawing it close and studying the handwriting—the same which had written the letter Hollis received all those weeks ago. This document was Venator Kephan's, then, not Nane's.

Ayleth's eyes flicked first to the date inscribed in the upper right corner. Only three days old. Well, perhaps it would offer a clue to the venator's current whereabouts and when he might be expected back. Ayleth let her gaze drop to the main bulk of the document:

Three deaths, quick succession. One man—Motte du Giote. Seventy years of age, cut his own throat. Two days later, a cat found dead from an unnatural fall, three miles from the du Giote farm. One day later, a cow found—impaled itself on an old fence post. Five miles from the site of the cat's death. No sign of shade blight in any host.

Ayleth shuddered. Venator Kephan was on the trail of what sounded like a body-jumping shade. Most shades, glad to be free of the Haunts, took special care of their host bodies, no matter how humble. During the Witch Wars, however, many of Dread Odile's lieutenants took to the practice of violently killing less desirable host bodies and shifting to new and better hosts. They would possess human slaves, selecting the strongest and most beautiful to be used for this purpose.

Since the war, such practices had died out as the witches themselves were killed or driven into the Witchwood. But now and then a shade would take it into its head that it could improve its lot via suicide and possession. Without the careful preparation spells worked by the witches, however, the possession process was erratic. A violently propelled shade had little control once separated from its host body and would be obliged to claim whatever new host it could find.

From the sound of it, poor possessed Motte du Giote had been driven to kill himself so that the shade might find a fitter host, but the spirit inside him had moved on, not to a human body, but a cat. For a cat to die from a fall was decidedly unnatural. And a cow impaled on a fence post? Ayleth drew an uncomfortable breath through her teeth.

She sat back in her chair. If Venator Kephan was following a new lead for this strange mystery, he could be gone for days. Would he want a new hunt sister to come out and join him? Or would he prefer for her to stay on at Milisendis in case word arrived of new shade doings?

And there was still the prince's command to consider . . .

Chewing the inside of her cheek, Ayleth set aside Kephan's document and reached for another paper from the back of the desk. This was still inclined to curl in on the edges from having been rolled and sealed as a scroll. She recognized the seal of Breçar—a message from the castra itself.

She hesitated a moment, conscience-stricken about reading another venator's correspondence. But Nane was dead, or presumably so. She needed to utilize any means possible in her bid to discover the truth of his fate. So, she opened the scroll and read quickly:

To Nane, Venator du Vincent,

I regret to inform you that the sample you sent for testing has been confirmed. The child you found is, as you suspected, inborn. You have full leave from the Council to do what must be done. Gather and prepare the ashes according to your training and send them on with your next shipment.

It was signed: *Esabel, Phasmatrix di Conradin. Domina of Castra Breçar*

Ayleth's stomach gave a sickening twist. She read the words again, hoping she saw them wrong, hoping she'd somehow misunderstood. But no. There was no mistaking those words, written in the Phasmatrix Domina's clear, precise hand: *The child you found is, as you suspected, inborn.*

"No," Ayleth whispered. "Please, Goddess, not that."

In all her years training under Hollis, she'd never heard her mistress mention hunting an inborn—a mortal born of a shade-taken mother or sired by a shade-taken father. But she knew about them from her readings. In such cases, a shade soul would grow right alongside the new mortal soul of the unborn child. These two souls were inextricably bound, and they could be difficult to recognize even for an experienced venator. Many inborn went undiscovered until they were older, often until adulthood.

As with all shade-taken, only the point of death could offer hope of separation for the two souls. But unlike with ordinary shade-taken, a violent, painful death was required to separate an inborn from its shade. No Gentle Death for these unlucky mortals.

A child, though? Ayleth shuddered. She knew the law. She knew the teachings of the saint. She knew that it was better ultimately to suffer a little pain in this world than eternal torment in the next. But . . .

With a forceful shake of her head, she pushed the document away. She drew a long breath, held it, then let it out slowly until her heart stopped racing. She checked the castra missive and noted the date: almost exactly six weeks ago. Very close to the time when Nane went missing.

Was his hunt for the inborn child related to his disappearance? Possibly. But the Domina's letter gave no indication as to the name of the child, her family, or where they might live. Nane certainly would have entered all these details in his logbook, which was no help if he'd had his logbook on him at the time of his disappearance.

She needed to figure out some way to track Nane himself. If she could just find a trace of him and put Laranta on his scent . . . It should be easy enough here in his own outpost if she could think how best to go about it.

"The curses," she whispered. Frustration burned in her chest. How could she have been so shortsighted? "You could have traced him using one of the curses!"

Broken and frayed though those tangled curse threads were, Laranta might have been able to pick up a thread leading back to the curse caster himself. Not while suppressed, but if Ayleth gave the wolf shade more freedom, relaxing the soul tether as much as she dared, it was possible. But here she'd gone and broken all those curses without a thought.

"There might be another curse somewhere in the outpost," she muttered thoughtfully. "Venator Nane wasn't stingy with his castings."

Leaning back in her chair, she rubbed her face and pushed strands of dark hair out of her eyes. The patches of sunlight were moving quickly across the room. She needed to get going if she wanted to make progress on this hunt today.

Ayleth frowned suddenly, looking back over her shoulder into the empty room. Where was that slugabed Terryn anyway?

She tilted her head, listening for some sound of him moving around upstairs. Nothing. This seemed odd. He had not struck her as the sort to sleep in late on his first day, desperate as he was to prove himself and prove his competitor's unworthiness. Was it possible he'd sneaked out and taken his horse while she was caught up in rifling through the desk? But no, she would have seen him at the door, surely.

Her brow knotted in curious concern, Ayleth got up and stood at the bottom of the stairwell. "Venator du Balafre?" she called up to the floor above. When no answer came, she climbed the stairs to the landing. The door to his room was shut fast. She knocked sharply. "Venator? Venator du Balafre?"

Still nothing.

She put an ear to the door, listening with her shade's

augmenting senses. Was that gentle snoring she heard? The latch gave when she applied pressure to it, and she carefully pushed the door open a crack and peered into the room.

"Oh, great Goddess above!" Ayleth cried. And burst out laughing.

Terryn lay on Venator Nane's bed, caught fast in a winding snarl of cursed sleep.

CHAPTER 15

SHE FOUND THE CURSE THREAD ANCHORED TO Nane's pillow. The curse itself was just as frayed and inharmonic as all the others, but it still held plenty of potency. One had to give Nane his due—he knew how to craft these curses of his.

Ayleth stood over the bed, arms folded, considering. She'd have to break it, of course, and free the venator. But, first and foremost, could she catch a thread that would lead her to Nane?

"It's worth a shot," she whispered, unsheathing her Vocos pipes. She began playing the Song of Unbinding. Slowly, carefully, she called to life the drone and melody, then began building layers of complexity into the song. The Unbinding song took years to master and must always be played with extreme delicacy so as to never fully undo the Suppressions.

Closing her eyes, she slipped into the pine forest of her mindscape. Laranta stood before her, shadowy and powerful, not quite contained in the form of a wolf. In this realm, Ayleth saw the shimmering tethers of the Binding song wound around her shade's neck. Using her pipes with care, she loosened those tethers, first a little, then much more.

Laranta tossed her head and snarled in wolfish delight, pleased by this unexpected liberty. She started to move, to bound away.

"*Wait.*" Ayleth shifted the melody of the Unbinding deftly into a variation of the Song of Command. "*There is another curse. I need you to find the curse thread that will lead us to the caster.*"

Ayleth then opened her eyes and, with another flare of

the song, urged her wolf shade to manifest in the room before her. The chamber was much too small to fit a being of Laranta's size, but she was spirit, not physical, so she warped the perceived reality of the space to suit her own needs. Huge and shadowy, she padded to the bed and sniffed at the curse.

She pulled back with a disapproving expression. *Sour. Breaking*, she said.

"*I know*," Ayleth answered. She saw well enough how bad the curse looked, heard the discordant hum of its unraveling. She needed to break its hold on Terryn soon or it might unravel completely, leaving him still asleep but without means to wake. "*I've given you your head, Laranta. Find the curse thread. Find the trail.*"

Laranta obediently plunged her magic senses into the snarl. Ayleth watched as her wolf shade carefully sorted through the shimmering tangle of sound and magic. At last, with a satisfied growl, Laranta took something in her teeth and backed away from the rest.

Ayleth, looking with shadow sight, saw the curse thread, faint but still detectable, caught in her shade's grip. "*Good girl*," she said. "*Now I need you to hold onto it, tight. I'm going to break the curse, but we need to follow this thread back to its source. Can you do that?"*

Laranta tilted her massive head, like a shrug. *I'll try.*

Ayleth couldn't ask more than that. She finished playing and sheathed the pipes once more. Then, blinking back into her own mortal sight, she studied the sleeping venator lying on Nane's bed.

He was not wearing a shirt. On a small chair under the window lay his uniform, folded neatly, awaiting service. Did he wear anything under that blanket? The question appeared in her mind despite her best efforts to suppress it, and Ayleth's cheeks heated. She had little enough experience with young men, and the last thing she needed just now was to be curse-breaking for a naked man who was practically her enemy. Nevertheless, she took a step closer to study the situation.

For as tall and slender as he was, his shoulders were well muscled, as was the one arm sprawled over his head, across the top of the pillow. His skin was even darker against the pale linen, and in sleep he looked oddly peaceful. Innocent, somehow. Black hair framed his face in a dark halo, curls falling over his forehead. But the effect was spoiled by the ugliness of that strange, circular scar across his right cheek.

How had he come by a scar like that? Certainly not in the field. It was too precisely made, too perfect a circle. Had he carved it there intentionally?

Ayleth took a step back, her brow darkening as she noticed something she'd not recognized before. Venator Terryn looked remarkably like . . .

"Like Prince Gerard," she whispered, the name slipping unconsciously through her lips.

The difference in their complexions was great enough to disguise the similarity at first, but now that she'd seen it, she couldn't pretend she hadn't. It was as though the same artist had sculpted both men, inspired by a single idea. Terryn was the first, raw attempt, with his wider, rougher mouth and sharper jaw and cheekbones, while Gerard was the more polished, finished image, elegantly refined and beautiful. Two separate statues born of the same inspiration.

The image of Queen Leurona's ice-cold eyes in the portrait flashed across Ayleth's memory. Eyes which had felt strangely familiar . . .

She frowned and backed away two more steps, uncertain where this trail of thought might lead but quite certain she didn't want to follow it. "Maybe I'll just leave you here," she whispered, taking another step back toward the door. "After all, if I break the curse, it will be that much harder for Laranta to keep hold of the thread. And you're not causing any trouble where you are."

She began to turn away but stopped, conscience-stricken. Prince Gerard had been very clear that Ayleth and Terryn were to work together to solve the mystery of Nane's disappearance. While she much preferred the idea of following this trail, discovering the answers, and presenting her findings to the prince all on her own, she couldn't shake the nagging guilt brought on by these imaginings.

"Haunts damn it," she muttered. Leaving Laranta holding tight to the shimmering curse, she knelt beside the sleeping venator, took hold of the pillow and, with a single jerk, pulled it out from under Terryn's head. Looking at it closely, she thought she could almost discern traces of a sigil painted in blood. Or she might have been imagining it. Either way, thinking of the stone under the gate and the slat in the gate itself, she tore the pillow apart, scattering goose down in a flurry of white.

The curse held. The anchor was gone, but the sleeper did not wake, and the fraying curse threads remained in a snarl all around him.

We hunt now? Laranta asked, seated by the door.

"*You just keep holding that curse thread,*" Ayleth told her, scowling down at the gently snoring venator. She studied the shape of the curse. Without an anchor it should dissipate, but there it remained in defiance of all reason.

"Oh, Haunts damn it all," she muttered, her shadow sight quickening. There, faintly shimmering, were five distinct threads reaching into the venator himself. New bindings which had formed the moment he put his head down on that cursed pillow. He himself was the anchor.

So, what was she supposed to do now? Take out her knife and carve the curse out of him? He had scars enough as it was . . . and those threads were coming straight out of his mouth. She couldn't very well cut into his tongue, could she?

Ayleth crossed her arms, narrowing her eyes at him. "Well, I'm *not* kissing you, so get that idea out of your head."

There had to be another way.

A stand in the corner of the room held a pitcher and basin filled with water for Terryn's morning ablutions. Ayleth snatched up the pitcher and poured its contents over the venator's face in a long, cold stream. His dark curls plastered to his forehead, but he did not so much as flinch.

"Hmmm." Ayleth set the pitcher back down with a *thunk*. Then she marched downstairs, grabbed one of Nane's big copper pots and a wooden spoon, and bore them back up to the bedchamber. "Wake up!" she shouted, pounding the pot just next to the venator's ear. "Wake up, wake up, wake up!"

Nothing.

She tried pinching. She flicked his long nose. She blew in his ear, used a feather from the torn-up pillow to tickle his upper lip. All to no avail.

The minutes passed. And Laranta still patiently held onto the curse thread. The wolf shade said only, *It's fading.*

She needed to follow the curse soon before it vanished entirely, taking with it what might be her last link to wherever Nane was now, dead or alive.

With a huff, Ayleth sat down on the edge of the bed. Her fingers trembling more than she liked, she pushed loose hair out of her own face, tucking strands behind her ears. Then, very gently, she stroked a damp curl back from Terryn's forehead.

She was stalling. Time to act.

"No offence, Venator du Balafre," she said. With that, she bent over him and gave him a quick peck on his parted lips. Pulling back quickly, she watched for the effect.

Nothing.

Well, no. Something. The anchor gave a little shudder, the threads vibrating the air with a distinct, magical hum. But a kiss like that was not going to suffice.

"Festering saints!" she cursed. Then, closing her eyes and bracing herself, she bent again, and this time pressed her mouth more firmly against his. She'd never done anything like this before—she'd never dared so much as kiss Hollis on the cheek back when she was a child. On further recollection, the entirety of her kissing experience involved Chestibor's velvety soft nose.

But . . . it wasn't so difficult as all that. For such a cold, unfeeling sort of man, his lips were surprisingly soft and warm. At first, they were very still beneath hers. Then, with a shivering scatter of curse threads, they moved, and she realized with a jolt of something like lightning down to her gut that he was kissing her back.

She opened her eyes—and Terryn opened his.

With an inarticulate cry, the venator sat bolt upright in the bed, pushing her so hard that she landed in a sprawl on the floor. He clutched at the blanket like some blushing and offended maiden and yanked it up to his chin, uncovering quite a lot of his bare legs in the process. "What do you think you're doing?" His outraged roar nearly raised the roof.

With as much dignity as she could muster, Ayleth picked herself up, straightened her jerkin, and schooled her furiously flushing face into an imperious mask. "I'll have you know I got no pleasure from doing that," she said, then turned away from his open-mouthed, wide-eyed stare and marched to the door.

There she paused, tossing back over her shoulder, "I've got a lead on Venator Nane, and I'm going to follow it. If you want to come with me, you'd better hurry. I'm not waiting around for you to polish your buckles."

With that, she whistled to Laranta and made her getaway down the stairs, following the curse thread as fast as she could go.

CHAPTER 16

AYLETH MADE READY TO RIDE IN RECORD TIME, saddling her horse, arranging her weapons, and stocking her saddlebags all within half an hour. When she led Chestibor out of the stable, she cast a glance back at the blockhouse, but there was still no sign of Venator Terryn. He must not have recovered from his shock swiftly enough to accompany her on the hunt.

Well good. She didn't want his glacial company.

So, she opened the heavy outpost gate, led Chestibor

through, and, refusing to look toward the blockhouse again, pulled the gate firmly shut behind her. Swinging into her saddle, she whistled to Laranta, who stalked in wolf shape beside her. *"Do you still have hold of that curse thread?"*

Yes, Mistress, Laranta answered around her mouthful.

"Follow it then," Ayleth commanded, pulling her hood up over her head. *"Let's see where it takes us."*

Laranta released the straining, fraying thread of discordant magic. With a sour trill of sound, it whisked away, spraying sparks in its wake. Ayleth's shadow vision wasn't quick enough to follow it, but Laranta, her suppressions lifted to a greater degree than usual, leapt into action. Her smoke-like form lost all wolfish shape and streamed across the landscape in a formless shadow. The soul tether connecting her to her host body strained, and Ayleth spurred Chestibor into motion, galloping him as fast as she could in pursuit before the yank of the soul tether could pull her right out of her saddle and haul Laranta to a stop.

The stony valley in which Milisendis Outpost stood looked no more welcoming in the light of midmorning.

They left it behind swiftly enough, Laranta chasing after the curse through a grove of spindly pines and up to the high ground beyond. The sun shone bright on Ayleth's face, for they rode due east. There was no venator's circuit to follow—the curse thread did not lead by a winding route, but straight to the location of the venator. Ayleth pushed Chestibor as fast as she dared across the open landscape, all too aware that a wrong step on this unfamiliar ground could send him crashing and her flying, bringing their chase to an abrupt end. The thread led straight across fields and pastures, thankfully never drawing too near any established centers of living. Ayleth caught only occasional glimpses of distant rooftops and the stone bell towers of shrine houses. Few people dared to live this far east in the borough. Not with the Witchwood looming so near.

Abruptly, a stretch of autumn-gold forest loomed ahead, casting deep shadows beneath its many interlaced branches. The sight of that forest, however natural and tame it might appear, made her stomach clench with dread. The Witchwood waited just on the other side of those trees.

But she had to follow the curse thread. If she lost it now, she might never find another lead to Nane's whereabouts.

"Come on, boy," she muttered to Chestibor, urging him faster, closing the distance between them and her wolf shade. Laranta ducked into the fringe forest and away, vanishing into the shadows, but the soul tether pulled Ayleth along in her wake. Chestibor could not continue his galloping pace through the trees, but they progressed as swiftly as they could, Ayleth guiding her beast around the thicker underbrush.

Suddenly Ayleth felt a *buzz*, a strange, dissonant hum of music, deep down in her bones. The vibration of spirit and physicality combined unlike anything she'd ever before experienced. This had to be the song of the Great Barriers. The enormous working of magic created by Dominus Fendrel du Glaive nearly twenty years ago. The power of the song spell jarred her, and she shuddered, dizzy and half afraid she'd double over in her saddle and vomit.

The first wave of sensation passed, however. With a quick shake of her head and shoulders, as though she could shake off her own discomfort, she focused again on following Laranta. The forest undergrowth seemed to close in on either side. She could no longer discern a trace of the curse thread they pursued. Judging by the decreased tension she felt in the soul tether, Laranta was starting to lose it as well.

Dismounting, Ayleth took Chestibor by the reins and continued on foot, taking care where she led him through the uncertain terrain. Laranta's pace had slowed significantly as well. She'd reassumed her wolf shape, picking her way one footfall at a time.

Then, with a flash and fizzle of dying magic, the curse thread vanished. Though Ayleth could not see it, she felt its sudden dissolution and recoiled back a half step.

Ahead of her, Laranta simply sat down and tilted her head at Ayleth.

"Festering Haunts," Ayleth cursed. That was the last of her lead. She'd known all along it was an unlikely lead at best, but it was the only one she had. "I shouldn't have delayed," she muttered, her eyes flicking back and forth as she scanned the shadowy forest, as though she could somehow force her vision to detect a trace that was not there. "I shouldn't have delayed. Should have left that stupid venator sleeping . . ."

Still, the curse had led them in a nearly straight line from the outpost to this point. Could they simply forge on ahead, as straight as possible? Nane's remains might lay but a few yards from where she now stood.

"*If* he's dead," she reminded herself. "If—"

A sharp crack of a branch breaking.

Ayleth jumped and spun around. Something large pushed through the branches and crunched on twigs on its way through the forest. Sensing Ayleth's unease, Laranta paced to her side, growling softly, her wolf shape blurring on the edges into curls of darkness. Ayleth put out a hand, resting it atop her shade's head—a useless gesture in that there was no physical form for her to actually touch. But her shade responded nonetheless, relaxing her tense stance and leaning into her mistress.

Using her shadow vision, Ayleth peered through the trees, not allowing her eyes to be dazzled by the contrasts of sunlight and shadow, but gazing beyond into the spirit realm. Through the weird, stationary yet vibrant spirits of the tall, drowsy trees, she saw two active spirits approaching swiftly. One untaken and one definitely shade-taken, though of the shade she could get no clear sense.

She knew who it was.

"Had enough of your beauty sleep, Venator du Balafre?"

The sounds of approach stilled. The shade-taken spirit quivered in response to her voice, flashing with some strong emotion she didn't bother trying to identify. Her head ached from straining her shadow sight, so Ayleth switched back to her ordinary mortal vision, crossed her arms, and waited. The sounds of approach started up again, and within a minute, the tall venator appeared through the trees, leading his red mare behind him. If she'd thought his eyes cold before, they were veritable ice daggers now, freezing the air as they looked out from the shadow of his hood to fix in frosty fury on her face.

She smiled. "You're certainly looking rested."

His gaze searched her up and down and seemed momentarily to flicker to that space where Laranta stood. He could not see the wolf shade in her assumed shape, but he detected her presence, the level of ascendancy which Ayleth had granted her. No doubt he disapproved of her giving her shade such free rein.

He said nothing, however, merely returned his attention to Ayleth. She was almost certain his gaze didn't linger for a moment longer than necessary on her mouth, just as she was almost certain any blush staining her cheeks was well hidden beneath her hood. She tilted her head and said nothing, waiting for him to break the silence between them. She would maintain her peace for as long as necessary, just to prove that his stubborn silence did not intimidate her.

He didn't make her wait long. Breaking her gaze, he looked off into the space over her left shoulder in the direction she and Laranta had been charging through the forest. "So where is this lead you claim to have found?" he demanded. "Or was that a ruse on your part?"

Ayleth resisted the urge to roll her eyes. As if she would waste her valuable time inventing leads and rushing off into nowhere on a whim! "The curse you so conveniently located in Nane's bed," she said dryly, "was still connected to its source. To Nane, presumably," she added, in case he didn't understand her point. "My shade followed it out here."

"Your shade can trace broken curse threads?"

Ayleth's cheeks heated again, but this time with a much more pleasant warmth. The venator sounded impressed. And well he should! A skilled venatrix might use her shade's power to trace an established curse thread while it was fully intact. But to trace a broken thread required a Feral shade such as hers and the skill to control its powers. Most servants of Evander's Order, no matter the years of their training, never boasted such a level of control. But most Evanderians never permitted their shades the level of freedom Ayleth allowed Laranta.

Maybe she toyed with fire. Maybe she even, as Venator Terryn had suggested, danced on the edge of heresy. But, by the Goddess, she did get results.

She moved her shoulders in a dismissive shrug as though the venator's words didn't please her at all. "The curse is completely unraveled now, and the thread vanished. Unless you think you can find us another curse back in Milisendis, this trail has gone cold."

The venator said nothing. With a tug on his horse's reins, he led the beast past Ayleth, so close that their shoulders almost brushed. Laranta growled and backed away from him just before he walked directly through her immaterial form.

"Where are you going?" Ayleth demanded.

"The thread led you straight from the outpost to here," the venator tossed back over his shoulder. "Broken or otherwise, the trajectory is the same."

He was right of course. It was the same plan she'd been mulling over a moment before his arrival. But she didn't like the way he said it, the way he assumed she hadn't thought of something so basic, and she wished she could think of some reason to contradict him.

"The Barrier," she spoke to the back of his head. "Keep going that way, you'll run into the Great Barrier."

He didn't look back, didn't bother to answer, simply kept on his way. The thick undergrowth soon hid his passage, and Ayleth would need to start moving if she wanted to keep up with him.

She grimaced. Barrier spell or no barrier spell, if this was the direction the curse thread led, they had to follow it. But that sick sensation she'd experienced only a few minutes ago still hovered in her memory. She didn't want to go any nearer to the Great Barrier than absolutely necessary. The fringe forests were bad enough, but the Barrier marked the edge of the Witchwood. And that place she had no desire to see up close. Her view from the distant hilltop had been more than adequate to satisfy any curiosity she'd ever felt about Dread Odile's final curse.

But did she want to become Venatrix of Wodechran or didn't she? If she intended to take this borough as her own, she would have to learn to work in proximity to the Witchwood.

"*To me, Laranta,*" she commanded, and her wolf shade fell in step at her heel as she led Chestibor after Venator Terryn. He and his mare had cleared something like a path through the dense foliage as they went, making Ayleth and Chestibor's progress easier. She pulled her horse along behind her, wincing when the buzzing whine of the barrier spell struck her bones, making them hum like the plucked string of an instrument.

She switched again to shadow sight, peering ahead. Soon she spied the Great Barrier shimmering like a silvery web, a complex pattern of magic, of song spell. She could feel the deep, dark pulse of the drone anchoring it into the earth, the trilling of the melody rising to form all those complex woven threads. They wound between tree trunk and tree trunk, more delicate than spider silk and a thousand times stronger. The mighty spell crafted by Dominus Fendrel all those years ago, still throbbing with power, still vibrant, still vital. And beyond it . . .

Beyond waited the Witchwood itself.

There Ayleth dared not look. Not yet. So, she focused her attention instead on the spell, on the brilliance of the magic performed. It was truly astonishing. Fendrel du Glaive was by far the most accomplished venator in all Perrinion, possibly in all Gaulia. It was no wonder the Goddess had selected him to guide and direct the Chosen King into the fulfillment of Her prophecy.

But something was wrong here. A spell woven with such care and complexity shouldn't leave this sick feeling roiling in the pit of the stomach.

Ayleth spotted Venator Terryn standing a few paces away from his horse, which he'd left to nose her way into a patch of long grass. He seemed to be studying the spell, one hand fingering the Detrudos pipes in its sheath at his belt. His face was obscured by his hood from this angle, but something in the set of his shoulders struck Ayleth as uneasy. Confused.

Terryn had studied under Fendrel du Glaive. No doubt he had been trained in the complexities of this particular song spell as Ayleth had not. She understood the basics, but when she listened to the hum of that intricate webbing, she couldn't decipher the variation of the original melody. This was not music as the mortal ear perceived music but a multifaceted power of the spirit realm. Her shade-augmented senses were finely tuned to hear it, but not finely enough to comprehend it.

She drew up beside the venator. "Well, there we have it," she said. "Can't go any farther than this. The lead is cold."

He didn't look at her. He didn't acknowledge that she'd spoken.

Ayleth sighed and turned from him, eyeing their surroundings. The fringe forest seemed to draw back slightly from the spell, leaving a clear space of several yards between the natural trees and whatever grew on the far side of the Great Barrier. Blue sky arched overhead, unobscured by interlacing branches and autumnal foliage.

No one passed beyond the Great Barrier. No one save the most desperate of shade-taken fleeing pursuit. Anyone could cross—the Barrier did not prevent passage through. But to step over that line of spell was to be trapped in the curse beyond. A venator properly trained in the barrier spell could make an opening to return, but such a move would be dangerous. Even a small opening would attract whatever beings lived on the far side, drawing them to it like flies to scat.

Yet, the curse thread had led unerringly this direction. Was it possible . . . could Venator Nane have . . .?

Ayleth shook her head. No. No, she wouldn't think it.

"*Laranta,*" she called to her shade, "*see if you can pick up a trace of blood. Mortal blood. It could be that his body is—*"

"There was an opening here."

Ayleth shuddered at Terryn's cold voice, turning him slowly. "What did you say?" she asked, hoping she had misheard.

"There was an opening. Right here." He pointed straight ahead into the song spell. Directly where the curse thread would have led them had it not frayed too soon. "It's been repaired. Badly. By someone who did not know the correct variation."

Ayleth shifted her shadow sight back to the spell song, studying the webbing. The unpleasant discord struck her senses again. She couldn't see a difference in those shimmering strands of magic, but she could hear it. The wrongness in the song, the unsuitable variation that did not blend correctly with the rest of the vast complexities of the Great Barrier. As though some novice composer had tried to insert a measure of music into a master's orchestration.

"Who could have done this?" she asked. Poorly conceived or otherwise, it had to be Evanderian work. Only members of the Order knew the song spells to make magic of this kind. "Venator Nane?"

"Not Nane," Terryn answered sharply. "Nane was trained by Fendrel. He would know better than this."

"Venator Kephan?" Ayleth suggested next. "Could he have put a temporary repair in place since Nane disappeared?"

Terryn did not answer. He pushed his hood back from his head as though to better his view, one hand running through his dark tangle of hair. Striding forward, he drew as near to the spell as he could without touching it. Though its webbing was immaterial, invisible save to shadow sight, he put out one long finger, gently running it along the length of one of the humming threads.

Ayleth drew in behind him. "If there was an opening, someone on the far side made it," she said. "Someone with knowledge of the song. Could Kephan have entered the Witchwood for some reason and, on his return, tried to close it? He may have hoped to find Nane and get him to do a proper fix later."

"But why then did the curse thread lead you here?" Terryn said, still speaking in a low voice as though she wasn't present. She had to strain to catch his words.

"Perhaps the curse was Kephan's and not Nane's?" Ayleth suggested. "We've assumed all this time that Nane set the curses on the outpost, but there have been two venators serving here in Wodechran."

"Venator Kephan du Tam is possessed of a Feral shade." At this, the venator cast her a sidelong glance brimming with such scorn, she wished he'd go back to ignoring her. "You ought to know that if you have any thought of becoming his hunt sister."

Feral shades, like Laranta, were not curse casters. The magic they worked was of a different variety entirely, pertaining to the augmentation of strength and natural senses.

Deciding Terryn's snide remarks weren't deserving of an answer, Ayleth faced the barrier spell again. Her pulse jumped, and she realized what she was about to do. The intention was there before she'd quite planned it, but now there was no going back. She needed to look beyond the spell. She needed to look beyond the magical webbing, into the world on the far side. She was too close now to avoid it. She had to see.

Taking a step nearer, she peered through into the Witchwood.

Her heart twisted with horror, and her stomach heaved, bile burning as it slid up her throat. She backed away quickly, twisted to one side, and bent over, gagging. Nothing came up, but that was worse. The sickness merely pooled in her gut and stayed there. Stayed along with the image in her mind that she wished—desperately wished—she could somehow unsee.

Terryn watched her. She felt the icy coolness of his eyes on the back of her head, soothing in a strange way. Something about his disdain for her gave her heart, and she pulled herself back upright and faced him, refusing to let her voice tremble when she spoke.

"Someone is there," she said. "Just on the other side. I think it's Venator Nane."

CHAPTER 17

TERRYN STARED AT HER AS THOUGH SHE'D LOST HER mind. Ayleth, drawing deep breaths, struggled to calm the roiling in her stomach and met his eyes, unblinking. "What do you mean, you think it's Nane?" the venator demanded. "Do you mean . . . his body?"

Ayleth nodded. "I couldn't see a face. Not that I would recognize Nane's face. But there was a hood. A red hood. And a Detrudos pipe." She closed her eyes, wishing she could banish the image of what she'd glimpsed. The

Witchwood was no mere forest, of that she was certain. She'd known it would be dark. She'd expected a sense of evil, of predatory malice.

She'd not expected the *foulness*. The sordid repulsiveness of fleshy trees clutching the ground with ravenous roots, sucking at the air and spewing back thick, poisonous fumes. This was evil, but not evil in a theoretical, distant sense. It was evil made tangible.

And all waiting just beyond that thin webbing of magic.

Why would Nane enter that? Why would anyone, no matter how desperate? She closed her eyes, her stomach heaving again despite her best efforts to calm it and herself. How many of Dread Odile's servants had fled beyond the Barrier by choice? The Crimson Devils, her lieutenants. And others hounded down by the Order. Would it not have been better to accept their fates? To die and leave this world behind?

But to die meant entering eternity in the Haunts. Ayleth thought of the brief glimpses she'd caught through those gaping holes in reality when she helped Hollis drive souls from this world back into that hellish realm. If a shade once escaped the Haunts, it would fight with everything it had never to return.

It might even choose the Witchwood as a better fate.

This did not explain Nane's actions, however. If indeed it was Nane she had seen, fallen on his face mere steps from the Barrier. So close to freedom! Had he pursued a shade-taken and simply not realized where it led him? But no. Even Ayleth, inexperienced as she was, would not make such a mistake. The Barrier was too obvious, too powerful. Nane must have chosen to follow his prey beyond.

She looked again at Terryn, who once more studied the Barrier. His face was a mask of ice, revealing none of the confusion she herself felt. Nevertheless, by the way his eyes swiveled sharply back and forth, up and down the magical webbing, she suspected he was considering a host of his own questions, all rather similar to hers.

With a sudden firming of his jaw, he stepped up to the Barrier and, like Ayleth had a moment before, peered through. With a sharp, hissing breath, he pulled back more quickly than she had, his lips curled, the puckered skin on his scarred right cheek tensing as he clenched his jaw.

"Did you see him?" Ayleth asked, whispering though there was no one to overhear her. Somehow, now that she'd seen the Witchwood, she felt as though it might listen through the Barrier.

Terryn nodded then shook his head. "I saw a body. It may or may not be Nane. We . . ." He backed up one pace then another, his eyes squinting as though against a bright light. "We should report what we have seen to the prince, and—"

"Report what?" Ayleth demanded. "Report that we didn't find anything? That we saw what *might* be a venator's body but we're not sure? That we found the Barrier tampered with but have no idea who did the tampering?"

The venator's hard gaze swiveled to meet hers. He did not speak. She could see calculations running in the depths of his eyes.

"We are servants of Saint Evander," Ayleth persisted. "It is our duty to protect this borough. And to do so we must find answers, not more questions. We can make all the reports you like, but the prince will send us right back here. Right back to this spot. And the answers we seek may be beyond discovery by then."

Terryn blinked slowly, drawing a long breath. "Venator Kephan—"

"Kephan is not here. You and I are. Are we Evanderians or aren't we?" Ayleth took a step nearer to him. She did not like what she was saying. How could she? Her rational mind urged her to turn and run as hard and as fast as her extraordinary shade strength could drive her.

But another, less rational but equally powerful part of her mind urged: *The hunt. The hunt. The hunt . . .*

Laranta's growl rumbled deep in her brain.

"This is our hunt," she said, her hands tightening into fists. "This is our task. To find what happened to Venator Nane. To make certain whatever happened to him does not happen again." She indicated the Barrier with a nod of her head. "Our brother lies just beyond. Or something wearing his hood and carrying his pipe."

"Let me make certain I have understood you correctly," Venator Terryn said. "You propose to cross the Barrier into the Witchwood. With me. Is that right?"

"He's only a few steps in," Ayleth said. "I can carry the body, bring him out. It won't take long. Only as long as you need to make the opening. I will stand guard while you work the spells. Can you or can you not repair the Barrier once it's opened?"

The muscles in his throat constricted as he swallowed, but he answered firmly, "I can. I can open and close the Barrier as necessary. I can repair this . . . mess." His gaze darted to the ill-played section of the song spell.

"Very well," Ayleth said, and turned from the venator to face the Great Barrier. To face the Witchwood.

"The minute an opening is made, every shade-taken within miles will sense it. They'll feel the shift in the magic. They'll come."

Ayleth thought of those names Hollis had listed in her book. The Warpwitch. The Phantomwitch. The Corpsewitch. And more. All those terrors of the Wars, the fiends who had held Perrinion in thrall for two hundred years, empowered by their dark goddess queen.

Did they wait just on the far side of the Barrier, hidden behind that first stand of repulsive trees?

"It's a good thing we're in this together then," she

said, her lips twisting into a wolfish grin. "Isn't it, Venator du Balafre?"

Terryn didn't answer her. He faced the Barrier. She saw his hand move to his Vocos pipes and wondered if he would take out the instrument and call up his shade, relinquishing some of the profound bindings holding it at bay. But he did not draw the Vocos from its sheath.

"Have you power enough to open the Barrier?" Ayleth asked. She was not about to step through that song spell unless her partner was properly prepared to enact his role.

"I can accomplish what I must, Venatrix." He shot her a quick look. "Don't presume to tell me how to manage my own shade."

Her jaw clicked, but she didn't press the issue. If he wanted to pass into the Witchwood with only partial access to his shade's abilities, let him.

"*To me, Laranta,*" she said, and her wolf shade again stepped to her side, her whole being simmering with strength and vicious cunning. Ayleth put out a hand and rested it on her shade's immaterial head. She was ready.

Standing shoulder to shoulder with Terryn, Ayleth looked into the Barrier spell. For an instant she felt the terrible reality of her own *smallness*. The enormity of the evil waiting just beyond those thin strands of magic was so overwhelming, and she herself, so weak by comparison. If she stopped and let herself think about it a moment longer, she would never find the courage to go on.

"Now!" she said, before she could stop herself. And that word was enough to spur her into motion. She took a step, not waiting to see if Terryn stepped with her. She crossed into the webbed spell and felt the silken strands of magic flutter across her skin, not breaking but somehow permitting her to pass. A burst of light like the final flash of the sun sinking beyond the horizon burst on the edges of her vision, and she was suddenly hyperaware of the blue sky arching overhead.

Then the light was gone. The sky overhead was not blue but gray, heavy, low, and streaked with red like lesions. She stood in the Witchwood.

Though she'd taken that first stride bravely enough, she slammed to a halt as though struck with spirit bind. She could not think, could not fully comprehend that on which she looked. The first thing her awareness truly felt was the solidity of the Barrier at her back. Whereas a moment before she had walked through it as though it were made up of nothing more than airy filaments, it was now a wall of solid, powerful magic.

She could not retreat. She could not escape. If Terryn did not follow, she didn't know how to make an opening.

These thoughts flashed through her brain before she'd taken a breath. But just as she sucked a gasp of air into her lungs, Terryn stepped through to her side. She let her breath out in a gusting sigh of relief as he also stopped stock-still, struck with the same horror she had experienced a moment before. Ayleth left him to deal with his own realizations and dared to peer ahead into the world stretched before her.

The darkness was not absolute. It would be better if it were. Instead, the sun overhead diffused through the thickness of the air, its light rendered a sickly pale sheen, highlighting sharp edges, emphasizing deeper shadows. The trees were like warped reflections of those on the other side of the barrier. A careful eye could discern the shapes of oak leaves and the curl of birch bark. But there was a strange fleshiness to the wood. A fleshiness scored with deep, seeping wounds. Pus rolled down trunks and dripped from branches, soaking into the ground beneath.

And everywhere . . . everywhere were choking, strangling vines, ripping into the trees and feeding on the oozing infection.

Dark motes floated in the air before Ayleth's vision, now and then flickering with strange glints of light. She knew what they were—*oblivis*, an element not of this world. The "air of the Haunts" as Saint Evander described it in his writings. The atmosphere here was thick with it. To breathe too much *oblivis* into one's lungs was to breathe in pure poison.

Ayleth hastily twitched her hood so that it covered the lower half of her face, a small protection. That one simple act of hers seemed to bestir Terryn, who shook himself out of his stricken state and quickly followed suit, adjusting his hood like hers. They looked at one another, each recognizing the horror reflected in the other's gaze.

This was a big mistake.

Terryn's hand moved for his Detrudos. But Ayleth reached out quickly, catching him by the wrist. "We're here now," she said, her voice oddly thick through her hood and the dense, *oblivis*-laced air. "We should get the body."

Terryn's arm tensed under her hold, and she saw that he was on the verge of fighting her, of throwing her off. The moment passed, however. His expression shifted into grim understanding. He nodded, and the two of them turned to find the corpse.

It lay sprawled only a few paces away. The red of the hood stood out starkly in the eerily colorless world. One hand was outstretched, what was left of its gloved fingers still curled around the bone-white Detrudos pipe.

Terryn took a step, but Ayleth, holding onto his wrist, restrained him from taking another. "Wait a moment," she said. She flicked her gaze to Laranta, who stood in wolf shape on her other side. "*See to the body,*" she commanded. "*Make certain it is real.*"

Laranta leaped into action, floating across the ground, more smoke than wolf in her movements. She lowered her muzzle to the corpse, sniffing with interest, searching for some sign of illusion. Witches lived in this place. Witches who hated Evanderians more than anything. Who was to say they wouldn't set a trap for unwary venators, baiting it with the body of one of their own? She didn't bother explaining her suspicions to Terryn, but he did not question her, merely waited. No doubt he sensed her reaching out with her shade's powers to test the body.

After a few tense heartbeats, Laranta looked up, her eyes gleaming red pinpoints in the dark. *It is mortal,* she said. *It is dead.*

Not an illusion then. *"Any sign of a trap?"* Ayleth asked.

No trap. None that I can smell.

Ayleth met Terryn's eye and nodded. Together they headed toward the corpse. Within the first two steps, the ground beneath made a sick, wet, squelching sound. Ayleth grimaced and looked down in revulsion to see that her boots had sunk several inches into the sodden soil. A sour reek seemed to be set loose under the pressure of her foot, and she gagged again, her whole body spasming.

Best to get moving and get out again as fast as possible. She quickened her stride, still holding onto Terryn, no longer to restrain him but simply to feel that human connection here in this inhuman place. He remained close to her as well, only stepping away from her once they reached the body, crossing to the other side of it and crouching.

"*Keep watch for shades,*" Ayleth told Laranta. Her wolf shade nodded understanding and backed away several paces, turning her bright eyes to the forest. Then Ayleth crouched as well beside the fallen man.

The body was weirdly still intact. Considering how long it had been since Nane was first reported missing— more than a month—Ayleth would have expected his dead remains to have rotted significantly more. Or had he not died all that time ago? Had he simply wandered lost in the Witchwood, only recently meeting his end? The corpse looked no more than few days old, but that may have more to do with the abnormal atmosphere of *oblivis* influencing the natural process of decay.

The face was turned away from her, toward Terryn. She glanced up at her fellow venator, watching his eyes as he took in the features. "Is it him?" she asked.

Terryn nodded. He didn't speak. She could not see his mouth, covered as it was by the lower part of his hood, but something in his eye told her that he *could not* speak, could not find the words.

More than anything, Ayleth wished to heave the body up and carry it out of this place. But what if the minute they crossed the Barrier, away from the weird preservation of *oblivis*, it began to disintegrate? Better to take a few extra moments and see if she could discern anything, pick up any clues as to how Nane had ended up like this. Laranta was on watch. She would alert them if any shade-taken drew near. They had time.

"Find his logbook," she said.

Terryn met her gaze, his eyes blanked out with horror. He blinked, shook himself, then nodded and set to work, carefully reaching beneath the spread cloak of the dead man, searching in the satchels still draped over his shoulder. From the way he moved, Ayleth could tell he was trying to touch the body as little as possible. She couldn't blame him. Every movement on their part, every shift of their weight on this toxic soil, made the air around them explode in vile stench.

The corpse itself was cold as though frozen, though the air was not freezing here, simply very, very still. While Terryn searched for the logbook, Ayleth studied the body for some indication of a death wound. Something must have killed the venator, after all. Unless he'd simply breathed in too much *oblivis* and fallen dead on the spot. But that seemed unlikely—surely he would have been conscious of the effects of *oblivis* on his body and taken care to retreat before it was too late.

Besides, the way his limbs were spread indicated that he'd been struck from behind, his right arm outflung, the Detrudos still in his fingers, the other arm twisted beneath him. There was no sign of tearing in the cloak on his back, no indication of an arrow wound or sword stroke. No claw or teeth marks.

Something about the way his hood lay over his head seemed odd. Ayleth reached out hesitantly and pulled the hood back. She hissed, and her stomach turned over in her gut. A gory wound opened at the back of his skull. Black blood crusted his hair, and pus bubbled up before her vision. Vines crawling along the forest floor reached into the wound on all sides, latching hold and plunging down inside. Now that the hood was pulled back, Ayleth could see tendril shoots of those same vines climbing through the venator's sagging mouth, his eyes, his nostrils, crawling into his skull.

It was too horrible.

She turned away, unable to look closer, staring into the forest around her. Was she mistaken, or were the shadows deeper than they had been? Were the vines more densely clustered in the low-hanging limbs?

"His logbook isn't here," Terryn said. His voice seemed muffled, as though he spoke through a wall. Ayleth did not look at him, keeping her gaze fixed on the trees. "His satchels have been tampered with. Someone took the book off his body."

Laranta, standing guard only a few paces away, put back her ears and growled deep in her throat. Her voice rumbled in Ayleth's head: *Coming . . . coming . . . .*

Ayleth's heart jumped. "We need to get out," she whispered.

Coming . . . here . . . .

Her eyes straining with shadow sight, Ayleth stared into the forest. She saw no souls, no gleam of spirits. Only darkness, absolute darkness, and whirling motes of *oblivis.* But down underneath the soil, deep down, lower than the plunging roots of those wounded trees, something . . . pulsed.

Boom.

Boom.

Boom.

Ayleth sprang up. The soul tether between her and her shade snapped taut, and Laranta turned and leapt back to her side, phasing out of this world into Ayleth's mind, crouching in the forefront of her consciousness. *Shade! Shade! Shade!* she snarled.

"We have to get out of here. Now!" Ayleth said.

Terryn was on his feet already, his Detrudos out and snapped into position. "Get the body," he said and turned to the Barrier. He put the pipes to his lips, calling to life the reverberating drone. The melody of the Barrier song spell poured from the other pipe head, not the variation to build and sustain the spell, but a unique variation, one Ayleth did not know. The variation to create an opening, no doubt.

But she could hardly hear the song. Not above that deep, earth-plunging pulse.

Boom.

Boom.

Boom.

She bent over Nane's body. *"Laranta, give me your strength!"* she commanded, and immediately felt the power of her shade coursing through her limbs. Though she hated to touch the cold corpse, she caught Nane under his arms and heaved.

The clutching vines reared up from the soil, casting gobs of rotten earth aside in huge clouds. Coiling over the dead man's arms, his legs, his torso, they refused to let go. Ayleth screamed.

The song spell faltered, and Terryn turned to her.

"No! No!" she cried. "Keep playing! Get it open!"

Boom.

Boom.

BOOM.

She hauled against the hold of the vines. Bones broke. The vines pulled. The corpse twisted in her grasp, drawn back down into the ground, and still more vines sprang up and covered it, eager, ravenous, like so many long and licking tongues. Ayleth let go and staggered away, her hood falling back from her head.

BOOM!

Something touched her foot.

Ayleth's eyes widened. She stared down to see one long vine coiling up from her ankle, to her calves, to her knee, to her thigh.

"*Laranta!*" she screamed in her mind even as her mortal mouth shouted, "Terryn!"

The song spell stopped. Her heightened senses heard a gasp, and the next moment strong arms wrapped around her. She felt warm breath on her cheek, felt the strength of Terryn's body as he caught her close, felt the thud of his heartbeat against her shoulders.

Then she was yanked from his grasp, down onto her back, dragged along by one leg. She screamed, twisted, tried to catch at the ground, which gave away beneath her scrabbling hands. Shadows, branches, vines, and glimpses of red-streaked distant sky flashed across her vision as the Witchwood pulled her into its depths.

CHAPTER 18

TERRYN LANDED HARD, FACEDOWN IN THE SOFT SOIL. Slimy dampness soaked his front, seeped beneath his collar and up his sleeves, and the earth made sucking sounds as he struggled to get back upright.

"Venatrix!" he cried, his voice muffled in the thick air. He staggered onto one knee, his hand sinking wrist deep in oozing dirt, but he was up again in an instant, flinging himself after that writhing mass of vines as they vanished into the forest. The trees tossed and waved in terror like so many manic limbs, and the vines laced through their branches, shooting from tree to tree, weaving together into a tight, impenetrable curtain of parasitic foliage.

Terryn was two paces too slow. Or perhaps he was just slow enough. Had he been a little faster, the vines might have crushed his bones to powder.

"Haunts damn!" he snarled, striking at the vines with his fists. He pulled back before a tendril could wrap around his wrist and tried to peer through the interlacing stems, tried to catch some glimpse of the venatrix. At his last sight of her, she was writhing in the grasp of the vines, clawing at the ground, her cloak and long braid of hair trailing behind her as she vanished into the forest.

She was gone. Dead, or as good as dead. The Witchwood had devoured her.

His breath came too fast, sucking in great gasps of *oblivis*-tainted air. He felt the motes accumulating in his throat, a thick coating. With a shudder, he pulled his hood back around his mouth, his hand trembling. His hand . . . his empty hand . . .

His Detrudos! A thrill of terror shot through his heart. He'd dropped his Detrudos! When the venatrix screamed, he had whirled and, seeing the vines climbing up her leg, leapt to her side. And his instrument? He turned this way and that, his eyes bulging as they searched.

He caught a gleam of white bone and lunged for it, plucking the pipes from the soil into which they had partially sunk. Relief flooded his whole being as he used his cloak to wipe the instrument clean. He could still open the Great Barrier. He could still escape this place with his life. The Witchwood seemed to have no interest in him so long as he did not try to penetrate that wall of vines. It had taken its toll, and he could walk free, carrying word of the deaths of both Nane and the venatrix back to Gerard . . .

His hands moving of their own accord, he slid the Detrudos into its sheath. Facing that wall of ghastly trees and vines, he pulled the Vocos free, snapping the instrument into position. He did not realize what he was doing until he'd lifted the mouthpiece to his lips. Only then did his brain catch up with what his will had already determined.

He was going to find the venatrix. In order to do so, he would call up the power of his shade.

Deep down inside him, beneath layer upon layer of suppressing spell song, the spirit stirred. It knew what he intended.

Terryn closed his eyes, closed out the terrors of the wood around him. He concentrated his mind, his soul, and began to play the Song of Searching. He cast himself into the music with everything he had, purging all thought of the vanished venatrix, all thought of the wounded trees, of the devouring vines. He channeled his awareness inward, following the flow of the spell song.

When he opened his eyes, it was not the physical world he saw around him but the realm of his own mind. A landscape more real than any view made up of material substance—a harsh, barren world that existed only inside him.

He stood on dark stone cracked in a million thin crevices that seemed to plunge down for an eternity, none of them wide enough for him to catch a foot in. Overhead, an iron sky weighed heavily upon the landscape, dark save for a thin streak of glowing heat on the far horizon, as though some powerful light was on the verge of bursting through.

Terryn never allowed himself to look at the horizon for long, fearing what he might see should the sun of this world ever rise.

The Searching song surrounded him like a cloak as he strode through this realm. He made his way to an enormous, lumpen bulge on the otherwise flat terrain. If one looked at that bulge from a certain angle, one could almost discern the outline of a vast draconian body, fallen hard and encased in stone.

Encased in the bindings of the Suppression song spell.

Despite the strength of that binding, Terryn approached his shade with caution. The nearer he drew, the more he heard the faint whisper of what might be a voice, deep down under the suppressions. He took another step, and the voice seemed to clarify.

What is my name?

Do you know my name?

It was a hiss of, not sound, but meaning, slithering down into his awareness. Terryn shuddered. He knew better than to answer.

"Never speak your shade's name," Fendrel had told him long ago, early in his training. "Never even think it.

To allow it a name is to give it power. To allow it a name is the first step in your own destruction."

In the physical world, Terryn switched the Searching song into the Song of Command. He played it with harsh accuracy, lashing at that stone-bound form. The voice ceased its whispering. But there was a quivering expectancy to its silence that Terryn did not like.

The power of this shade was far beyond anything he could hope to control were it ever to get free of the suppressions. He must take care. He must take only the power he needed and not a sliver more. Otherwise, he risked the shade working its way free, rising to full ascendancy and ousting his soul. Or worse.

He switched from the Command to yet another, more unusual melody—the Song of Harvesting. Shooting that spell directly into the stone form, he chipped away with absolute precision, like a sculptor at a marble block.

The being under the encasing rock stirred. Around the weird, bulky head, the stone quaked, moved—and a single blazing eye opened, staring out at Terryn.

What is my name?

Terryn braced himself. Moving in spirit, he reached

out a hand. He hesitated, then plunged his fingers down into the eye.

A shriek ripped the air. Once more the massive body tried hopelessly to move, to shrug off the binding stone, to escape. Terryn's fingers closed around a fistful of pure, brilliant light. He pulled it free and staggered back, cupping that brilliance in both hands.

In the mortal world, he opened his eyes and let the Vocos melody fade away and die. Magic pulsed through him, and he grinned despite himself at the sensation.

The sensation of light—pure, beautiful, inexplicable light.

Now he was a force to be reckoned with.

He collapsed and sheathed his pipes, then squared off before that wall of vines. Stretching out both arms before him, he aimed his hands, palms out, at the place of thickest growth, the place where the venatrix had disappeared.

The veins in his hands pulsed with a living glow, building up in his fingertips.

With a cry, Terryn let go—and a blast of light so blinding it would have burned his mortal eyes had he not closed them at the last instant shot out from his palms, from his fingers, and struck the vines. A thousand unnatural voices chorused in the air, a cacophonic song of shrieking, wailing. The trees shook though there was no wind to move them.

Terryn closed his hands, and the blast subsided, light still burning in his veins, so hot that it might boil his blood. Blinking hard against the dazzle still flaring in his vision, he peered ahead.

A path now opened before him. Curls of putrid smoke licked the air, rising from burnt and shriveled remnants of vines. The trees stood mostly bare. Sluggish gobs of pus oozed from their gory wounds, but they were somehow less menacing without their choking mantle.

Adjusting the hood around the lower half of his face, Terryn raised his right hand, holding it before him as a weapon. He strode forward into the Witchwood.

Oblivis surrounded her, whirling and thick. Too thick to see through, too thick to penetrate.

Ayleth dared not take a step. She couldn't see where it

would take her, couldn't know if even a single step would send her plunging over some precipice. And she dared not breathe for fear of the poison coating her lungs. She could only stand there in the dark.

Then suddenly, there was . . . something.

Ahead of her. A figure emerging in silhouette.

"Hullo?"

Speaking was a mistake. Ayleth choked on the *oblivis*, coughing and sputtering painfully. She waved the air before her face, sending the thick dark motes whirling but unable to clear any space before her. Still, something inside her—some need for human connection in this lunatic world—made her take a lunging step toward that figure. "Hullo, can you hear me?"

The figure turned. The *oblivis* seemed to part around it, like a veil drawing back.

Ayleth saw her clearly—a woman, more beautiful than any woman she had ever before seen. Dark hair flowed down her back; dark eyes sparked like lit coals in her face. She was naked except for a scarf draped across one breast and her nether regions. Each limb was perfectly proportioned, gracefully formed, and her neck was long and swanlike save where it bled from an ugly gash. Black blood poured from that wound, streaming down her shoulders, her breasts, her arms.

She wore a crown of some dark metal on her head.

Ayleth stopped. Her eyes widened, and though the *oblivis* stung them painfully, she could not blink. She knew who it was. She did not doubt for a moment.

"Odile," she whispered.

The woman looked at her, her expression like stone. Then she closed her eyes, bowed her head.

Ripples of light pulsed through the dark metal crown. Like veins of shining blue blood spreading, expanding, they covered the entire surface of the crown until it writhed around her brow, no longer solid but moving, liquid, only just contained within that shape. It glowed brighter and brighter, until Ayleth had to raise her hand to shield her eyes from that glow.

The woman faded away, her beauty, her majesty subsumed in shadow. There was only that crown, only that living, brilliant light.

Something looked out through that glory of power, something without form but contained within that form.

A shadow voice appeared in Ayleth's mind.

At . . . last . . .

Ayleth screamed.

Her eyes popped open, and her lungs heaved, coughing up a huge glob of slime and mud and rot. Her stomach clenched and shuddered, and more foulness spilled from her mouth, falling to the forest floor far below.

She blinked blearily. And realized she was wrapped in vines, suspended from a tree branch a good ten feet above the ground.

CHAPTER 19

THE VINES COILED AROUND HER LIKE SNAKES, pinning her arms against her body. Her left leg was lifted at an odd angle a little higher than the rest of her body, and the result left her not quite upside-down, but not level either. Her right leg was free, but kicked uselessly in midair, unable to reach the nearest branches or tree trunks for leverage.

Craning her neck, Ayleth looked down at the distant ground. Festering saints! She was strung up in these branches like some holiday pendant, dangling and useless. She drew several breaths, each more putrid than the last. Some of the stink was her own sickness spilled onto the front of her jerkin.

The heavy shadows and weird half-light were more oppressive here, deeper within the boundaries of the Witchwood. No sign of Venator Terryn anywhere. But what did she expect? If he had any sense at all, he'd made good his escape through the Barrier. A small, cowardly part of her mind dared hope that the venator might come for her. That he might feel the hunt brother bond.

But that was stupidity itself. No use thinking that way. They were not hunt brother and hunt sister. They were competitors. She was nothing more than an obstacle standing in his way to success. If anything, he was probably relieved that the Witchwood took her.

She would accomplish her own escape.

Closing her eyes and drawing another gag-inducing breath through her nostrils, she concentrated first on her own body. No bones seemed to be broken. A small mercy, but one for which she was thankful.

"Laranta?" she called next. *"Laranta, are you there?"*

Here, Mistress, her wolf shade spoke in her head. *You woke up.*

"*Yes, I did. I need your help now. We've got to get down.*"

Shade. Laranta shivered and whined, oddly pathetic for such a ferocious being. *Shade in our mind. Evil shade.*

Ayleth shuddered again. Faint memories of what felt like a dream flickered behind her mind's eye. An image of a tall woman in a crown . . . of living blue metal pulsing with possession . . . a voice . . .

She shook her head. There was no time to try to decipher such mysteries, not now. Not while tied up high above the ground in a noxious forest, far from all friends and allies. She needed to focus. She needed to get the festering-Haunts out of here.

"*Laranta, give me your strength,*" she commanded.

Her shade obeyed without murmur, and power flowed through Ayleth's limbs. She began to tense her muscles against the constricting hold of the vines. From her neck and shoulders down through her arms and her back, everything strained. The vines gave slightly, relaxing their hold, and she redoubled her efforts, pouring out more of Laranta's tremendous force.

The vines struggled, quivered—then suddenly they broke. Ayleth swung loose, still caught by her leg, now completely upside-down. Her long braid whipped the air, and her cloak fluttered like a flag. But this was better. She could work with this.

With an animal growl she tightened her stomach muscles and, curling her torso, tried to pull herself up and grab her own leg, to reach her bound foot. The first attempt didn't work, but she tried again, the burn of shade magic firing her blood. She succeeded in catching hold of her own boot and, bending her knee, clawed up to get a hold on the vine.

Something caught her right wrist. Ayleth, startled, tried to pull away, but too late. A vine wrapped tightly around her forearm. With her other hand she grabbed it, tearing, but just as she was about to yank free, yet another vine swung down from the trees above and twined around her left elbow. She struggled, falling back into the upside-down suspension.

Her right arm was caught again, and both arms pulled out to the farthest extension so that she splayed in the air like a star, one leg still kicking uselessly. A single tug more, and her bones would begin to dislocate.

With a roar, she concentrated Laranta's strength, pulling at her restraints. She felt a give on the end of the right-hand vine, as though she'd uprooted something far away. But no sooner did she feel that brief slackening than another vine shot out at her and another still. Something coiling and sinuous wound round her neck, and she screamed in pure rage and terror.

Movement down below.

Ayleth's gaze flicked, not fast enough to catch sight of whatever passed. A wind of action stirred the leaves and her hair, the only sign that something had been there.

Another blur. A flash of red, Ayleth thought, this time scaling the tree on her right.

Suddenly, the vine holding her leg gave way. With a cry, she swung down, suspended now by her arms. The vine around her neck tightened its hold, choking her. She kicked frantically, struggling to draw breath.

The vine fell away, slithering free from her throat and falling in a pile far below. Ayleth blinked, a mere instant of closed eyelids. When her eyes opened, someone stood over that pile.

It was a woman clad in the remnants of a red cloak, with a hood pulled over her face. As she tilted her head back to look up at Ayleth, that hood fell back over her shoulders, revealing her face. A deathly pale face, mottled with strange, black, tumorous growths crawling up her neck and jaw and cheek. Eyes burning with shadow-light peered out from hollow sockets.

Across her forehead, stark against the pallor of her skin, was a tattoo of five vertical slashes over a single horizontal line.

Ayleth's heartbeat seemed to still, the world around her seemed to fade away. Everything inside her, her own awareness and Laranta's, focused entirely on that one image, that mark. The mark of a Crimson Devil.

The witch, staring up at her, seemed to mirror Ayleth's own horror and surprise. Her eyes, already wide, widened still more, and her mouth opened to reveal gums black with shade blight and teeth far gone to rot. Her lips moved, and she spoke in a quavering voice, almost like a child's: "It . . . it can't be . . ."

A vine launched out from the shadows straight for the witch's face. It passed through empty air, for she was already gone. Ayleth gasped and twisted, still suspended by both arms. Then the vine holding her left arm broke, and she swung down, all her weight now on her right arm, straining at the shoulder socket. She cried out, kicking the air, swinging her free arm, trying to move herself closer to one of the branches hanging just out of reach.

The last vine gave way. She fell to the ground ten feet down, landing hard and momentarily stunned. Laranta's power surged in her limbs, however, and she pushed herself upright, ready to fight, ready to run, her teeth flashing in a wolfish snarl.

Something struck her from behind, and she fell back onto her knees. Then a whirlwind of motion, so fast it stole the breath from her lungs, and something wrapped around her arms, pinning them to her body. At first, she thought it was more vines. But there was a strange quality to this binding, unlike anything Ayleth had felt before. She looked down and saw . . . nothing. And yet that nothing was strong beyond her ability to break. It was as though the air itself had hardened, become solid. A rope of wind.

A yank, and Ayleth spun around on her knees as she struggled to get her feet under her, to rise. With a roar, she lurched to a standing position.

She faced the tattooed witch.

The woman's hands extended before her, grasping at emptiness as though she held the end of a rope. Shade power flowed through her arms, out from her soul, and Ayleth realized that this wind binding stemmed from the witch herself.

Grimacing, Ayleth braced her feet and strained. The wind was stronger than the vines, but Laranta's power surged through her. She felt the bindings give, and then she felt them break as her arms tore free, her fists upraised.

The witch's eyes widened. "What . . . are you?" she breathed, her voice raw and broken as it scraped through her corded throat.

On impulse of training, Ayleth's hand moved to the quivers of darts on her chest. But those were long since broken and scattered across the Witchwood floor. So, she curled her hands into fists, fastened her gaze upon the witch, and lunged.

She missed entirely, careening into one of the fleshy trees. A spurt of infected sap blood rolled down over her hands and arms. Her stomach heaving with disgust, she pulled back.

A burst of pain exploded in her chest. She gasped, choked, as all her air whistled out through her mouth, her nostrils. Her lungs flattened in desperate need, and she clawed at her throat, clawed at her chest, turning as she fell to her knees.

The witch stood over her, hands upraised, fingers curved, wrists rotating slightly back and forth as she pulled the air out from between Ayleth's lips and coiled it like invisible string in her grasp. Darkness closed in on the edges of Ayleth's vision.

She collapsed senseless at her enemy's feet.

The ground breathed.

Terryn felt it—the rise and fall, more pronounced the deeper he ventured into the forest. He could not quite see it happening, no matter how hard he strained his gaze at the ground or the towering trees. But that didn't make the sensation any less real.

He kept his right hand up, his fingertips flaring with white light, serving as an effective torch in the darkness. His initial blast had cut a quarter-mile path into the forest, but he soon came to the end of that and faced more of the thick vines. They did not try to impede his passage, however, wary now that they knew what sort of power he wielded.

His quick eyes, trained for tracking, discerned signs of something being dragged along the forest floor. He could see where a hand may have clawed at the loose, wet soil, where a body had bent and broken lower branches in its passage. Terryn concentrated on these details and carefully progressed, all the while too aware of vines gathering on the periphery of his vision.

His arm burned with the need to set off another blast. But to do so was dangerous. He could not use this magic at will, must save it for only the most vital moments. At most he had a total of three blasts available to him from the amount of magic he had harvested. And he'd already used one. To try to use more would be to draw on more magic, magic not carefully taken but impulsively grasped.

This would weaken the suppressions currently holding his shade in check, might break them entirely.

Searching with his shadow sight, he watched for sign of other shade-taken but saw none. Nothing but foul forest as far as his eye could see. How any being, shade-taken or otherwise, could survive in such an atmosphere, Terryn could not guess. The poisonous *oblivis* in the air alone must kill them eventually. Perhaps they had all died off over the years.

Beneath his feet, the forest breathed again. And deeper still, he felt the pulse of what might be an enormous heartbeat.

"What kind of a curse is this?" he whispered. Fendrel had taught him that the Witchwood sprang up from the last words spoken by Dread Odile in the moment just before the Chosen King cut off her head. But this did not feel like a curse.

It was too . . . alive.

Had Fendrel misled him all these years? Or did the Venator Dominus not fully understand that which his Barrier song spell restrained?

Terryn continued along the trail left in the venatrix's

wake. He must now be close to a mile in from the forest's edge. How much deeper had it dragged her? He shook his head, a terrible urge suddenly overwhelming his senses, an urge to look back the way he'd come. To peer through the branches and shadows and vines, to search for some sign of the Great Barrier at his back. He forced himself to take several more paces as the urge grew inside him. He was almost shaking with the need to turn, to look.

At last, with a gasp that was almost a prayer, he whirled on his heel, his hand outstretched, light flaring almost out of his control. He clenched his fist, gripping back the blast.

The trees had drawn close behind him. The vines, thick as a woven blanket, obstructed his vision. The whole forest had shifted, penning him in.

Terryn's breath caught in his throat. Then he grimaced, tensing, getting ready to let out another burst of light. But did he really plan to use up his available power to cut a path back to safety? Before finding the venatrix? Would he abandon her here in this poisonous place? True, she might be dead already.

But if she wasn't, and he turned his back on her now,

he doomed her for certain.

He swallowed with difficulty, his throat thick and dry. Then he turned back, facing the way the drag marks led.

The forest had closed in on this side as well. He blinked and saw the rise and fall of the land like a deeply drawn and expelled breath. The trees crept in closer, blood and infection pouring from their wounds, vines reaching out from their limbs.

He was trapped.

CHAPTER 20

AYLETH BECAME AWARE OF THE DARKNESS. NOT darkness like a dream or darkness like night. This was the familiar darkness of just behind her eyelids. She was awake, or nearly awake, her conscious awareness slowly returning to that time-bound place within her mortal body.

She tried to open her eyelids. But she couldn't. They were so heavy, much too heavy to move. And the back of her head throbbed painfully. Well, she wouldn't let that worry her. Not yet, anyway. She drew a deep breath, let it out slowly, and tried again to open her eyes. Still no luck, so she tried instead to lift her hand and rub it down her face.

But she couldn't feel her arms. She couldn't feel . . . anything.

"*Laranta?*" she called inside her head. No answer. She searched deeper down, but all was too muddled and murky. Once more she tried to move, but her limbs wouldn't obey her. Though she felt the heaviness of her mortal body, her spirit wore it like a heavy, leaden garment.

She was drugged.

Someone had dealt her paralysis poison, the very poison she would use were she to hunt a Feral shade-taken. She was paralyzed and utterly, utterly helpless.

Though the paralysis kept her body inert, refusing to let her open her eyes, her other senses slowly came into focus. She heard a familiar *patter-patter-patter*, the sound of rain on a rooftop. So, she was indoors at least. Concentrating her senses as best she could, she thought perhaps she lay reclined on a stiff, uncomfortable surface.

Not a bed, perhaps a table. She smelled something sour. Rotten sour.

"We should kill her."

Ayleth's heart jumped at the voice—a reedy male voice, which broke off in a harsh cough before it finished speaking. The coughing lasted for some time, almost drowning out the sounds of rain. When at last the fit subsided, the voice spoke again. "I see no reason to keep her alive. We can gather her blood."

"We have no means to keep it fresh," a rasping whisper answered. "The blood must be fresh. We have no bottles of *oblidite*. They're all at Cró Ular, if those Haunts-damned venators didn't destroy them already. No . . . she may be our last chance. We cannot risk mishandling this gift."

"We cannot risk keeping her alive either," the man answered. An impatient sound like pacing followed, a dull thudding of footfalls. "She can as easily mean our end as our salvation. And . . . Oromor wants her. We can't let it have her."

"Zarc, Zarc." The whispering voice was heavy with long-suffering patience. "You always were much too short-sighted. Kill now, think later. Look where that has gotten you."

"No better nor worse than you, Zilla," the man's voice responded with a grim, sickly chuckle. "We share the same lot, you and I. And without me, Oromor would have devoured you long ago."

Their voices continued, biting bitter words at one another. Ayleth, her pulse thundering in her ears, could scarcely hear them now. The names she had just overheard whirled in her poison-numbed brain. Zarc. Zilla.

She saw again the list written down in Hollis's skin-bound book:

Zarc d'Utrehd – The Stormwitch
Zilla d'Utrehd – The Windwitch

The twins. Two of the most feared and terrible Crimson Devils, who had survived the purge of Perrinion following the wars and managed to escape beyond the Great Barrier.

It must have been the Windwitch she had faced while

trying to escape the vines. And this man sharing the room was her brother, the Stormwitch. They had fought side by side under Dread Odile just as they had once fought side by side for the Order of Saint Evander. Long ago, before they turned to heresy.

Ayleth thought of the marred, growth-covered face she had glimpsed. However powerful the Windwitch once was, her existence here in the Witchwood had reduced her physical body significantly. And though the spirit of Zilla d'Utrehd had once jumped with wild abandon from host body to host body, there were no such options to be had now. Presumably Zarc was in no better state than his sister, which meant, if she could just get her feet under her, Ayleth might stand a chance against them.

But the paralysis poison held her in its thrall. Had Zilla found one of Ayleth's lost darts? Had a trail of darts led the witch to her location, bound up in vines? Once a venatrix herself, the Windwitch certainly knew how and when to use those poisons.

They could kill her. They could carve her into tiny pieces, and she would be aware of every moment, and there was nothing she could do to stop them.

"*Laranta!*" she cried again. But her wolf shade had fallen under the influence of the paralysis as well.

"Your storm is weakening." Zilla's voice broke through Ayleth's numb terror.

"I can't sustain it forever," her brother answered, choking out the words as though trying to restrain a cough. "It'll do for now. And I'll raise a fine mist following. Oromor won't get through for several hours. There's nothing it can do to save her, if we act fast."

"So, we have until the rain ends and the mist dissipates to make a decision," the Windwitch mused. "Do we keep her alive or do we drain her blood here and now? Do we trust Ylaire to succeed in her task and return for us?"

"If your message carried through, the others should arrive soon," said the Stormwitch. "We should give them a vote and let the numbers decide."

The others? Ayleth's throat tightened. What others could they mean?

Only the Crimson Devils. The seven Devils of Dread Odile, all gathering to decide her fate.

Terryn lifted his hand, ready to expend one of his two remaining blasts. At the last second, he curled his fingers into a tight fist, restraining himself. What good would it do him to cut a path leading only deeper into the Witchwood? No, he must try to carve a way either forward or back.

But in this darkness, with the trees and vines closing in and the *oblivis* thickening in his throat with every breath taken, he suddenly wasn't certain which way was which. It all looked the same—any distinct landmarks by which he could have discerned his position had vanished as the wood shifted around him.

Panic pulsed in his veins. And, responding to that panic, the spell songs binding his shade trembled. He must keep himself in check, must put a guard on every stray emotion. If he could not master his own emotions, how could he hope to master the foreign spirit inside him? So Fendrel had taught him when he was still a young lad, newly possessed and struggling to find the control he needed to survive. A venator must be master of himself first and foremost.

Drawing deep, careful breaths, Terryn repressed his fear, tamping it down fast. He felt it encased in stone within his soul, just like the shade itself. Still present, still simmering with molten power, eager to erupt. But for the moment at least, both his shade and his own traitorous feelings were contained.

"Always remember," Fendrel had often said, impressing the lesson into the very core of Terryn's being, "no matter where you go, no matter what enemies you face, no foe is greater than that which you carry inside you. It is up to you to keep it at bay for as long as you are able. Never trust it. Never give in to its subtleties or its power. You must be stronger than it at all times."

Terryn dropped his hand, his second blast held tight in his palm. He controlled this moment. He would make a rational decision based on reason, not terror.

He would not give his shade even an instant of mastery inside.

With his careful gaze shifting in and out of shadow sight, Terryn studied the forest, slowly reorienting himself. In this weird half-light, in this haze of poison, this miasma of putrid rot, he could not distinguish east from west. But looking down at his own feet, he could still just see something of his own footprints in the wet soil. He'd moved around too much in this small circle for anything to be clear, but he made an educated guess of which way he must send his blast in order to carve a path back to the Great Barrier.

The trees crept closer, roots rippling under soil. Branches pressed in upon him, twisting like eager fingers into the fabric of his cloak.

Terryn lifted one arm then the other. The first he pointed before him, back where the Great Barrier waited. The other he pointed the opposite way, deeper into the forest, the direction he believed the venatrix was taken. He could only choose one. Power mounted inside him, soon to reach the point of no return; he would have to let it out in a burst of white-hot light before it melted his very bones.

He must decide. Now. Go on after the venatrix, or retreat and attempt to save his own life. Vines reached out and tickled his fingers, leaves licking like hungry tongues.

Then the ground beneath him drew a breath. Terryn almost believed he heard a deep, deep exhale. The forest moved, not before or behind him, but off to his side—south, unless he was much mistaken. Dragging their roots and their trailing vines, the trees parted to reveal a path. Even the soil solidified, no longer the pus-oozing mud on which Terryn had walked all this way.

It was a trap. It couldn't be anything but a trap. But . . .

Terryn's breath hitched. His eyes shifted from shadow sight to mortal vision, staring hard into the gloom. Down the center of the path lay a trail of darts—Evanderian, poison-tipped darts. Like bait.

Bait which could easily lead to the venatrix. Or to her body.

He swung his right arm out, supporting it with his left hand to keep it steady as he would support his scorpiona were it loaded. Though every instinct of self-preservation told him to let go of his power, to burn his way back to the Barrier, to escape, he could not live with himself if he did not investigate this trail. If he could only find some sure sign of the venatrix's death, that would be enough.

And perhaps . . . He grimaced. Perhaps, against all odds, he would find her alive.

CHAPTER 21

THE SILENCE LASTED TOO LONG, SECONDS MEASURED by the throb in her temples.

Ayleth guessed that the witches had moved away from her, presumably to continue their argument out of range of her hearing. It was a relief not to have to listen to them discuss whether to kill her, if *relief* was the right word. Would it be better to know which of them currently held sway over the other? And when it came down to it, who did she hope would win? While she certainly did not care for Zarc d'Utrehd's murderous intentions, somehow, she guessed that whatever his sister had in mind for her would be much, much worse.

And who was this person they kept mentioning with such dread? This . . . Oromor . . .

It didn't sound like a human name. When the witches spoke it, they did not merely use their lips, their throats, their tongues to pronounce it. There was a hint of shadow speech in their voices as well. If Ayleth were to try to speak Laranta's name out loud, it would sound much the same. Could this Oromor whom they dreaded be a shade?

And if so . . . what did it want with her?

It didn't matter. None of that mattered. Because she wasn't going to just lie here and wait for them to kill her.

Ayleth drew a long breath and strained the only part of her body she could *almost* feel—her right eyelid. It fluttered faintly, an indication that the paralysis might be starting to wear off, if only a little.

"*Laranta,*" she called again, to no avail. Her wolf shade was still too far gone under the influence of the poison. She was on her own. On her own, paralyzed, up against two of the most bloodthirsty, inhuman monsters to survive the Witch Wars.

She could handle this.

Plunging her awareness down inside her head, she searched for something she might use. But she could not find her familiar pine-forest mindscape. Only darkness, darkness, and more darkness, humming faintly with the echo of old spell songs. Surely there must be something in this darkness she could use! Some hitherto unused power or memory or . . . memory . . .

Nothing.

She had to regain control of her body. Her right eyelid seemed like the best place to start. She poured all her will into opening that eye. That one tiny proof that her body was still her own. That she was mistress here despite what any witches or woods might do to her. She fixed her entire being onto a single point and strained.

Her lashes fluttered against her cheek. Then, slowly, the darkness lessened as her lid pried open.

The relief at her success was so great, Ayleth almost lost her concentration and let her eye close again. She caught herself just in time, forcing the lid open wider and wider. It wasn't much, but it was good enough for the moment. For the next few heartbeats. If nothing else, she could take in her surroundings.

The sound of rain had faded to nothing, and the world was cast in a gray gloom which filtered through gaping windows. Long, tall windows, like those of a shrine house. In fact, Ayleth seemed to be lying in shrine-house ruins, judging from the shadows of the arched roof, the pillars, the crumbling stone. The Witchwood had grown up so fast following the death of Dread Odile, it had swallowed entire cities and towns before Fendrel du Glaive established the Great Barrier. It made sense that those trapped within these evil borders would try to take shelter in the ruins left behind.

Straining her one open eye as far as it would go, Ayleth tried to get some sense of the world beyond the windows. She saw nothing but mist, which oddly did not pour through the gaping window openings. Something didn't smell right about that mist. Even without her shade awareness, Ayleth could smell a burning sourness in the air. She remembered from Hollis's teachings on the Wars themselves that Zarc d'Utrehd did not conjure ordinary storms. His clouds spat a rain that burned like fire on contact. And his mists, creeping stealthily through unsuspecting ranks of warriors, bore devastating, mutilating effects.

While Ayleth studied her surroundings, sensation slowly returned to the left side of her face. Ayleth opened her other eye, and the world came into clearer focus. For a brief, exalting moment, she felt powerful indeed.

Then the witches' voices echoed on the stone. Her captors were returning.

Ayleth turned both eyes as far as they would go down the nave of the shrine house, trying to catch a glimpse of the brother and sister. Just as their shadows appeared in her line of sight, she realized she would be wiser shut her eyes and not let them know the poison was wearing off. She didn't know how many of her darts Zilla had found. They might poison her again. If they didn't just kill her outright. And what could she do to stop them? Blink them to death?

But she wasn't fast enough.

"She's coming to," Zilla said. Her bare feet padded on the smooth paving stones of the shrine-house floor. "We need to decide soon." A few more steps, then a hand grabbed Ayleth by the chin, squeezing hard. "Open your eyes, Venatrix. I know you're awake."

What use was there in resisting? Slowly Ayleth lifted her eyelids and looked up into that grotesque face marred by its many tumorous growths. A particularly large growth on the left side of her mouth pulled the witch's lips so that they could not close, giving her a horrible leering expression and revealing her shade-blighted gums.

"There, you see?" Zilla said, stepping to one side so that her brother could take her place. "How can there be any doubt?"

Another horrible face appeared, hovering over Ayleth. Zarc was only like his sister in that his forehead, too, was tattooed with the sigil of Dread Odile. Otherwise they were completely unalike, not even the same age. The two of them had changed bodies far too many times to be recognizable as twins anymore.

But . . . there was something in the expression. Though their features were unsimilar and so mutated, something about the lift of the eyebrow and the flare of the nostrils bespoke a certain kinship. And, like his sister, the Stormwitch wore a faded red hood draped over his head, the final remnant of his service to the Order of Saint Evander.

"No," he said softly, his voice rasping in his thin, corded throat. Horrible growths trailed down one side of his face, and red, oozing rash covered every inch of what may once have been ivory-pale skin. "There can be no doubt at all." He turned from Ayleth, looking over his shoulder to his sister. "We must do it now. You have no more poison. We have no choice. We cannot wait for the others."

"They'll be here," Zilla answered vehemently. "They'll come. This is a decision we should make together."

"It's a decision that will be taken from our hands if we wait. She's got fight in her eye. The moment she can, she'll summon her shade and attack, and we'll be forced to end her then. Better to do it now while we have full control of the moment. Waste as little of her blood as possible." As Ayleth watched, he withdrew a worn-looking waterskin from the front of his robes. "I can catch enough blood in this to serve our purpose."

Zilla moved around the altar stone to lean over Ayleth

opposite her brother. "But if Ylaire doesn't return," she breathed, "if she cannot summon Inren, we are trapped here for Haunts-knows-how-long! Her blood would spoil. We have no other source. We need *her* blood and we need it *fresh*."

Ayleth's eyes swiveled from one disgusting face to the other, her heart clamoring in her throat. She strained for some other feeling, some other sense, and with a magnificent effort managed to move her eyebrows up and down. Goddess help her, what was she to do?

"Laranta!" she cried. No answer came. She might as well be untaken for all she could sense her shade.

"How do you propose we keep her without poison to subdue her? You are strong, my sister, but you are not what you once were. You bested her in your first encounter, but from what you tell me, she carries a formidable spirit within. If I could sustain my rains, we might imprison her, but I am not what I once was either. We haven't the means to keep her alive. And if she were to escape, if she were to go to Oromor . . ."

Ayleth strained her eyes as far as they would go to watch Zarc set down his waterskin and lift an unsheathed knife. The blade was corroded with rust but sharp enough. "You know I'm right, sister," the Stormwitch said.

His hand moved. The blade plunged straight for Ayleth's throat, and she choked on her own terror.

But Zilla was too fast. Carried on her winds, she whipped around the altar stone, caught her brother, and slammed him against the far wall before his blade even grazed Ayleth's skin. The force of her speed was so great, it pushed Ayleth partway off the altar. One arm dangled, and she was in imminent danger of falling in a heap to the floor. She blinked and blinked, as though, somehow, by activating the one part of her body over which she had control she could catch herself.

The Windwitch's voice echoed to the arched roof above. "Do not touch her, Zarc! We will wait for Gillotin, Scias, and Crisentha! We will decide together! If you make one more move to spill her precious blood, I'll—"

"You'll what?" Zarc's voice barked, then gave way to a fit of hoarse coughing. The fit took him so hard, his sister backed away, letting him slump to his knees, his shoulders shaking, one trembling arm preventing him from falling on his face. At last, wiping black blood from his lips, he glared up at Zilla. "Will you kill me?" he rasped. "Will you damn my soul after all we've been through?"

The Windwitch turned from him so sharply that her red hood fell back from her head and over her shoulders, revealing the bald patches where her fair hair had fallen out in clumps.

"You need me to survive in this place," Zarc said, chuckling bitterly. "Without my rains, Oromor will—"

Zarc broke off in a scream instantly echoed by his sister as a brilliant flash of white-hot light burst through the gloom and pierced in lancing rays through every crack and crevice in the stone wall. Ayleth would have screamed as well, and she was thankful she could at least shut her eyes, though she could not cover them with her hands or turn her face away or duck behind stone for shelter. The flash came and passed in no more than a breath, but it seemed to last much longer, leaving a burning glare inside her head.

The burning faded, and Ayleth feared to open her eyes again, feared to discover that she had been blinded. Her other senses screamed with alarm so profound that it reverberated down the soul tether connecting her to her shade. Despite the poison, Laranta stirred in response. Still out of reach, but present.

Ayleth dared crack her eyelids open. At first, she could perceive nothing with any of her senses. Then, slowly, her dazzled vision began to clear, and with the clearing, her other senses came into focus.

The witches were gone. Her ears just detected the echo of their running footsteps leaving the shrine house.

Vines crawled along the borders of the path on either side, sinuous as snakes, tendrils and leaves hissing softly. They were as thick as Terryn's forearm and moving like a predatory pack in synchronized undulations.

Terryn refused to look. Fear mounted inside him, struggling to escape the stone in which he had encased it. If he paused now to look to his right or his left, that fear would surely burst free, and he would use up one or both of his remaining blasts. No, he must maintain his calm, progressing along this narrow path with sure, steady strides.

There were too many darts, he realized as he passed another one lying on the path. The Venatrix could not have carried this many on her person. It was possible that the vines themselves were picking up the darts as he proceeded, then shooting on ahead and placing them in the path before him once more.

The sentience of this forest was nightmarish.

"This is no curse," Terryn whispered as he passed yet another dart without stooping to retrieve it. "This is no curse. This is something else. Something . . . wrong."

The weird half-light murkiness seemed to darken ahead of him. Was that a low mist creeping through the trees? Terryn took another step but stopped abruptly when a vine coiled around his ankle. For a heart-thudding moment, he feared the vine would yank him off his feet and drag him away into the forest the way he'd seen the venatrix dragged. But it simply restrained him with a firm grip.

Terryn parted his dry lips. "What then?" he whispered. "What do you want of me?"

He got the distinct impression the Witchwood was listening.

Suddenly the vines on either side of the path spilled out from the trees and merged in a dark, twining mass before him. Terryn wanted to step back, to run, but the tendril gripping his ankle kept him rooted in place. He swung his hand up before him, fingers tensing, and light built up in his veins, pulsing to his fingertips. If he did not let loose soon, it would be too late.

Before he could act, one of the vines rose above the mass like a snake rearing its head. It turned away from Terryn and zipped forward into the waiting mist.

A hissing screech pierced the air, sending bolts of horror up and down Terryn's spine. The vine withdrew again, and Terryn watched it melt away into nothing all along its writhing length. The rest of the vine mass scattered back into the forest, even the one holding Terryn by the ankle.

Terryn stood still as stone. His heart pounded too hard to allow for rational thought. Then, slowly, his mind forced its way through the miasma of fear, and he whispered: "The Stormwitch."

One of the Crimson Devils trapped within the boundaries of the Witchwood was known for his burning mists and rains. A single drop of rain could sear through flesh to the bone. His mists could maim whole battalions of seasoned warriors, leaving them blind and begging for death in their agonies.

He took one step back then another. He was not prepared to face the Stormwitch. And who was to say that the venatrix waited at the end of this path? It was a trap. Perhaps the Witchwood was trying to drive him here, to force him into this mist.

But then why had that vine burnt itself to warn him?

No. The Witchwood wanted something of him. What, he could not guess, but he knew when he was being used. When he looked back over his shoulder, he saw once more the incredible density of the vines twining between tree branches, blocking his retreat. He had no path but forward, into the mist. If he tried to blast his way through the vines, they would only close in again and again.

Had he harvested enough power to reach the forest's edge? He doubted it.

And there was still the chance, unlikely though it was . . . the chance that the Witchwood was in fact guiding him to the venatrix. If she lay within that mist, she could still be alive. Burned beyond recognition but alive. If nothing else, he could give her the Gentle Death and separate her soul from her shade. He could save her from damnation.

If he could only get to her.

Squaring his shoulders and bracing his legs, Terryn raised his hand and focused into the mist. If the venatrix was close, he risked killing her with the force of his blast. But what choice did he have? He drew a long breath, closed his eyes, and summoned up the power inside him. It boiled through his veins as though his very blood heated. Everything channeled along his right arm, down to his palm, his fingertips.

With a cry, he let go—and the flash of pure shade power and white light tore out from his core. The blast was so great it pulled him off his feet. He landed hard on his knees but kept his arm up, kept the bolt as steady as he could.

It was all over in the space of three heartbeats.

Terryn, blinking and shaking his head, felt raw. As though his heart had turned into a torch and blistered his insides. But the magic of his indwelling shade kept him whole and safe. Or as safe as he could be while containing such a spirit.

He pulled himself up onto his feet, swaying heavily, and looked ahead to see what he had done.

The darkness of the Witchwood had retreated. Before Terryn stretched a swath of nearly open land. No fleshy trees with pussing sores. No vines, no seeping soil. Instead, he saw heaping mounds of what once might have been timber buildings now reduced to rubble and rot, leaving behind only the outlines of their foundations. Terryn saw only one standing structure—a stone shrine house, much dilapidated but still stubbornly holding its ground.

Terryn's senses quickened. If the Stormwitch had, as he suspected, summoned the burning mist, was he still somewhere near? Was it possible that the venatrix had taken shelter somewhere among these ruins, that she'd managed to burrow in deep enough that the mist could not affect her? Or, if he sought her among the rubble, would he find her covered in melting burns?

He couldn't stand here forever, waiting for the Stormwitch to attack. There had been no subtlety in his approach, and he needed to act fast, to find some sort of defensible ground.

He sprang into the clearing, relieved to leave the Witchwood behind. The vines did not follow him, and he walked under a clear sky for the first time since crossing the Great Barrier. For a few moments he dared revel in the openness of his surroundings and the air which, though sour with the residual aroma left by the mist, was at least clean of *oblivis*.

But he'd scarcely progressed ten paces into the clearing when a wind picked up. At first, it merely blew a few leaves and bits of dust around his feet, but it strengthened by the moment, billowing his cape out behind him. Debris flew in his face, dust stinging his skin, and he put his hand up to shield his eyes.

As a result, he almost didn't see when the wind suddenly intensified in one quarter, heaving up a fallen, rotten beam in an invisible hand and hurtling it straight for his head. The tail of his eye caught sight of the incoming projectile at the last instant. He dived to the ground, narrowly avoiding a braining. The beam flew on over his head and crashed into a tottering foundation wall ten feet away, sending stones flying.

Terryn covered his head with his hands and spat curses: "Haunts damn, Haunts damn, Haunts *damn!*"

The Stormwitch wasn't alone.

The wind plucked at him, trying to get under him, to scoop him up as it had lifted the beam. He pressed his body into the dirt and, only rolling enough to give his hand access, slipped a dart from the quivers on his chest. As he tried to slot it into his scorpiona, the wind caught it and sent it flying from his fingers. "Haunts damn!" he growled again. He had only so many darts effective on Elemental shades.

Grimly, he pulled out another and this time firmly slotted it into place. Crawling on his stomach, he took shelter behind a low foundation wall. The wind roared around and over him, so vicious it would soon bring the stones toppling. He needed to get a sight on the witch, needed to find some way out of this wind so that he could take the shot. Even if he peered over the wall and spied her now, firing the scorpiona would be useless. His dart would never make its mark.

The sky rumbled overhead. Terryn looked up and saw

clouds forming. The Stormwitch was entering the action now, his storm blown in on his sister's winds, whirling into a thundering vortex overhead. Any moment, the heavens would open and burning rain would fall.

The shrine house. Terryn's mind clamored with single focus. The shrine house. He had to get to the shrine house, the lone standing building in this clearing. He was fairly certain he'd seen its roof still mostly intact. But how could he possibly reach it in time?

The wind died down. The Windwitch wouldn't want to blow her brother's storm away from its intended victim, after all. A drop fell, hissing as it burned into the stone wall only inches from Terryn's face. He had seconds, no more.

He sprang up from behind the wall, his scorpiona upraised, aiming in the direction from which the wind had blown. He spied a figure at least fifty yards distant, almost out of range. There was no time to steady his arm. There was no time to make certain of his shot.

The witch turned her head, looked him right in the eye. He stared into her hideous face, saw the black growths covering her neck, her cheek.

The next instant, his dart whirred through the air where she had been. The witch herself stood at his side.

"Nice shot, Venator," she said, just as her fist connected with his jaw.

The body containing her spirit was not strong, and the blow startled more than hurt. Terryn turned with it then offered a return blow, the iron spike on his left arm bracer flashing as he swung it straight at her face. She was on his other side before his arm had finished its swing, her fingers catching in his hair and yanking his head down as her knee connected with his stomach.

Terryn gasped, winded—but again, her blow was not strong. Pushing off with his feet, he lunged at her, tried to catch her in his arms. If he could just lay hold of her, she might not be able to tear from his grasp, no matter how swiftly she moved. Terryn's fingers brushed the edge of a cloak, but his arms closed around nothing.

The witch was behind him, and her foot connected with the small of his back, sending him flat to the ground.

"Zilla! Move!" cried a hoarse voice, almost immediately drowned by a roar of thunder.

Terryn looked up, saw the Windwitch standing over

him, saw her mutated face twist in a grin. Then, with a gust of dusty air, she was gone.

Rain speckled the ground. A drop fell on his outstretched hand, and Terryn cried out, bolting upright. He had to run! He had to get out of this! He had to—

A terrified scream cut through his senses. Terryn whirled, his rain-burned hand clutched to his chest. Spilling out from the forest came a whole tentacled mass of black vines. Like some hideous monster from a realm of pure nightmare, it hurtled into the clearing. One tentacle lashed above the others, and Terryn saw a small male figure clutched around the waist and waved around like a ragdoll as he shrieked.

The storm overhead scattered.

In the blink of an eye, another figure appeared before the writhing mass. The small form of the Windwitch looked pathetically weak facing such a monster. But her arms raised high as she summoned a gale-force blast of wind which somehow took on solid form and sliced into the vine holding her brother aloft. He fell, a vine still wrapped so tight around his waist it looked as though it would cut him in half. His sister caught him in her arms, and her winds carried them away just before another vine caught her by the foot.

It all happened so fast, Terryn scarcely had time to realize what had taken place. Then it struck him—the Witchwood was giving him a distraction. A distraction that would not last much longer.

The next moment he was running, instinct driving him toward the shrine house, the only possible shelter he could take against either wind or rain.

CHAPTER 22

COULD IT HAVE BEEN VENATOR TERRYN WHO CAUSED that blinding flash?

No. No, surely not.

Ayleth blinked up at the ceiling above her, raising and lowering her eyebrows as sensation crept back into her face. Did she feel a tingling in her fingertips, or was she imagining it?

But she hadn't imagined that bolt of light. It was real. And it could not have come at a timelier moment. It was certainly magical, and it did not seem like something caused by the Witchwood itself. Some other shade-taken then. Some other dweller of the forest? It couldn't possibly be . . .

Ayleth closed her eyes, sinking back into the darkness of her mind. The faint outlines of pine trees were murky but just discernible. The poison was fading. But fast enough to matter?

"*Laranta!*" she called into the shadows of her mind. The poison was so numbing, she could not conjure a mental image of herself. She floated disembodied in this realm of emptiness.

But the soul tether between them tightened. Laranta heard her. Laranta was active again, fighting against the numbness.

"*Laranta, come to me!*" she cried.

The soul tether tensed again. Ayleth couldn't tell whether her shade answered her or not. Haunts damn this poison!

She opened her eyes. Balanced precariously on the edge of the altar, she struggled to get a view out the window. Storm clouds gathered and dispersed, and thunder echoed overhead, reverberating among the stone arches of the shrine-house ceiling. She waited for another flash of light, but it didn't come. Whoever was out there held back on unleashing that incredible power again.

Wind blasted the world outside, one gust striking the shrine house so that it groaned on its foundation. Ayleth's heart thudded, and she half feared she'd end up buried beneath stone walls and tin roofing.

Then a horrible shriek—a man's voice?

"Terryn?" Her lips formed the name. Goddess above, she had control of her mouth again! Could she speak? Would it matter?

"Terryn!" she gasped, the sound no more than a whisper. She tried again. "Terryn! *Terryn!*" Each time, she put a little more force into her voice. It was stupid, hopeless. But she didn't care. She couldn't just lie here waiting for the witches to return and end her. She had control of her eyes, she had control of her voice, and maybe, *maybe*—

"TERRYN!" she cried.

"Venatrix di Ferosa, is that you?"

It was his voice. His deep, dark voice, strained with

fear but firm nonetheless.

Her heart thudded, and a spasm shot through her arms. She felt them—she felt her arms! With a gasp that was almost a sob, she managed to move the index finger of her left hand.

"Terryn, I'm here!" The words came out strangled and struggling, but loud enough. The pounding of boots on stone rang in her ears. Then the venator loomed over her, unruly curls falling in his dark face, his eyes two shining orbs of ice.

"What have they done? Have they bound you?" he demanded, his hands running up and down her arms, searching for ropes or restraints.

"No!" Ayleth choked. "No, they've poisoned me. I'm paralyzed."

His eyes, already round, widened still more with realization. His jaw tensed, and the muscle in his cheek jumped, pulling at the puckered skin of his scar. She watched his hand move to the quivers on his chest, searching.

"What are you doing?" she demanded.

"I know a trick," he said, sliding what looked to be a

dart intended for Anathema shades free of the quiver. He paused, met her gaze. "This will hurt."

Before Ayleth could protest, he stuck the dart into her throat, just under her jaw. Her eyes bugged, and her tongue seemed to swell in her mouth, blocking off her breathing.

Then came the pain.

Dealing the wrong poison to a shade-taken is always disastrous. Ayleth had discovered that truth herself when she shot the Lure in Godelieve Abbey with a poison meant for an Apparition. The pain caused to both the host body and the indwelling shade spirit is so extreme, it will drive the shade to madness, activating a blast of power so intense, it can spell the end of the venator who made the mistake.

The wrong poison rushed through Ayleth now like slicing knives cutting through her arms and legs, piercing down to her soul. She screamed. She could not help herself—and her scream was not human, not natural at all.

Laranta shot to the forefront of her mind, roaring and slavering. Had she been capable of taking physical form, she would have sprung from Ayleth's head and torn out Venator Terryn's throat on the spot. As it was, she shattered all the suppressions of the partially faded paralysis. Through the pulsing of her own agony, Ayleth felt the paralysis break, felt the life returning to her limbs. It was a life of fire and blades, but she felt it, every throb of it.

She sat upright on the altar stone and swung a fist at Terryn's face. He stepped back just in time, and she fell off the altar and landed on the floor. Sweat dripped from her forehead and saliva from her foaming mouth. Every muscle shuddered, and her bones quaked as Laranta's strength surged through her, desperate for an outlet.

Her senses exploded with shade awareness. Nostrils flaring, she inhaled and smelled . . . witch.

Ayleth's head shot up. Still flat on her stomach, she looked between Venator Terryn's boots and saw the Windwitch appear at the end of the long shrine-house nave. A gust of wind flowed in her wake, mounting in power. In the next instant, the witch crossed the space, her arm plunging as she brought her brother's rusted knife down in an arc aimed at Terryn's throat.

Her blow never landed.

Ayleth, propelled by the power of her shade, lurched to her feet, her hand darting out and catching the witch's wrist. Every muscle burst with magic and strength. Ayleth looked into Zilla's eyes, saw the horror wash over her face.

A wolfish grin pulled at Ayleth's lips. "Welcome back," she snarled.

With a screech, the Windwitch whirled her free arm, summoning up a wind that wrapped them both in a tornado of power. It should have wrenched Ayleth's hold loose, should have sent her flying across the open chapel to break her bones against the wall. But the pain of the wrong poison still burned through Ayleth's veins, and her shade flared with magical potency and rage. She did not let go.

Instead, with a yank, she pulled the witch close, wrapping her free arm in a stranglehold round her neck. Zilla gagged and flailed her arm again. The wind caught them both in its embrace, lifting them off the ground, hurtling them higher and higher. Still Ayleth did not release her grip, only tightened it, applying more force on the witch's trachea. She had just time enough to realize they were nearing the ceiling, just time enough to hunch her shoulders, to duck her head.

Then she slammed into the rafters and burst through the tin roofing, out into open air. It should have shattered her neck, crushed her spine, but the power of her shade was too far ascendant. She felt nothing, and her bones, wrapped in Feral shade force, did not break.

The whirlwind spun them out into the empty sky, and Ayleth's vision swam with views of the clearing, of the ruined town, of the shrine house below. She saw the Witchwood surrounding them, and still the wind bore them higher, spinning them wildly. She thought she caught a glimpse of the Great Barrier, of the world beyond the darkness of the forest.

She wrapped her legs around Zilla's and squeezed her neck harder. The witch choked, gagged, and went limp in her arms.

The wind whistled away. And they fell.

The fall seemed to last forever. Long enough for Ayleth to wonder if Laranta's strength would be enough to keep her from shattering into a million pieces when she struck the shrine house again. She turned in the air, trying to angle herself feet first, and her boots hit the tin roof and broke straight through. They passed in an instant through the empty air of the vaulted chapel, and Ayleth turned again.

Her back slammed into the floor, breaking the stones, breaking the foundation, burrowing deep into the rock on which the shrine house was built. She lay there with the Windwitch on her chest, breathing hard, not believing that she still lived. Not believing the coursing energy of magic flowing through her limbs. Not believing that her body wasn't smashed into a bloody pulp of nothing.

Laranta roared in her head.

Ayleth closed her eyes against that clamor. "*Down, Laranta!*" she scolded. "*It's not that bad.*"

Hurts! It hurts! her shade howled savagely.

"*I know it hurts, but it's better now. We must get up. We have to get out of here.*"

She opened her eyes again, and Terryn's face came into focus, peering down into the hole she'd made in the shrine house's floor.

"Venatrix!" His eyes looked as though they would

drop from his head. "You're alive?"

She couldn't blame him for his disbelief. She could hardly grasp it herself.

"Get this witch off me," she growled, shoving at the limp weight on top of her. Terryn crouched, reaching in to help. He caught the witch's arms and hauled her out as Ayleth picked herself up, shaking off dust and debris. All things considered, she wasn't too battered or bruised.

Terryn tossed the witch's body on the floor without care. Not dead yet, apparently; Ayleth's shadow sight detected both the human and the shade spirits still twined together in the center of the host body.

"The Gentle Death," she said. "Now!"

Terryn's hand moved to his quiver but came back empty. His gaze met Ayleth's. "I don't have any."

Ayleth ground her teeth in frustration. "Then we'd better get out of here before she wakes!"

Terryn nodded, and the two of them turned and ran down the broken nave, aiming for the open doorway. As they approached, the sunlight pouring through the door suddenly darkened, as though clouds rolled in thick overhead. They skidded to a stop in the doorway, peering out.

The Stormwitch stood at the base of the shrine house's steps. Clouds gathered over his head, formed at the beckoning of his hands. Eyes bright with shadow-light, darting like lightning between his lashes, fixed on Ayleth's face.

"We should have killed you when we had the chance!" he wheezed and drew back his hand.

He stopped mid-action.

His eyes widened, and he coughed. One hand slowly rose to finger the dart quivering where it stuck right between his eyes.

Terryn lowered his scorpiona. The poison ordinarily required time to take full effect—but a creature like Zarc, so weak in this ruinous host body, had not the means to fight off its influence.

The Stormwitch fell to his knees and slumped onto his side.

"Come on, Venatrix," Terryn said. "We're not out of this yet."

Together they sprang down the steps, Terryn's long legs struggling to match Ayleth's shade-propelled stride.

She reined in Laranta's power, allowing him to catch up. Only when they had left the shrine house far behind did she realize they should have killed the witches. Should have slit both their throats where they lay. There were no potential host bodies out here in the Witchwood for their violently expelled souls to possess. They would have flown uselessly within the boundaries of the Barrier until the Haunts inevitably dragged them home.

It was a mistake, a costly mistake to leave their enemies alive. A mistake Ayleth hoped she wouldn't live to regret.

Too late now, though. The Witchwood loomed before them, and they needed to penetrate that darkness and return to the Barrier. Terryn skidded to a halt a few yards from the forest's edge. "I don't know which way to go," he said, his face tense, his voice edged with desperation.

Ayleth gave him a look. The instincts of her shade had driven her west the moment they left the church doors behind. They were aimed the right direction, she was certain.

"This way," she said, speaking with such confidence, Terryn believed her at once. He moved to her side and took hold of her hand. She blinked down at his fingers interlocked with hers then blinked up into his eyes, too surprised to speak.

"We must not be separated," he said shortly. "This forest is dangerous."

Ayleth didn't try to argue.

Dark vines poured out of the Witchwood on all sides of the ruined town. Without the Stormwitch's burning rains to hold it back, the forest would soon reclaim what they had pried from its many fingers. With this grim thought in mind, Ayleth dragged Terryn into the shadows beneath the wounded trees. The stench of the Witchwood assaulted her nostrils, and she gagged but hurried on. The trailing vines seemed to watch them as they ran, alert and venomous.

Laranta's senses pointed her true, however. Ayleth, gripping Terryn's hand, led him straight through the forest, heading west. Even when the vines crawled in thick masses, even when the trees seemed to slide into their path to obstruct their progress, she dodged and ducked and continued stalwartly forward. They didn't have to find their original point of entry; if they just continued due west long enough, they would reach the Barrier somewhere along its winding extent. Then, Goddess willing, Terryn would be able to open it.

A sudden weight hauled on Ayleth's arm. She tightened her grasp on Terryn's hand, and as a result was pulled right off her feet. Landing hard on her shoulder, her hand grasping at empty air, she rolled over, pushing her head upright.

And saw a mass of vines wrap Terryn into their clutches, coiling around each arm and leg. His eyes darted to meet hers just before vanishing in a black writhing swarm.

CHAPTER 23

"NO!" AYLETH ROARED AND LEAPT AT THE VINES, Laranta's fury hot in her veins. She ripped, she tore, she uprooted long strands.

More came, faster and faster. No matter what she did, no matter what she tried. Long, black slitherings poured down from the branches, wrapping the venator tight.

In the back of her mind, behind her fury and fear, Ayleth wondered why none of them reached for her. But she ignored that thought, pouring all her concentration, all her power into reaching the venator.

He shouldn't have come after her! He shouldn't have left the Barrier, shouldn't have ventured into this cursed place! He should have given her up for lost, said a prayer to the Goddess, and moved on with his life. That's what any sane man would have done in his place. Haunts damn it, she wasn't even his hunt sister! She was his festering competition, for haunt's sake! He should have left her behind.

"No, no, no!" she screamed at the vines, screamed at the forest. "You're not taking him! You're not, you're not! I won't *let* you!"

Laranta snarled inside her, empowering her limbs, and Ayleth drove herself faster and harder. But she could make no headway. How long had it been? How many moments, how many heartbeats? Had he already smothered under that constricting tangle, had the breath already been crushed from his pulverized body?

Something shone in her eye. Ayleth flinched and drew back, surprised. She put up a hand to shield herself against the mounting glow. White light streamed through the snarl of vines, and the outermost tendrils and leaves trembled, shivered.

At the last possible moment, she flung herself away, planting her face in the wet soil of the forest floor, covering her head with her hands. Still, with her eyes shut fast and pressed into the muck, she saw the brilliant flash, felt the intense heat of it roll over her head. Her cloak, her boots, and the hood covering the back of her head were all singed.

It was over almost before it began.

Ayleth lifted her mud-crusted face, her senses assaulted by a stink worse than the stench of infection from the wounded trees. That stench was still present, but added to it was the greater funk of scorched *oblivis*. The air seemed to shiver with its own rankness.

She pushed herself upright, turned in a crouch. Venator Terryn lay in the center of the blast radius, surrounded by the ashes of burned vines. For as far as Ayleth could see, the trees were blackened from about three feet off the ground and higher.

Ayleth crawled to his side and turned the venator over. Light moved in weird bubbles under his skin, flowing in his blood. Using shadow sight, she peered into his soul, making certain the potent spirit he carried within was still properly suppressed. The last thing she needed just now was an ascendant and powerful shade taking possession of the venator's body.

But miraculously, Terryn's suppressing song spells still held. He must have accessed only a limited amount of that incredible power, a feat of complex spell-working Ayleth could hardly comprehend in theory, much less practice. No wonder he was the favorite of Fendrel du Glaive.

"Wake up," she growled, smacking his face. The Witchwood was quiet for the moment, but with a tense sort of stillness that told her it was watching. They didn't have long before it came at them again. "Wake up, du Balafre. I'll kiss you again if you don't."

He didn't stir. Only the pulsing light of his spirit inside him and the ongoing hum of his song spells told her he still lived.

Shades, Laranta said. *Shades coming. Fast.*

Ayleth's head popped up. Her shadow senses were keener than she'd ever before experienced, spiked by the Anathema poison. She drew a deep breath of the putrid air, swiftly sifting through the layers of rank and rot and ruin to find that new scent, that scent that didn't belong.

Shades, Laranta said again. *Shades, shades, shades.*

Three shade-taken. Approaching through the forest. Ayleth smelled them and knew better to than to doubt her senses. She remembered what she'd heard the Windwitch say: *We will wait for Gillotin, Scias, and Crisentha . . . they are coming . . .*

The other Crimson Devils.

With a hissing curse, Ayleth shoved one hand under Terryn's shoulder, the other behind his knees. He was tall, and so densely muscled that it took much of Laranta's strength for Ayleth to heave him up in her arms. She took several steps but knew she would not be able to run with him draped like an enormous sack in front of her. Breathing hard through her teeth, she shifted him up and over her shoulders, bowed under his weight.

Then she began moving—walking at first, as she found her balance. Shade power coursed inside her, and she quickened her pace until she was running. Running as fast as she could through the light-blasted trees, through the burned remnants of vines. Running until she reached the place in the forest where the blast had not penetrated, running on into the shadows and the poisons and the lurking evil. Running, and knowing that every step could well be her last. The witches on her trail could catch her. The forest could ensnare her, devour her. She was as nothing compared to these foes, and *oblivis* thickened in her throat with each gasping breath.

But she had Laranta. And Laranta gave her strength to sprint onward, faster and faster. Her shade senses reached out ahead, and she could feel the thrum of the Barrier song spell. She was close, so close.

Both sooner than expected and long after she'd given up hope, the woven spell threads shimmered ahead of her in the shadows. She was within sight. And the witches . . . no. She would not seek them with Laranta's senses. It would do no good. She focused everything she had on that gleam of song. They would make it. They would escape!

Her feet carried her right up to the spell, and she could not make herself slow down. At the last moment, she turned to the side, striking the Barrier with her shoulder and rebounding to collapse in the muck. Terryn rolled over several times and lay still, and Ayleth panted, propped up on one elbow, staring up at that impenetrable brilliance of magic and song. Summoning the last of Laranta's strength, she crawled through the squelching black mud to Terryn's side.

"Come on, du Balafre," she gasped, turning his face toward hers. "You've got to wake up. I don't know how to open the Barrier."

He moaned. His eyebrows puckered and his mouth twitched beneath a layer of grime. But he did not wake.

"If you'll wake up," Ayleth said, clasping his cheeks in her trembling hands, "I'll renounce my candidacy. I'll give you the post at Milisendis, I swear. I'll ride straight back to Gillanluòc, and I'll tell Hollis she was right, I should never have left. You can have your destiny; you can have it all. Just wake up!"

Nothing. Only another faint twitch at the corner of his mouth, pulling at the scar on his cheek.

Shades, Laranta growled. *Shades, shades.*

Ayleth drew a shuddering breath through her nose, glancing up into those dark shadows. She swallowed hard. Using the side of her hand, she wiped some of the mud from Terryn's mouth, smearing it along his cheek.

"No offence, Venator," she murmured.

Then, with a desperate gasp, she pressed her lips against his. Not just a rough connection of their mouths smashed together, but a collision of souls. As she clutched him by the back of his head, pulling him up, pulling him closer, she sent her spirit diving down inside him, screaming his name, begging him to answer, to respond.

Something warm bloomed inside. Whether inside of him or within her own breast, Ayleth could not say. For the moment they were much too close, much too mingled for her to discern a difference. Her fingers tightened in his hair, her hand on the side of his face tensed, fingers digging into his temple.

His body moved, convulsed.

Then he sat straight up, grabbing her by the shoulders to push her away. Her lips parted from his, but her hands still gripped his head so hard, she almost pulled him back in for another kiss without meaning to.

"Festering devils!" Terryn roared, choking on the words as his wild eyes stared into her face. "What is it with you and kissing?"

Ayleth could say nothing, her mouth open, her lips parted. She could not draw a breath. Her hands moved downward before she realized what she was doing, grabbing at his belt. He yelped and tried to slap them away, but with Laranta's strength still inside her, she knocked his hands aside easily enough.

She pulled his Detrudos pipe free of its sheath.

"Play!" She pressed it into his hands. "Play, now! Open the Barrier!"

"Wh-what—" Terryn did not finish his question. Realization flooded his face, and with Ayleth's help, he scrambled to his feet. She clung to his elbow, holding him upright as he raised the instrument to his lips and called the drone into life.

The first variation of the song spell spilled out, too tentative, too quavering. Ayleth, inexperienced though she was, knew at once that it would have no effect on the powerful spell of the Venator Dominus.

She looked back over her shoulder into the Witchwood. Did she see movement in the shadows?

Shades, shades, shades—

"Haunts damn it, Laranta, I know!"

Terryn, sensing her tension perhaps, shrugged off her hold on his elbow, braced himself more firmly, and started again, this time a stronger variation of the song. She felt the flow of shade power going out from him. Not the intense power he must have accessed for those light blasts, but the power of an ongoing connection between human soul and shade necessary for the working of the Detrudos pipes. He did not need a lot of power to work the spell. What he lacked in ascendant magic, he more than made up for with skill.

Gaining confidence and conviction in the variation he explored, he trilled more and more complex notes in bright contrast to the ongoing boom of the drone. Ayleth, turning her back to the wood, stared up at the gleaming Barrier, the impossibly complex webbing of music. Slowly, carefully, threads unwound. Down near the ground, a hole opened—a mere slit in the vast wall.

"Good enough!" Ayleth cried, and tugged Terryn's arm. He resisted a moment then seemed to agree with her. Playing a resolving whirl of notes, he ended his variation abruptly. The opening he'd made was less than a foot tall, but it didn't matter.

"Go!" he barked, and Ayleth didn't wait to be told twice. She flung herself flat and crawl-scuttled on her belly through the mire, spitting disgusting mouthfuls from her teeth as she went. She felt the weight of the spell overhead, felt the power of the Barrier as though it would come down hard and cut her in two. But on the far side—Oh! On the far side she glimpsed sunshine and caught a taste of fresh air, free of *oblivis*. Stretching out both hands, she grabbed hold of the ground beyond and pulled herself through, popping out like a cork from a bottle.

She rolled out onto firm, solid dirt, staring up at a sky so blue, it dazzled her eyes. If all was right with the world, she would have lain there for hours, not moving, simply drinking in that sight of heaven, those trailing tails of distant white clouds.

But Terryn's grunting voice brought her back to reality. She whipped around and saw the venator struggling to push himself through the too-tight opening. Leaping at him, she caught his arms and applied Laranta's surging strength to pull him free. Terryn shouted, cursing her to all kinds of horrible ends before he, too, slid free, dragging a trail of foulness behind him.

With a wordless cry, Ayleth hauled him onto his knees and wrapped her arms around him, their bodies a mass of gross mud and slime and pus.

Terryn pushed her away, crying, "No time! No time!" He still gripped his Detrudos in one hand.

Shades! Laranta cried.

Ayleth sprang to her feet as Terryn, still kneeling, put his instrument to his lips and began reversing the variation he had just performed. She stepped up to the Barrier, peering through the webbing back into that horror of forest. Her experiences had not hardened her to the sight. Her soul trembled with panicked terror, but she clenched her fists, pulling at Laranta's strength.

If the witches came too soon—if they got through— Goddess help her, she would pummel them to dust with her own two hands!

They appeared. Three shadowy figures moving out from the darkness of the forest and rushing up to the Barrier. The light of the spell song illuminated their faces, the black tattoo of Dread Odile stark against their foreheads. Ayleth saw the same growths she'd witnessed in the other two, saw the same signs of weakness and decay. She saw the remnants of their red hoods.

She knew them at once. She did not have to be told which name belonged with which hideous visage. Scias du Sibb—the Legionwitch. He was the short one with the broken arm dangling uselessly from one shoulder, his jaw covered in fungus like a nightmarish facsimile of a beard. Crisentha di Bathia—the Crystalwitch. She wore a woman's body, skeletal, all trace of femininity leached out by pain and suffering.

And Gillotin du Visgarus—the Corpsewitch. The tallest and broadest of the trio, he seemed hardly affected by the malice of the curse in which he lived. He strode right up to the webbing, a tall man with dark skin and long, long hair, still thick, still lush even after all these years of imprisonment. His eyes, black as the Haunts, landed on Ayleth through the Great Barrier and stayed there, gazing with an expression of pure, unabashed wonder.

The Barrier shuddered violently, struck from the far side. Ayleth shrank back several paces. She saw Crisentha backing away from where she had flung herself bodily into the spell. Hard, gleaming stone encrusted every visible inch of her skin, and protrusions of sword-sharp crystal burst from her knuckles. She punched the Barrier again and again, and Ayleth backed away further still. If this witch was this vicious in her reduced state, what must she have been like in her glory days?

Terryn's song resolved. He let his instrument fall to the ground and sat back on his heels. "It's done," he said. "It's repaired. They're not getting through."

Ayleth's gaze darted to the place where the opening had been. The Crystalwitch, on the other side, must have seen where she looked, for she leapt to the spot, pounding with everything she was worth, trying to find a weakness. But Terryn's spell was strong. The Great Barrier might as well never have been opened at all.

She moved to his side, just behind him. She wanted to put a hand on his shoulder, to say something congratulatory. Nothing felt right. They could only stay as they were, silent, watching as the witches on the far side of the Barrier watched them. The Crystalwitch made obscene gestures, gnashing her teeth. The Legionwitch ran wildly up and down the Barrier, desperate to find some weakness that wasn't there.

But the Corpsewitch only stared out at them, unblinking.

"Five," Ayleth whispered.

At the sound of her voice, Terryn started and shook his head. "What? What did you say?" he asked, his words heavy with exhaustion.

"Five," Ayleth whispered again. "Seven Devils fled into the Witchwood. We've only seen five. Where are the other two?"

Terryn offered no answer.

CHAPTER 24

THEIR EXIT POINT THROUGH THE BARRIER WAS approximately two miles north of where they'd entered. Ayleth, using the last shreds of Laranta's poison-enhanced strength, reached out with her shade senses and caught a trace of Chestibor.

"This way," she said to Terryn and started walking. He followed silently in her wake, and Ayleth wondered if he was as aware as she was of the watching eyes of the three witches fixed upon them.

The relief of stepping into the chilly shadows of the fringe forest was so great, Ayleth's knees nearly buckled. It took all her willpower to keep going. She didn't want to spend a second longer than necessary in such close proximity to the Witchwood.

Terryn kept his peace as they pushed their way through the crisp underbrush, their boots crunching dead leaves with every footstep. Ayleth almost wished he would speak, just to fill her head with something other than her own spinning thoughts.

Too many things fought for supremacy in her mind. The strange conversation between Zilla and Zarc, debating whether they should kill her or not. The three witches still following them, contained behind the Barrier and yet somehow far too threatening.

The fact that the Witchwood had let them escape.

Because there were no two ways about it: any step of their flight back to the Barrier could easily have been their last. They could fight, but ultimately they could not have saved themselves from a power like that. They'd only made it out alive because the Witchwood allowed it to be so.

But . . . why?

She couldn't puzzle through these mysteries. Not now. Not until she'd washed some of this putrid muck from her skin, not until she'd purged some of the *oblivis* from her throat and lungs. Not until she'd found her horse and put miles between her and the Barrier song spell. Otherwise, the very weight of her confusion would crush her.

Could she bear to stay on at Wodechran Borough?

The thought brought her up short so abruptly that Venator Terryn almost walked into her from behind. He stopped close enough that she could feel his breath on the back of her head. Still he said nothing.

Did he sense the sudden turmoil in her soul? Did he sense her indecision? Her cowardice? Because, more than anything, she wanted to get in the saddle and ride and ride and ride with the speed of a Haunts-bound spirit for the Skada Mountains. To throw herself at Hollis's feet and beg her forgiveness. To vow never, ever to venture beyond Drauval Borough again. To be content with her humble lot, serving alongside the venatrix of Gillanluòc.

More than anything, she wanted to give in.

"Venatrix?"

The deep voice in her ear sent a tremor straight to her gut. She drew a long breath and began walking again without a look back at the venator. The single word spoken with that questioning lilt was enough to decide her.

She would not back down. She would not surrender to her fears. She would stay on at Wodechran and fight for her position with everything she had to give. And if Venator du Balafre still ultimately won the day, at least she would know she'd made him earn it.

They found their horses eventually. Laranta tracked down Chestibor not far from where Ayleth had dismounted and left him. Terryn's red mare had stayed close to the brown gelding for companionship, and neither steed looked the worse for a long afternoon of waiting and nosing about in the forest foliage.

Ayleth caught her horse by the reins and prepared to mount. A hand on her shoulder restrained her, and she looked around to meet Venator Terryn's icy gaze.

He held his Vocos pipes in his other hand.

"Yours were lost," he said. "Use mine. Suppress your

shade."

Ayleth looked at the bone-carved instrument. Part of her wanted to refuse the offer. Laranta was far ascendant inside her, true, but she didn't feel unsafe. Throughout the horrors of that day, her shade had served her well. She'd shown no sign of wanting to take control of their shared host body. Indeed, she'd been a loyal comrade throughout every battle and every flight.

But the law of Evander was firm—no venatrix might leave her shade ascendant when the battle was over. She must bind the spirit down with song spells, protecting herself against the malevolence she carried inside her.

With a heavy sigh, Ayleth took the pipes and, turning her back on both Terryn and her horse, began to play the Song of Suppression. Laranta growled in her head, and Ayleth saw a flash of blazing eyes in the darkness behind her closed eyelids.

Why, mistress? the shade demanded in her sharp, barking voice. *Why? Why, why?*

"*Because it's the law,*" Ayleth answered, and wound the spell song tight.

When she finished playing, and as the final boom of

the drone faded from her ears, she realized another song spell was currently being wound behind her. She turned and, through a curtain of leafless low branches, saw Venator Terryn standing close to the Great Barrier, working to repair the poorly rendered patch of song spell. Even if the witches found this place, they would not be able to break through. Not after Terryn had done his work.

Ayleth, leading Chestibor by the reins, pushed through the foliage and took up a position just behind Terryn. When he finished his spell-crafting and turned, lowering the Detrudos from his lips, she held out his Vocos to him.

"I don't suppose you want to try again to fetch Venator Nane's body?" she said dryly. His eyes flared wide, and Ayleth hastened to add, "No, no, I'm not serious. It's gone. We can't get it now."

He swallowed hard, his Adam's apple bobbing. Then he snatched the Vocos from her outstretched hand, sheathed it, and stalked over to his waiting horse. He mounted in a whirl of foulness-encrusted cape and spurred the mare into motion almost before he'd settled into the saddle.

Ayleth rolled her eyes at the venator's grimness. Did he think she was poking fun at him with her bad joke? Calling his devotion to duty into question? She shouldn't have said anything, but . . .

Haunts damn it, he was an impossible sort of man.

She climbed up onto Chestibor's back and nudged her horse to follow the red mare's trail back through the fringe forest. How strangely lonely she felt inside with Laranta suppressed. With no way to judge the passage of time beyond the Great Barrier, Ayleth could not guess how long they had been gone. The sun through the tree branches above indicated late afternoon, but of what day she couldn't know for certain. Only the fact that Chestibor and the red mare were close to where they'd been left indicated that no more than a few hours had passed.

Emerging from the forest into open country, Ayleth spied Terryn a good distance ahead. Part of her wanted to let him ride on back to the outpost without her. But a larger part of her didn't want to be alone with her thoughts.

So, she squeezed Chestibor's flanks, pushing him to a canter, and soon drew up alongside the venator and his mare. His icicle gaze shot her way, then fixed on the horizon again.

Ayleth drew a long breath and expelled it slowly. She could almost feel the motes of *oblivis* pouring out of her. Her head cleared, and some of the pressing worries and mysteries discovered beyond the Barrier retreated for a time.

"I have to thank you," she said after a while.

He didn't look at her. He didn't so much as grunt.

"For coming after me," Ayleth pressed on. "Back there in the Witchwood. You should have escaped, of course. It was completely stupid for you to venture deeper. But . . ."

Her face heated. She wasn't doing her own gratitude justice. And had she actually just insulted him in the process of offering thanks? She bowed her head and, in a quick gesture, pulled up her hood until it at least partially covered her blush. "I just want you to know that I appreciate what you did," she finished lamely.

No answer. She stole a look his way. It was hard to

discern any distinct expression beneath the layers of grime on his face. Nothing but stony indifference.

Her lips twitched and, on an impulse, she added, "In case you're worried, Venator du Balafre, I have no intention of kissing you again anytime soon."

The muscle in his jaw ticked.

It wasn't much. But it was a reaction.

Hiding her grin behind the drape of her hood, Ayleth urged Chestibor back into a canter then on to a full gallop, putting distance between her and the venator. The wind rushed in her face, blew back her hood, and whipped her long, dirty braid behind her. The hunt was not over. Yes, they'd found Venator Nane, but they still didn't know why he had been killed or who dealt the killing blow. They would need to find answers before they could report to Prince Gerard, before they could know if the borough was truly safe. But for now, in this moment, her world was made up of nothing more than cold autumn air in her face, a good horse beneath her, and broad open spaces stretching before her.

She gave herself over to the pulse of her heart and rode for the horizon.

EPILOGUE

D<small>RY</small> <small>LEAVES WHISPERED ABOVE</small> H<small>OLLIS</small>'<small>S</small> <small>HEAD AS SHE</small> rode her gray gelding up the winding track to Gillanluòc. Autumn drew toward its end in the mountain country, bringing hard on its heels the fierce winters that plagued this borough. She would not be venturing back into the wilder regions again until after spring thaw.

No matter. She'd succeeded in her most recent hunt— a wild boar, which she hauled in the cart behind her. He'd proven a difficult quarry to run down. She'd spent weeks in the mountains rather than days. But she'd killed him at last and driven the violent Feral shade inside him back to the Haunts where it belonged.

Her gelding stumbled on a rough patch in the road, and pain shot up Hollis's leg. The boar's cruel tusks had caught her with a gash to the thigh. Nothing serious, but enough to keep her quiet for another week or so as it healed.

No matter. Once back at the outpost, she'd get Ayleth to help her tend the wound. And she would return to work soon enough. There was always more to be done, unending labor in the service of the Goddess until the day the castra told her she was through. On that day she would select a venator or venatrix to deal her the Gentle Death, separate her soul from that of her shade, and speed her on to Heaven. Only . . . she did not believe she would live that long.

Ayleth was nearly of age now. The time of the last hunt was near . . .

Hollis looked up and saw the tower of Gillanluòc ahead. No light in the window, though the day was lengthening. Strange. Ayleth would ordinarily set up a light as a welcoming beacon to her mistress out on the road.

Hollis was tempted to pull out her Vocos pipes, call up her shade, and reach out with its powers to sense Ayleth's mind. But the girl hated such invasions. And it never behooved a venatrix to use her shade's powers without good reason. So, she rode on up to the gate, dismounted, opened it using the secret lock, and led her horse through to the yard.

A terrible stillness held the outpost captive. No sign of life anywhere.

Had Ayleth run off again on some mission?

Hollis's face darkened as she settled her horse in the empty stable and hung up her tack. Ayleth's gelding was missing. Not a good sign. She made her way to the blockhouse in limping strides, favoring her wounded leg. As she burst through the front door, she called sharply, "Ayleth? Where are you?"

But the blockhouse was empty. Ayleth was gone.

"Haunts damn," Hollis muttered, turning back toward the door, of half a mind to saddle up and ride out after the fool girl. As she turned, a parchment nailed to the doorframe caught her eye.

It was the letter from Venator du Tam. The letter informing her of Nane's presumed death. The letter which told of the opening at Wodechran Borough.

Hollis stared at it—displayed there so prominently where she couldn't miss it. Her heart seemed to swell up in her throat, choking her.

"No," she breathed. Then louder, *"No!"*

She pounded a fist on the doorframe. The whole house seemed to shake, but she pounded again. Then with a sob, she bowed her head, leaning against the wall. No tears came—she'd not wept real tears for many, many years now.

But her heart slowly tore in two.

"Was it all for nothing?" she whispered. Lifting her head, raising her eyes to the sky outside the open door, she entreated the heavens themselves. "Was it all for nothing in the end?"

A NOTE FROM THE AUTHOR

Thank you so much for taking the time to read *Daughter of Shades*. It's been such a crazy ride writing Ayleth's story, and I am so excited to share more of this unfolding adventure with you!

Reader reviews are so important to an independent author like me, so if you would take a moment to leave an honest review on Amazon, I would be so grateful! It doesn't have to be long—just a few words can be enough to help another reader decide if they want to read my story.

Each review is like gold to me, so I hope you'll consider helping me out!

Thank you,

Sylvia Mercedes

ACKNOWLEDGMENTS

I have so many people I need to thank for helping me take The Venatrix Chronicles from dream to reality. The journey has been long and sometimes so exhausting . . . but these individuals made it all worthwhile.

—Jill. My editor and #1 supporter. Because of you, I've learned to tighten my prose and reduce superfluous wordiness. I am very, very, very, very, very, very, very grateful for your patient instruction. (Don't choke, please!)

—Papa. This book . . . this world . . . would not exist without all those hours of intense brainstorming. Plus you sustained me on a life-giving flow of "bad" coffee all the way. I couldn't have done this without you. (Raises the unicorn mug in salute.)

—Esther. I feel a little guilty to admit it . . . but your tears are highly motivating! Seriously, knowing something I wrote could make you cry THAT hard was just the encouragement I needed when I was ready to throw in the towel.

—Stephanie. You will be glad to know that, due to the great respect I bear for you . . . I removed the gold flecks. (And-lots-of-hyphens.)

—Candace. You were willing to read for a total stranger and give me objective feedback . . . and it made all the difference! Thank you for telling me what I needed to hear so I could fix that confusing first chapter and make the whole book stronger.

—Ariel. You were Ayleth's first honest-to-goodness fan. Your enthusiastic Wattpad comments gave me LIFE. Girl, you don't know how I jumped for joy at every one of those little notification *dings* on my phone!

—Emily. My NaNoWriMo buddy, you were there for

those crazy weeks of November 2017 when I wrote the first draft of this book. Thank you for all the encouraging notes and updates. I cannot wait to celebrate your book launch someday soon. You know I'll be shouting it from the rooftops!

—Kim and all the folks at Deranged Doctor Design. It was a thrill to get to work with such a talented group of people. These covers you created for me are gorgeous, and I love them to pieces.

—Frank. Sir, your artistry truly knows no bounds. The map design is out of this world! I appreciate the hours you put into creating such a stunning image, bringing my world to life.

—My Advance Reader Team. Your interest for this project, your typo-crushing skills, and your reviews mean the world to me! Thank you for having my back and helping me to launch this series.

—Baby Lady. You're not such a baby anymore! These last

three years you've grown into a little kick-butt heroine in your own right, and I couldn't be prouder.

—Handsome. You inspire and delight and motivate me by turns. This has been a long couple of years, but you believed in me even when I couldn't believe in myself. You will always and forever be my hero.

ABOUT THE AUTHOR

Sylvia Mercedes makes her home in the idyllic North Carolina countryside with her handsome husband, sweet baby-lady, and Gummy Bear, the Toothless Wonder Cat. When she's not writing she's . . . okay, let's be honest. When she's not writing, she's running around after her little girl, cleaning up glitter, trying to plan healthy-ish meals, and wondering where she left her phone. In between, she reads a steady diet of fantasy novels. But mostly she's writing.

After a short career in Traditional Publishing (under a different name), Sylvia decided to take the plunge into the Indie Publishing World and is enjoying every minute of it. The Venatrix Chronicles is her first series as an independent author, but she's got many more planned!

Don't miss the continuation of Ayleth's adventures in
Book 2 of The Venatrix Chronicles!

The hunt is on.
But who is the hunter
and who is the hunted?

VISIONS OF FATE

Meanwhile don't miss Song of Shadows:

Visit www.SylviaMercedesBooks.com
to get your free copy.